MODERN BUDDHA

AN INCREDIBLE JOURNEY OF TRANSFORMATION

Biswajit Jha

STERLING

STERLING PUBLISHERS (P) LTD.
Regd. Office: A1/256 Safdarjung Enclave, New Delhi-110029.
CIN: U22110DL1964PTC211907
Phone: +91 82877 98380/ +91 120-6251823
e-mail: mail@sterlingpublishers.in
www.sterlingpublishers.in

Modern Buddha - An Incredible Journey of Transformation

ISBN 978-93-93853-49-3
Cover design by Mohit Suneja

Printed and Published by

Sterling Publishers Pvt. Ltd.,
Plot No. 13, Ecotech-III, Greater Noida - 201306, Uttar Pradesh, India

For those who show that
it isn't over 'til it's over

Author's Note

All human beings have a vague idea about what their life ought to be like. And, in a majority of cases, these vague ideas start to shape how we become, what we achieve and most importantly, what we give back to our society. Ultimately, everything boils down to a simple fact that our lives become exactly how we perceive it. So, it is important that we have the right perspective of life. But unfortunately, most people, including the so-called educated ones, don't have the right perspective. They don't know how to lead a 'happy and fulfilled life' despite becoming 'successful'.

I have come across many people who have everything -- money, property, beautiful bungalows or apartments, high-end cars, social reputation, etc. -- but they are still cut-off from their roots and are leading a miserable life without peace, happiness, contentment and good health. The most interesting part that I have seen about these people, is that they all repent when they sense that the end is somewhere nearby. The youth with audacity and adventure, peopled with familiar faces and unfamiliar mysteries, is far... far behind.

Everything in life is connected. When we lead a life without any purpose, or lead a life looking only for transient pleasures, it affects our mindset, which in turn, impacts the path we choose in life. If we go to sleep late, we would wake up late. This awakening, if it comes earlier saves us the troubled path. Material success seizes our mindscape so much so that we only think of all the comforts and luxuries of life. We unknowingly create a comfort zone -- a cocoon around ourselves. And it destroys us in every way possible -- physically, psychologically and ethically. Our ego gets the better of us; it destroys our overall attitude, which then spoils our relationship with everyone.

However, once we step out of that comfort zone or that cocoon, positive changes happen within us. We become completely different – full of energy, with a positive outlook, humble, but not servile, and committed to working for fellow human beings – in fact, for all sentient beings.

Of all the blessings that I have received so far, my biggest blessing came at the end of 2018, when I met Lhato Jamba, President of Gyalphozing College of Information Technology, Bhutan's first IT College. I was amazed by his humility, innovative ideas and simplicity. Impressed by my writing, Jamba took me to his college and requested me to teach social media communication to his students. He even awarded me an honorary position -- Adjunct Professor-- at his college.

The visit to Bhutan threw open a hitherto unexpected opportunity to know Bhutan, a tiny Himalayan country, known for its happiness and its peace-loving people. Before COVID-19 broke out, I went to the college three times and stayed there for quite some time. The time I spent in Bhutan completely changed my ideas about life. I learnt so much about Bhutan and Tibetan Buddhism from Lhato Jamba that I cannot thank him ever enough. Bhutan and its people taught me that to be happy you don't need so many material things. 'Happiness is all about how you perceive your life and the world around you, and how content you are with what you have.' I was surprised by their care for Mother Nature, and their history, religion, art, culture, heritage and the sense of community.

I also met some Buddhist monks from whom I learnt some life-altering lessons. After returning from Bhutan, I read quite a few books on Buddhism and some books written by Swami Vivekananda. Paramahansa Yogananda's *Autobiography of a Yogi* also significantly shaped my thoughts.

When COVID-19 broke out and lockdown was declared in March 2020, I decided to make use of the time to write about this transformational journey. Modern Buddha is to a great extent autobiographical, or in parts experiences or events that happened to someone close to me.

I hope this book will have the same impact as it did on me while recording the experience of change. It may provide an alternative perspective to a life, which is 'content.' The book may refine our understanding of 'success' and 'happiness', the meaning of the words that I myself had never understood before I took the journey to Bhutan. I would consider myself fortunate if this book helps you realise the 'true meaning of life.'

1

Winter has its own charm in the forests. Everything is misty and tranquil. I love this season here. Actually, I love everything about it – the chilly breeze, the grey look, the mossy fragrance of mist and wood and the absolute tranquility. It is so silent here that I can only hear the chirping of crickets, the songs of birds, the flapping of a bird's wings and sometimes, the mooing of cows. Usually I don't keep any engagements after lunch, till evening sets in. This is my time, purely my own time, for reading and contemplation. The villagers know this. They rarely disturb me at this hour of the day. Looking at the mountains that surround this beautiful village, I am always overwhelmed with a deep sense of contentment.

I flipped through the pages of The Razor's Edge. I don't know after how many years was I reading this book by Somerset Maugham. Whenever I had this feeling of emptiness, I found comfort in my books, which are my companion of loneliness. Sometimes, I lose myself in some stray thoughts from my past that creep upon me, despite my best efforts to keep them at bay.

But today, my peace was broken by a sudden clamour of the village boys. I could easily sense that something unusual had happened. I saw some of my students rushing towards my small room.

"Great news, Sir!" Arjun burst into the room, barely able to contain his excitement.

He was almost gasping for breath as he spoke. He was the first one to reach among the lot. As I looked askance, other students followed him and barged into the small room, which had only a small bed, a wooden rack for my books, a chair and a table. Students often keep coming to my room for advice or complaints. They filled up my day, but hardly had so many of them barged in, all at once. A few of my books fell on the ground as they jostled for space. Even as I instinctively rose from my chair to pick up the books, one of the boys placed them back on the shelf.

Though I rarely get amped up by anything these days, I just couldn't figure out what had happened, as the boys were all talking at once, all of them jabbering about the same thing – "great news."

I turned to Jitesh Bhujel, the 15-year-old, Nepali boy of our football team, whom I knew to be pretty level-headed.

"What's the news? Boys, please stop shouting for a moment. Jitesh, you tell me what exactly has happened."

As the others stopped talking, Jitesh, his face aglow, announced enthusiastically, "Sir, our school has been selected as the best sports school in the country and our village, as the 'model village'!"

As soon as Jitesh gave me the news, the other boys started whooping and jumping in joy, shouting 'hip hip hooray', as if they had won a do-or-die football match.

Our senior players Shibu, Mantu and Bipin also chipped in to explain what they had seen on different news channels.

Gradually, other residents of the village, the Adivasis (tribals), and people of Nepalese and Bhutanese origin, crowded into my room. As there was no place to accommodate more people, some villagers thronging at the door of my room, tried to nudge their way in. Looking around, I decided that it would be best to step out of the room, so that we could all talk freely.

"Let us go outside," I said while moving out. They followed me like the disciplined soldiers of a military regiment.

Once we were on the lawns outside my room, they encircled me, and everyone started congratulating me, as though I was a hero coming back from battle front.

"All credit goes to you, Sir," smiled Ganesh Oraon, a skinny tribal, in his mid-forties. "You have changed my life and so many of ours. It's only after you came and started staying with us that everything began to change," he said. His weather-beaten face lit up with joy as he articulated his feelings.

"We have got this award because of you," Ram declared and everyone present there nodded. Ram was my co-coach of the football team. Passionate, highly energetic, Ram had a good physique.

"We owe a lot to you, Sir. You are God to us," said a visibly emotional Naresh, unable to control his tears. "Nobody knew about us before you came here. We were cut-off from the entire world," he continued, as tears rolled down his cheek. Choked with emotion, he could barely speak beyond those words.

"Sir, you will be surprised to know that the Prime Minister has especially praised the work of the self-help groups of our women weavers for producing high quality textiles," said Geeta, beaming with joy. A charming tribal woman in her mid-thirties, Geeta is diligent, and her leadership skills have helped her in managing the team of women weavers efficiently. It's under her leadership that the women of this village could change their fortune. "The

Prime Minister has asked all the women of our country to follow our example," she added with pride.

As she said these words, my mind went back to the day when I had met her for the first time, about nine years back. She had just lost her husband, an alcoholic, who had been suffering from cirrhosis of liver, and with him had died her hopes and dreams of a better life. Not only Geeta's, but the stories of all the women of the self-help groups of our organisation are more or less the same. They have all overcome one tragedy or the other to become stand on their own feet. They have, rather, sculpted their own destiny by sheer grit and a never-say-die attitude.

Long back, when I made this village my home, the women of this area had only one means of survival: collecting wood from the forest and selling it as firewood, either at the local market or using it as fuel wood in their homes. Then most of the villagers were very poor. To manage two meals a day for their families was a challenge in itself. Most of the villagers depended on the small plots of land they owned on which they cultivated mainly paddy and maize. But, that too, were often destroyed by the wild elephants.

I returned to the present when Magra, another tribal, bent down to touch my feet and started crying.

"What are you doing?" I shouted, feeling embarrassed. I get extremely uncomfortable when anyone touches my feet.

"You don't know what you have done for us," he continued, as I pulled him up and hugged him.

When I finally decided to settle down in this obscure village in Alipurduar district of West Bengal, near the Bhutan border, Magra's entire paddy field had been destroyed by a herd of rampaging elephants. He was at a loss, wondering how he would feed his family of eight throughout the year. He was not alone and most of the villagers who were farmers faced this problem year after year. They would cultivate paddy but the elephants would come out and destroy it.

He, along with other villagers, is now engaged in community farming, which has changed the fortune of the villagers. Those who did not own land would catch crabs or small fishes from the Buxa River or nearby ponds, as their livelihood. But today, almost all the villagers are cultivating the unused lands and sharing the profits among themselves.

"You inspired us to start community farming in the barren lands of our village. You taught us how to use technology in farming," said Bimal Bhujel, a fifty-year-old man of Nepali origin. A level-headed man, he commanded respect from everyone in the village by his sheer gravitas. That's why he had been elected as the Sarpanch of this village. "The idea of planting medicinal plants also worked wonders for us," added Bimal. His son Arjun had recently been awarded the best player in the Subrata Mukherjee Cup in New Delhi.

Amidst all these congratulatory words, I hardly had a chance to open my mouth. I was feeling a bit awkward.

"But all these are your efforts.... Why are you giving me credit for your achievements?" I asked in dismay.

"What are you saying, Sir? Earlier, we used to think that neither we nor our children have any capability or worth. But you made us believe in ourselves over the years. Did we ever think that one day almost twenty boys from our village would be selected in the Indian Army through its sports quota? Had any of us ever dreamt that our children would play for the academy teams of the big football clubs of India? Nobody gave us hope before you came here. But under your training our boys have won the Subrata Cup tournament thrice," said Ram.

Their words took me back to my initial days here, when these people were not ready to accept me as one of their own. It took time to earn their trust, as I was a total stranger without any identity. They still harbour a lot of questions about me, which I have no inclination of satisfying.

"I am very happy for all of you. This award is the result of all your hard work and dedication! I have just supported you," I said calmly. I really didn't feel that it was my success. It was their efforts.

I was extremely happy for these people, who had without any apparent reason made me a part of their community, their life. But these days, awards, adulation or the limelight seldom excite me. I feel comfortable in helping out the villagers, re-igniting their dreams and guiding them in improving the quality of their lives. If we can instil self-belief among the lowest strata of our country that they too can achieve great heights like the 'privileged' of the society, our country would never be the same again.

"Sir, without you we could not have done any of these things in life," said Geeta.

"We never knew that we could achieve so much," Bimal added.

As they were busy talking to each other and celebrating their success on the national stage and the rosy future of their children, the winter sun dipped further. Days in winter seem so short that once you are done with lunch, the day is almost over!

A cold breeze had started and I could see some people shivering.

"Go home now, all of you, and let's meet at 6 p.m. at our Buxa Development Society building," I told them.

"Okay Sir," said Bimal.

"We would discuss our future course of action then," I said, patting the shoulders of some of the villagers.

In twos and threes, the villagers made their way back to their homes in a celebratory mood. Their body language, as they were leaving, gave away their sense of pride and excitement. When you achieve something important, there is an automatic swagger to your walk. Every evening at 6 p.m. I went to Buxa Development Society (BDS) building, which we built after receiving a grant from the Central Government seven years ago. I teach the poor students of this village in the evening at the library, which is located inside the building. Among other subjects, I also teach them computers, and they have responded well to those classes, much to my delight. After that, I sit with our core team of BDS to plan the development activities of the village.

"Boys, there won't be any classes for you in the evening. Go home and study. We will meet tomorrow at the ground at 6 a.m. sharp," I told the football academy boys, who were listening to our conversation. They went away running, boisterously shouting 'hip hip hooray', again. Seeing them, I couldn't help but laughed out loud. Truly, these unblemished children have kept me alive!

Now alone, I sat down on the green lawn and took a deep breath. An eerie silence had fallen on the entire place after the departure of the villagers and my students. My eyes finally fell on the mountains that were now looking magnificent, with the slanted rays of the setting sun falling on them. The Buxa river, which is now nothing but a few dry streams in the vast river bed, flowed through the base of the mountains. This river wears an entirely different look in the rainy season when the region witnesses heavy rainfall.

The huge mountain range filled me up with the necessary strength to work silently and patiently, without any selfish motive, for these marginalised people, while the ever-flowing water of the river motivated me to carry on this tenuous task day in and day out. This is the reason I liked my small wooden room so much, as by simply sitting there I could see the mountains and the river; they made me more compassionate and selfless as the days go by.

Not only this village, but the Dooars and the Himalayan region of West Bengal, which is in the northern part of the state, comprising Darjeeling, Jalpaiguri, Alipurduar and Cooch Behar districts, are picturesque, full of natural beauty. With dense forests, three national parks (the Garumara National Park, Neora Valley National Park and the Jaldapara National Park), one tiger reserve (the Buxa Tiger Reserve), the Darjeeling hills and many small and big rivers – Teesta, Torsha and Jaldhaka are prominent among them – covering the region. This area is a heaven on earth. Since the weather remains pleasant throughout the year, this is a tourists' paradise. I have visited many places in several countries in my life, but this region has captivated my heart like one's first love.

A sudden freezing gust of wind brought me out of my reverie. The sun had completely disappeared; the whole area was under a blanket of darkness, and the mountains and the forests had been engulfed by the evening mist. The biting wind pierced through me as I was not wearing enough warm clothing, and it did get very cold here at this time of the year, in end-December. I hastened inside for my jacket and muffler.

An eerie silence had engulfed the area; the only sound I could hear was the chirping of some insects, especially, crickets. Our society building is just a ten-minute-walk from here. I took out a big torch, the likes of which you would find in almost every villager's home here. Though the village had electricity connections, not all the lanes had street lamps. Moreover, power cuts were rather frequent here at night.

One of the reasons why people use these big torches at night was the presence of dangerous animals and venomous snakes here. When elephants came out at night to plunder the paddy or maize fields, the villagers use the powerful torch lights to keep them away. At night, villagers sit on the bamboo machans, keeping a lookout for the herds of elephants. Though the name of this area was Buxa Tiger Reserve, the tiger was rarely seen these days. Sometimes, a leopard comes prowling into the locality, throwing the villagers into a tizzy.

Switching on the torch, I started walking towards our society building through the zigzag lanes of the village. The fireflies accompanying me lent a mysterious charm to my journey, as if guiding me to my destiny. The light of the torch seemed diffused due to the dense fog. The forest village generally remains quiet, but at night, when the stillness and the mist collude with the darkness, it seems magical. It is so quiet that I can hear the sound of my own footsteps and the sound of the dry leaves as they gently fall on the damp forest floor. I like the woody smell of the forest when the fog envelopes its every nook.

Villagers and our core committee members had already gathered at the BDS building, and were waiting for me. The Buxa Development Society is a non-governmental charitable organisation that we had formed nine years back. We have a core committee of five people, comprising Bimal Bhujel, 44; Ganesh Oraon, 49, who is the team leader of community farming, and heads the anti-alcohol campaign; Ram Lama, 30, looks after the facility work of the football academy; Geeta Oraon, 36, is the team leader of the SHG weaving team; and Chilam Dukpa, 34, looks after the project of protection and conservation of forest. I meet them every evening before dinner, but it is a special day today, so, around fifty villagers had gathered here for an informal celebratory meeting.

"Sir, we have been waiting for you intently," said Bimal.

Bimal then informed me that Bikash had called from Bengaluru to congratulate me. "He called you thrice in the evening, but you did not answer the phone," he growled disapprovingly.

"You know Bimal, I don't carry my mobile phone with me all the time. I have not touched my phone since the time you people came over this afternoon. It must be somewhere in the room. I don't have it with me even now," I said disarmingly.

"Even your football academy students, who live elsewhere have requested you several times to use a smartphone, so that they can send you their photos on WhatsApp or Facebook," continued Bimal. "I want to stay away from all these modern-day gadgets and the temptations of the social media. I have had enough of those in my life. I am very content as I am now, leading a joyful life with all of you. These gadgets prevent me from connecting with nature and with my surroundings. I don't want that to happen. Do you want me to spoil myself like the young kids of today, Bimal?" I asked jokingly.

As we were talking, Ganesh handed over a phone to me, "Sir, Bikash wants to talk to you."

Bikash congratulated me and told me how happy he was. He informed me that he had spoken with all our senior footballers, like Godai, Manoj, Nimesh, Pradip, Sanjay and they were all ecstatic after hearing the news.

Bikash, whose house was at the far end of the village, hence from the ground, also reminded me of those days when he had joined the football academy, but did not have a bicycle. He would walk all the way to the academy. I still can see the delight and joy in his eyes when I bought him a cycle when he was ten years old. Bikash, Godai, Manoj, Nimesh, Pradip, Sanjay and Kalpana are my first batch of footballers, when I started the academy years ago.

They were all rickety, shy kids of around 10-12 years old. Now, I myself marvel at the skilful footballers and smart young men and women that they have grown to be. I felt so proud of them. I could not believe my eyes when I watched the final match of Durand Cup on the TV, when both Bikash and Nimesh were playing together in the national team of the Indian Army. When I had started the football academy, I had never ever thought that one day two of my students would play in the prestigious Durand Cup.

When Kalpana returned from Malaysia after representing the Indian women's national team, it was such a joy for me that I still cannot erase it from my memory. Kalpana, a very poor Adivasi girl, who grew up practising with the boys, lost her mother just two months before the tournament. But she fought it out and even scored the winning goal for our country.

"All our senior players plan to attend the prize distribution ceremony in Delhi, which will be held after twenty days," Ram informed me.

"That is great news. It's time to plan how to attend the programme in Delhi," said Bimal.

"Who all are going next month to receive the award in Delhi?" I asked Bimal.

"None of us has ever visited Delhi," he reminded me.

"If the players are going, it won't be an issue for you people as they are now good enough to guide you around in Delhi," I reassured them.

"Won't you come with us to receive the award?" asked Ganesh.

"No. You know, I keep myself away from these award functions and all. I have always sent you or our senior footballers to receive all the awards that we have got so far."

"But this time you have to come with us. We won't listen to your excuses," Ram said stubbornly.

"And this time you have to purchase a good blazer. Ever since you came here, we have seen you wearing only a tracksuit," Geeta said, teasingly.

The other villagers who had been listening to our conversation joined in the loud laughter that followed Geeta's cheeky observation.

"I am a player and a coach, and I feel comfortable in only tracksuits these days. I am fed up with suits," I replied in a matter-of-fact voice amidst their laughter. "I would rather buy a blazer for each one of you for the award ceremony in Delhi. In January -- it will be very cold there," I said in a lighter vein.

Seeing that we were drifting away from the main topic, I said in a serious note, "It's true that we have done very well in the fields of employability and sports, as apart from football, our boys and girls are also doing well in athletics, but I want more students to study well and get good jobs in different sectors."

"Sir, this time we have to do something about the education of small children. You are teaching the senior boys in our free coaching centre, but we have to start something for the primary sections also," said Chilam, who generally is a person of few words.

"Very good idea," I said, encouraging her.

"Some village girls, who have passed their Class X or XII Boards, have expressed interest to voluntarily teach the small kids in our coaching centre," she informed. "That's wonderful. I have always wanted more people from this village to come forward and take on responsibilities. I am very happy that young people are coming forward to work for their own village," I replied.

The villagers nodded in agreement when I said this, but I knew that there were differences among the people here. There were people who didn't like it when the deserving received accolades and appreciation for their painstaking good work. But that's part of life. There will always be naysayers and doubting Thomases. I have seen this everywhere in life. Wherever I have worked, from high to low, from corporates to the education sector, some people are always there to come in the way of good work.

"If you want to achieve more in the coming days, you have to bury your differences. This award has shown us what we can achieve if we work together. We can achieve much more if we sort out the little differences that we still have among ourselves," I told them, despite realising that these obstacles are somehow needed to win bigger victories in life.

"You are absolutely right, Sir. Earlier, we had so many issues in our weaving team and it was adversely affecting our performances, but ever since we started working together, for each other, our productivity has increased manifold," pointed out Geeta. "You taught us about working for each other. Now, I don't work only for myself; I work for others, which in turn has given my work a whole new meaning," she added.

Sensing that this discussion will not end if we continue to talk, I bid them goodbye.

Everyone trooped out, except Ganesh, as I was supposed to go for dinner to his house, which I have been doing regularly since I started living here. I know Ganesh has a soft corner for me. I also love this very simple and honest tribal man. Though he speaks very little, he can point out if there is any mistake in the work of our Society.

"Ganesh, you know how satisfied I am today and how happy I am for you people," I said as we headed towards his home.

"Sir, I know. The way you have worked for us, talking to the government officers, the forest department people… it has resulted in today's achievement. Take the example of the library, which you almost established single-handedly. You purchased all the books with your own money and with the help of your friends. Now our children can read so many books and learn so many things."

"What will I do with my money, Ganesh? I want to spend whatever I earned earlier for these children. I want to stay in the village for the rest of my life ," for the first time today, after many years, I felt a bit emotional in front of another person, but I managed to conceal it, somehow.

"Sir, what about your own family members? Don't they want to meet you? Why don't you keep contact with them? Where do they live?" Ganesh threw a volley of questions at me, as we reached his home.

I smiled, "You will come to know all these things, Ganesh, at the right time. Come, let us go inside for our dinner."

Tonight, the temperature had dipped very low. Most of the villagers would be in bed by now. Ganesh, shivering in the cold, accompanied me as we walked through the forest lanes layered by heavy fog, with mist dropping from the leaves like raindrops. Like every day, Ganesh saw me to my room and then, went back. I asked him not to come with me tonight as it was very cold, but he refused to listen. As always....

I know that everyone in this village is curious about my past – whether I have a wife, a child or parents. What do they do? Where do they stay? Where did I live before I came here? Where did I work? They are also interested about my educational qualifications, my earlier professions and all the stuff. Even the players of our football academy or my students are pretty inquisitive about my past, which I have successfully concealed from them during the last ten years of my stay here.

Mornings in Buxa Forest are very serene as well as inspiring. I don't wish to miss these amazing mornings even for a single day. I have developed the habit of waking up early, savouring the morning and listening to the twittering of birds, the buzzing of insects and the clucking of hens. Despite the bone-chilling weather now, my morning routine remains unchanged. Once you have developed a good habit, you should not break it even for a single day. Though fog sits heavily over the entire area at this time of the year at 5 a.m., which is my wake-up time, in other seasons the region becomes clear as the sun comes out by this time. But today, I can't see my favourite mountains because of the dense fog.

For the first 5 to10 minutes after waking up, I generally gaze at the mountains and listen to the soothing sounds of nature. It helps me start the day on a positive note. After that, I meditate for about 45 minutes, which allows me to focus and makes me even more determined to work for the villagers and their children.

As our football field is very close to my room, I can generally see the players practising from my window. But today, the fog is like a thick wall, cloaking the football ground. I can sense their presence on the field by the sounds of the footballs being kicked around or from the dull thud as they land on the ground. I find this particular sound very stimulating. It can draw any football lover towards the ground. The severe cold has not deterred the boys from reaching the ground before the scheduled time; their energy is fascinating and wonderful. If you are deeply passionate about something, no one and nothing can prevent you from being successful in that particular field in your life.

As I put on my tracksuit, I could see the seniors joining them one by one. Shutting the door of my room, I headed to the ground through the biting cold. For the last ten years, irrespective of the season, this has been my morning routine.

As soon as I reached the ground, all the boys stopped whatever they were doing to greet me. I could feel the extra enthusiasm throbbing in each player that day. The senior players also looked more confident, excited and proud. They gathered around me, probably with the expectation of discussing our success.

"Now our next target is to produce some players who will play for the Indian national team," I told the seniors who now train the junior boys with my guidance.

"Sir, what about your other target?" Shibu asked.

"What?"

"You dream of building a women's team."

"Kalpana's experience has somewhat shattered my dream of a women's team. Despite representing the Indian national women's team, the government has not given her a job yet. She is getting depressed day by day," I told him.

Ever since she had come back to the village after her ankle operation, Kalpana had been rather wistful. I kept telling her not to lose hope. She had stopped practising after recuperating from her surgery, but I had convinced her to start the comeback trail. Still, I couldn't bear the helpless look on her face.

"Has Kalpana come today?" I asked Shibu.

Shibu pointed out where Kalpana was practising alone, on the other side of the ground.

These days Kalpana comes to the ground and does her physical exercise and skill-training practice on her own. She joins the team only when the seniors play practice matches. She is quite stressed as she is not financially well-off. She helps her father – who drank hadiya (a type of rice beer) and was unwell most of the time – in running a small tea shop in the village and doing her home chores and what not. I really feel bad for this talented hard-working girl.

I asked Shibu to call Kalpana. In her early twenties, Kalpana has a strong physique and a good height for an Indian woman. She stood in front of me. There was innocence on her face and tenderness in her eyes. Though she is a very shy and an introvert girl, yet it's a different Kalpana altogether when she touches the football. Anyone who saw her on the ground was impressed by her football skills.

"How is your father now?" I asked her.

"Not very well, Sir. You know he has asthma, which is troubling him these days."

"Ask him to stop drinking hadiya."

"I keep telling him but he hardly heeds my words," Kalpana replied, with an obvious tinge of frustration in her voice.

"Have you talked to your national team coach Sunita Ma'am recently?"

"No, Sir."

I realised that she hardly has any contact with the national team.

"Keep in touch with your coach and teammates. Otherwise, it will be very difficult to get back into the team."

She listened, but had a faraway look in her eyes.

"Don't lose hope, Kalpana. You need to learn how to tackle failures. I myself have faced enormous setbacks in life, as I didn't know how to handle failures. Life is all about transformation, Kalpana. You can also transform your life from here on. You need to have the mental strength," I tried to inspire her.

Kalpana just looked at me and nodded as if she understood what I was saying.

"You have made history by playing for the national team from this obscure village. You are already an inspiration for many," I tried to reignite the fire in her. "You will regret in future, if you quit at this stage," I added with a smile.

When I started the first batch, I used to train everyone, but now the number of students has grown in our football academy. Some seniors have completed the C and D level coaching license courses and they are now training the junior boys. These days I only train the senior boys in the team. Since all the boys study in the Buxa High School, the school gets to enjoy name and fame, even though it does not have any role, apart from providing us the school ground where we practise every day.

After our practice, I asked the senior team members and the two coaches to take all the boys to a corner of the ground and sit together.

As all the boys sat down, I asked Shibu whether all the boys knew about our award.

Everyone nodded in agreement. Then he asked me to say something to them.

"As you all know about our success, I want you to continue to work hard and realise your dreams. I have always believed that our boys and girls have all the skills to do well in sports. Keeping this in mind, we started this academy with only ten boys. Earlier, nobody believed in us, but we have proved everyone wrong. I can see future Indian players from this group."

As I finish my sentence, Shibu shouts, "Hum kissi se…"

And the boys thundered back, breaking the silence of this forest, "Kam nahi!"

I had asked them to chant this slogan, which roughly meant, 'we are as good as anyone', every day before and after practice.

Yes, these boys and girls are inferior to none. They have the potential to become the best.

Actually, I have done only one thing in the last ten years. I have successfully instilled the self-belief in these kids that they can beat any team and this has worked like an elixir for them.

I asked the boys to sing the national anthem and leave for the day.

Among the coaches and the seniors, Shibu was my closest. I sat down with him on the ground after the boys left. Shibu asked me the same question that he often did.

"Sir, which team did you represent in your younger days?"

I know that all those who are close to me have many questions about my past. There's no harm in telling my story to them, but I don't want to talk about those dark days any more. It seems that this Siddhartha Lahiri is different from the Siddhartha Lahiri of the past. Sometimes, I am not able to match the two characters which now look diametrically opposite to each other.

As I strolled back to my room from the ground, the winter sun had dispersed some mist that was there in the morning.

As I moved closer, I could see Ranjit standing outside my room. Ranjit, a frail man in his mid-thirties, with average height and small eyes, was a very dedicated and hard-working reporter of one of the bestselling newspapers of West Bengal. At first sight, one may not take him seriously, but he has been a star reporter of not only this region, but of the entire state. Some of his stories have become so famous that he has been awarded many times by different organisations in Kolkata. Ranjit often came to me to gather information about the activities of our Society, community farming, football academy and the women weavers' self-help groups. It's due to his regular reporting on our projects that people have gradually come to know about this village.

"Congratulations, Sir," Ranjit greeted me with a warm smile.

"Congratulations to you, Ranjit."

"Why are you congratulating me, Sir?"

"It's for your effort that this village has been recognised by the Government of India."

"No, Sir, without you it would not have been possible," said Ranjit, countering me.

"Oh, please, Ranjit..." I protested but Ranjit cut me short.

"Sir, tell me one thing, how do you keep yourself so fit even at this age?" Ranjit suddenly asked me, as if he was seeing me for the first time. "With your good height, you look like a superstar!" he said with an impish grin.

"Because I lead a very dull and boring life," I smiled back. "I have no ambition, nothing to get in life. I stay here amidst nature with all these villagers."

"I have been working as a reporter for the last 15 years, Sir. I have developed the art of identifying people very easily," announced Ranjit solemnly.

"So, what's your take on me?" I asked him with a grin.

"What I have realised by talking to you and seeing your activities in the last 6-7 years or so is that you have a brilliant past," he said in the confident voice of a good reporter. "I always talk about you. Your eyes tell a lot about you. If anyone wants to know the definition of a truly happy person, he should meet you and take your recipe of how to stay happy and peaceful in life," said Ranjit with a sense of assuredness, as if he knew all about my past.

“Since I love to soak in the winter sun, I suggest that we sit on the lawn outside my room.”

“Sir, my editor in Kolkata has asked me to do a feature story on your life,” Ranjit said after we sat down, facing each other.

“But how does he know about me?” I asked, surprised, shrugging.

“He was asking me about the person who was behind the huge success of this tribal village. I could not hide your identity from him anymore, as he was sure that a very talented person is involved here. Till now, you have never allowed me to write about you in the newspaper. I have always highlighted the activities of the villagers, but this time my editor wants me to do a story on you. I can’t avoid his request. It will be published in our Sunday edition in the ‘Silent Influencers’ series. Now, you have to tell me about yourself, before you came to this village, because I know your story after you settled here.”

I tried to dodge him again.

I asked him, “Have you had breakfast, Ranjit? You have come so early today. Let’s go inside and have breakfast together. Let’s see what Fulmani has sent for me. We will share; she is extremely generous.”

But Ranjit was determined, “Sir, I have had my breakfast. You have been avoiding this for the last 5 to 6 years, since I started talking to you and covering the news of this village. My job is at stake this time. My editor has given me an ultimatum that this time I have to do the full story on your life. I won’t leave until you tell me!”

Ranjit had a special kind of affection for me and this village. Actually, he has been a faithful companion in the journey of success of this village, and lately, it has become difficult for me to turn down his request. He has done a lot for us. The beseeching look he now gave me 'sealed the deal' and more so, since his job was at stake, I was further obliged. Sighing, I gave in and agreed to tell him about my life. Of the days when I, like many youngsters, was convinced that the world was made just for me; of days of dejection, elation, fury, jealousy; and, dare I use the word, 'enlightenment'? At times we all need to be mentally very tough to win our battles against our inner demons. These are our own battles against us. Every one of us has to fight this crucial battle at some point in time. All alone. In one form or the other. This is a very lonely battle, never glorified in history books. But at some critical juncture of our lives, this battle is as important as anything because it is all about conquering this very personal battle.

I looked up at the mountains, seeking to gather the much-needed strength to revisit those grim days, which I had tried to leave behind unsuccessfully. I started unwrapping the life of Siddhartha Lahiri – of that Siddhartha Lahiri who had lived a completely different life before he decided to settle down in this obscure village, far from the so called 'madding crowd'.

****

2

It was almost 3 a.m. I couldn't close my eyes even for a moment. I had studied till 1 a.m. for the maths class test the next day. Mathematics has always been my favourite subject, along with the science subjects. Rathin Sir, our maths teacher in Siliguri Boys' High School, had taken me under his wings and mentored me. He was my father's classmate and a close friend of his. He had become more vigilant ever since I was promoted to Class IX a few months back.

He, along with my parents, had been telling me that that year and the year after were very crucial for me, if I wanted to fare well in the Class X Board examinations and become successful in life.

However, at the age of 15, I hardly understood the true meaning of 'success'. Probably neither my parents nor Rathin Sir realised the actual meaning of that word, though they kept repeating ad nauseam, it like a child who has just learnt to say 'Baba' or 'Ma'. For that matter, how many of us know the true meaning of success?

But in those wee hours of the night, I could hardly be bothered about my class test or my upcoming Board examinations, or the elusive idea of success or failure in life. Actually, two things had taken away my sleep that night. First, the agony of my favourite team's shocking defeat in the opening match of the on-going 1990 FIFA World Cup that particular night, which I had watched on TV a few hours back, and was still in shock. I was heartbroken. The humiliation of defending champion Argentina at the hands of the newcomer Cameroon was unbelievable.

I would have been happy if it had been any other team than Argentina in that situation, as I have always had a soft corner for the underdog teams and unheard-of heroes, when they played against strong, established teams. Seeing the rise of a dark horse and the birth of a new hero never failed to give me goose bumps. I always cherished those encounters where David beat Goliath, as I drew immense inspiration from those situations. In that sense, I should have been happier with the way Cameroon played, but I was completely devastated as it had happened at the expense of my idol, Maradona, and his much-celebrated team.

I had been waiting for this World Cup ever so eagerly as the last World Cup, in 1986, had ended with Maradona winning the cup 'single-handed' for his team. It left an indelible impression on my 11-year-old mind in such a way that I could not think of playing any other sports except football.

Once the match ended around 11 p.m., my father started shouting at me for being addicted to football and not giving enough attention to my studies. In spite of being upset, and after an exchange of some heated words with Baba, I got down to studying for the maths test.

The other reason which had kept me very tense that night was my sore ankle. I had hurt my ankle in the semi-final match against Nadia, in Krishnanagar, a week ago. Since that day, I had been religiously applying ointments and doing whatever my football coach had advised. But it still hurt, and the next day was the final match of the sub-junior state-level tournament of our district team,

Darjeeling, against Howrah. The match would take place at the Kanchenjunga Stadium in my hometown, Siliguri, which is the biggest town in northern part of West Bengal, although it is a sub-division under Darjeeling district. Located strategically, Siliguri is the gateway to Darjeeling, Sikkim and the entire north-eastern region… even Bhutan.

A beautiful town situated at the foothills of the Himalayas and surrounded by forests and tea gardens, Siliguri has never failed to mesmerise me since my childhood. Although it has become very congested these days, it was not so, thirty years back. It was a very serene and peaceful place with pleasant, temperate weather throughout the year. Another attraction of the town has always been sports. Though table tennis is the main sport for which the city is basically known, the popularity of football and cricket was always there.

I was worried, as my ankle injury was yet to heal properly; true, it was better than before, but it still hurt. If I couldn't take part in the final match, my dream of playing in the state team would be shattered as we had been told that the performance of that match would be keenly observed by the state selectors.

……………………

"Siddhartha, get up! It's already 8.30," I could hear my father shouting and knocking on the door of my bedroom.

But I didn't feel like waking up. I felt groggy and woozy from lack of sleep; I did not know when I had finally fallen asleep last night.

Baba knocked on the door again. And this time it was even harder.

Somehow, I got up hurriedly and opened the door. But no sooner had I put my right foot on the floor, I felt the pain once again in my ankle. Though it's not my natural foot, as my stronger leg while playing football was my left leg - just like my hero Maradona - I doubted if I would recover in time for the match, which was scheduled at 3 p.m. in the afternoon.

"Is this the time to get up?" Baba screamed angrily, standing just outside my bedroom.

I kept mum, looking down.

"Rathin called me in the morning," he announced, sounding annoyed.

"What did Sir say?" I asked, trying to understand the subject of their discussion, but I was sure he had complained against me for my lack of focus on studies.

"Your Sir was praising you," he said sarcastically, and went off on his customary, everyday trip to the morning bazaar to buy fish and vegetables.

Going to the fish and vegetable market every morning is a typical Bengali thing - if not a favourite morning ritual. Bengalis believe in buying and consuming fresh fish and a variety of fresh vegetables every day; it is as important as anything else in their lives.

When I was getting ready to sit down for my studies, my mother came in with a cup of tea.

"I hope you remember you have a maths test today," she told me, placing the cup on my table.

It was evident from her face and voice that she too was upset with me. My mother, who was an English teacher in a government high school, was a thin, shy and soft-spoken lady, who generally protected me from my father's ire, but being a teacher, she had also never liked my lackadaisical approach to studies.

"Yes, I know," I replied, testily. "What exactly did Rathin Sir tell Baba?"

"I don't know but he must have complained about you. I didn't ask your Baba as the mornings are so rushed with so much household work," Ma replied. "I have to reach school on time, you know.

"Get ready and reach school on time because you don't have much time left to study now. You should have woken up earlier. And you must study consistently throughout the year," she told me in a tone which was a combination of a little anger and frustration, not typical of my mother.

I could easily understand things were not going in my favour. I drank the tea as quickly as possible. As I tried to reach out to the book shelves to take out my maths book and copy, I felt the same pain in my ankle again. Every time I felt the pain, I saw my dream crumbling down, piece by piece.

Brooding, I again applied some ointment on my sore ankle. Despite my final match in the afternoon, I knew I had to do well in the class test that day to keep things under control. Otherwise, I would not be able to convince my parents and Rathin Sir that football was not hampering my studies. If I needed to realise my dream of playing for the country, I had to do well in studies as well. Though it sometimes seemed difficult to manage both at the same time, I did not have an option.

I went through some chapters of the maths syllabus for the class test. As I got ready hastily, it seemed to me that the pain had reduced considerably by then. I carried my football kit with me and cycled to school. I would go directly to the stadium from school as they were just half a kilometre apart.

When I reached the school, the prayer meeting had already started. I quickly stood behind the last student in the prayer line, but Rathin Sir saw me.

After the prayers, Sushanta, who was my classmate and also my teammate in the Darjeeling sub-junior district team as well as in the school team, walked up to me.

"How is your injury now?" he asked anxiously.

"It's getting better."

"Will you be able to play in today's match?"

"Don't know, Mayna Sir will decide."

Sushanta, a natural athlete and a very agile boy of 15, played as a forward with me in our team. Like me, he too was a very good striker and people spoke very highly of both of us. We scored many a goal together for our district, as well as the school team; sometimes, he scored and I assisted and at other times, it was the other way round. Opposition teams had a tough time tackling both of us together. Everybody praised our understanding on the field as we liked to hunt in pairs. The secret to our understanding on the field was our deep bonding outside the ground. We both were very good friends and would do anything for each other. But Mayna Sir, our district team's coach, had a softer corner for me, as he believed that with my good height and speed, I had a very bright future ahead.

"Sir will definitely keep you in the team," Sushanta said innocently.

I knew he wanted me on the football field as badly as I wanted to play; his success and that of the team depended on our partnership. If I could not play, his game would not peak, and that would ultimately affect our team's overall performance. It was the most important match for both of us and for our team.

"Let's see," I told him as I was really not sure about my participation in the match.

"I know he will keep you in the team," Sushanta insisted, which gave me hope against hope.

"Let's go to class. Our first period will start soon."

"Is it English class?" asked Sushanta, who came from a humble background and somehow, was not very good in studies.

Though his modest background was writ large on his face and untidy body language, I was fond of Sushanta, not only because he was a very good player and my striking partner in the match, but also because he was a good human being. I wanted him to succeed both in football and in life. He badly needed that to change his fortune and that of his family.

Our first class was with Saibal Sir, who taught us English language. He was a short, dark-complexioned, bulky man in his mid-fifties and notorious for his unrelenting strictness. Every day, someone or the other would be caned by him, which he carried all the time in the school. In those days, many teachers thought that they could turn any bad student into a good one through corporal punishment. However, teachers of that era could have positively changed the future of many students by being a little friendly with them, by believing in their ability and dealing sympathetically with them, or, perhaps, listening to their problems patiently and sincerely.

I, along with other good students in the class such as Arka, Rahul and Sourav, were in Saibal Sir's good books, because he would always get correct answers from us. Rather, he would hardly ask us questions knowing fully well that we would not contribute to his daily mission of caning students, for which he would come to school every day with full preparation, mental and otherwise.

Some backbenchers like Animesh, Akhil and others faced his wrath almost every alternate day. Sushanta also had a very tough time in his class, although other teachers were fond of Sushanta as he earned many laurels for the school team in football. They generally did not trouble him much in the class, despite his poor academic performance, but Saibal Sir would never give him any breathing space because for him, the only thing that mattered in life was learning the rules of English grammar, correctly.

That day was not an exception either. Saibal Sir asked Sushanta something about English grammar, and, like every day, he failed to answer. Sir beat him with his stick so harshly that he broke down in class, in front of us. I felt terribly bad and angry with Saibal Sir; I wanted to plead with him since Sushanta was going to play a very important match of his life in a few hours' time. But I did not have the courage, and neither did any of my classmates. After the class, I went to Sushanta and made him understand that he needed to be mentally fit and concentrate on the final match only.

"Don't be upset, Sushanta. You have to be strong today. It's a very important match for all of us," I tried to console him.

"I can't play today," Sushanta said, wiping off his tears.

"Are you mad? Today is our final match. I am still uncertain. You have to play well today and help us win the trophy," I tried to inspire him though deep down I was also in pain seeing him in tears.

"You know my father wants me to quit studies as well as football. He wants me to run the paan (betel) shop, so that he can work as a daily wage labourer and we can jointly earn more for our family. His income from the paan shop is not enough to run a family of six," Sushanta told me, in a tearful voice.

"You are a very good player. You can easily reach the top level," I continued counselling him, as I sincerely believed in this talented footballer.

"I know. I also dream of becoming a footballer. But I don't get support from my family," he lamented.

"I don't get any support from my family either. You know how my parents are where football is concerned."

"But at least your parents hold government jobs and you are also good in studies. If you can't become a footballer, you will, at least, get a decent job."

"That's true, but you know football is everything to me. I can't live without football for a single day. My entire life revolves around this sport only."

"I know that, but your situation and mine are poles apart."

Probably Sushanta was right. I knew it was futile to argue with him that day. He was already dejected. So, I tried to change the topic and asked, "Did you watch Argentina's match last night?"

"No. I don't have TV at home," he replied in an irritated tone.

I was about to say something when Rathin Sir entered our classroom. Rathin Sir, a good-looking man in his early fifties with an average height and fair complexion, was also strict but would never beat anyone. He was a teacher for good students only. He loved good students like me and proudly spoke about those who would score good marks in the Boards, including his own son. Perhaps knowing that it was a useless exercise, he would hardly interact with the weaker students in his class. So, the Sushantas and Animeshes had no problem in his class.

I am not saying that all our teachers were unsympathetic towards the students. There were, in fact, some wonderful teachers who would do everything for their students.

Immediately after taking his seat, sitting upright, Rathin Sir, in his high-pitched voice, asked me to stand up.

"Why were you late today?"

I kept quiet.

"Meet me after the class," he commanded sternly.

He then handed each of us a hand-written paper of five sums of total 25 marks. I submitted the papers along with all the students after 20 minutes.

While leaving the class, he reminded me to meet him in the teachers' room during the recess.

We had two more classes before recess, but I could not wait for the classes to get over for the day as it was becoming difficult to concentrate on studies. My entire focus was on the match which would start in a few hours' time.

I saw Sushanta sitting quietly on the last bench, perhaps feeling a little better by then.

I asked Sushanta to leave school during the recess and advised him to inform Mayna Sir that I would be at the ground after 15-20 minutes. I had to meet Rathin Sir, which I could not avoid though this was the last thing I wanted to do before the match. I was tense that if Sir continued to talk for more than 15 minutes, I would be in trouble.

As I entered the teachers' room, I found Rathin Sir sitting at the far corner, checking the test answer sheets. I went to him and stood in front of him. He fished out my maths answer sheet and handed it to me. I had made two silly mistakes. All the other bright students had answered correctly and got full marks. I was the only exception.

"Look at what you have done," he said, incensed.

I kept quiet. I stared at it very closely. I found he had given zeros in two places. But my mind was so engrossed in the final match that the zeros suddenly turned into two footballs in front of me! I tried to pretend as if I was repentant, but deep down I knew that my mind was not in studies that day.

"Sorry, Sir," I mumbled.

"Siddhartha, you are a very good student. Now you are in Class IX. Next year is your Board exams," Rathin Sir began, slightly frowning. "You know every year students from our school make it to the top ten. I know that if you study well, you can be one of them. Your father, Subhash, is an executive engineer with PWD. He was also a very good student. Your mother is a reputed teacher in Siliguri. And you are their only child. But you are spoiling your life by playing football and not concentrating enough on your studies," he told me, partly scolding and partly cajoling. "Siddhartha, nothing succeeds like success. This world only gives respect to those who are successful and earn a lot of money. You won't get that by playing football."

I wanted to leave as my heart had already started pounding in excitement for the final match which would start in an hour. I looked at the old, round, big clock which was hanging on the teachers' room wall and saw it was already 2 p.m., which was our reporting time at the ground.

"I promise you, Sir, I will concentrate on my studies from now on," I knew that if I argued, I would be late. This was the best thing to do as I had to reach the ground as soon as possible. Otherwise, I would get into trouble.

Rathin Sir, however, was in no mood to relent that day, but by then I was unable to register what all he was lecturing on. In fact, I could only see his lips moving angrily. He continued to tell me something but I was already on my way out as I could not hang around anymore, even for a second.

....

Kanchenjunga Stadium was about half a kilometre away from school. I started running through the crowded roads, forgetting that I had brought my cycle to school that day. While running to the stadium, I once again felt the pain in my right ankle which I had somehow forgotten while in school.

I was ten minutes late when I burst into the ground. Mayna Sir was anxiously waiting for me as without assessing my injury he would not be able select the final 11.

"How is your injury?" he asked me, looking visibly tense.

"Better, Sir," I replied, panting heavily. "A lot better. I have a slight pain in my ankle, but I will be able to play full time," I added, trying to convince him.

As all the boys were almost ready for warm-ups, Sir asked me to hurry up and get ready.

I quickly put on my boots and the team jersey.

Normally, with persistent rain, which cools down the weather even in summer, the month of June in Siliguri generally witnesses a stable climate. However, it was very hot that day with the summer sun blazing down really hard.

As we started our warm-ups and stretching exercises, I felt the pain again. I realised that I was really not hundred per cent match fit. But I was desperate to play as the state selectors were going to be present at the field and they would be finalising the sub-junior state team after this match. Those selected would get the opportunity to represent the state team to play in the national tournament, which will be held in Goa in September.

I could sense Mayna Sir observing me closely. After 15 minutes of warm-up exercises with the team, Sir drew me aside and again questioned me how I was feeling.

"I am fine, Sir."

"But I am not convinced," he told me, looking straight into my eyes, as he was almost my height.

As we were talking, there was an announcement requesting both the teams to submit the final 11 to the match officials. Time was running out. So was Mayna Sir's patience.

"Siddhartha, we don't have much time left. Be honest with yourself and with the team. I have to submit the team list and select the final 11 as soon as possible. I can't be late even for a minute. From what I could see during the warm-ups, you were limping a bit."

Being an experienced coach, he could make out that I was not fit enough for the full 90 minutes of play.

"Don't let your team down in the final," he told me, a hint of irritation in his voice, as he looked at his watch; just 15 minutes were left for the match to start. The spectators were pouring into the stadium.

I finally admitted that I was not ready for the full match as I had felt slight pain while running to the stadium.

Since he was very fit and lithe, even at fifty, Mayna Sir sprinted across the ground to the other support staff of our team to make the team list. He put me in the reserve bench.

I was out of the playing XI. I was crushed. My mind went back to the semi-final match of the on-going tournament. After that match, Sushanta and I were treated like heroes for scoring three goals between us. Sushanta had scored the first two goals and I had scored the final one. So, my expectation from this match was higher. I had spent many a sleepless night thinking about this match and dreaming of scoring the match-winning goal to win the trophy for my team.

I suddenly felt I had no strength in me to even walk out of the ground. As I slowly moved towards the team tent, I could hear some of my friends, unaware of my non-participation, shouting at me from the gallery, "We want goals from you today!"

I was about to break down. I felt like crying. When I reached the team tent, all the boys came running out of the ground after warm-ups. Only the final XI would now enter the ground for the final showdown of the tournament. For the first time in the whole tournament, in which we had remained undefeated, I would not be a part of the first XI. I wished good luck to Sushanta and the boys.

Dejected, I sat on the bench with the other extra players and our support staff to watch the match. Mayna Sir would never sit. He would stand near the side lines and keep shouting at the players – this was his habit during a match.

The referee blew the whistle indicating the commencement of the match. Howrah started very well. But we pegged things back after 15 minutes or so. We had even created some chances. Sushanta missed a sitter just before the half-time break. It was an evenly fought first 45 minutes as both teams played well and did not allow their opponents to gain any foothold. It was 0-0 at half-time.

During the break, Mayna Sir explained to the boys the mistakes they had committed in the first-half. Since most of the opposition attacks were coming from the left-wing, he asked our right-back and right-winger to be very alert. He also gave Sushanta an earful for missing an easy opportunity.

I tried to cheer up Sushanta.

"Don't worry, you will definitely score a goal in the second half," I said while patting his back.

"Actually, I am missing you. Atul and my combination is not working on the field." Atul was playing as a forward in my place.

Sir made two changes before the team entered the field for the second-half. He replaced our right-back Madhu, as he was not able to control their left-winger, and also midfielder Sudhan, for his inability to supply the ball more often to our forwards.

The Howrah boys started the second-half superbly, creating a lot of chances. Our players, especially the defenders, looked absolutely clueless. Within 15 minutes, our goalkeeper Binod had to make three very good saves, which would have been certain goals otherwise.

In the first-half, they were attacking mostly from the left-wings, but in the second-half, their attacks were coming from all corners. After 25 minutes or so into the half-time, it was fairly certain that they would get a goal any time. Finally, we gave in and conceded a goal at 75th minute of the match. We were one goal down with just 15 minutes of play left.

Mayna Sir looked very upset and was livid with all the players. He had already made two changes. Only one more change would be possible now.

Sir looked at me and instructed, "Get ready."

He knew I was his last trump card. I sprang up as if I was only waiting for his instruction.

"Don't worry, Sir. I will score," I said confidently.

I completely forgot the pain in my right ankle. I had waited for this opportunity. I wanted to play in the final. I wanted to score. I wanted to lift the trophy.

"Best of luck," Sir told me as he asked the linesman to indicate the change, I was to replace Atul.

As I entered the field, I could hear a roar from the gallery, which was silent after we conceded the goal. Some people started shouting my name. I felt a sudden adrenaline rush in me. Sushanta also looked confident after I took the field. I asked the boys to go for the counter-attacks.

Our left-half Sanjay forwarded the ball to me, which I received in the middle of the ground and passed it to Sushanta, who returned it to me as I ran swiftly towards their penalty box. I dodged their right-half and then centre-half to send the ball to the net.

It was an equaliser.

Just 5 minutes were left for the final whistle.

All the boys were hugging each other and celebrating.

I could see Mayna Sir jumping in excitement. We came to huddle after this goal. I told everyone that the momentum was with us now. We must score one more goal in the remaining time.

When play resumed, I could see the body language of our team had changed dramatically while the Howrah team suddenly looked very down. Before our goal, they had thought they would be able to hold on to the lead and win the match. A kind of complacency had already crept into them.

As soon as the match started again, I crossed one ball from the left-wing to Sushanta who, with his speed and agility, dodged their centre-half, but the centre-half, unable to control him, chased Sushanta from behind and tackled him in the penalty box. Sushanta collapsed in a heap and there was no denying that he was in intense pain. It was a clear-cut foul. The referee awarded us a penalty kick.

The way I was feeling right then, I asked everybody to let me take the penalty kick. Just a minute left. If I could score, we would be state champions for the first time and would make history. What if I missed? Probably, I would never ever be able to forgive myself for letting my team down.

But I kept aside all the negative thoughts. As I kicked the ball with full force with my left foot, the ball hit the right-hand corner of the net. Their goalkeeper had no option but to helplessly watch the ball flying over his head to the net. The crowd roared in joy. That was it. We had done it. I had realised my dream. Everyone came and hugged me. I fell on the ground as everyone tried to pat me, congratulate and hug me.

When the referee declared that the match was officially over after a few seconds, we started jumping in celebration.

Mayna Sir came running in and hugged me.

"Siddhartha, it's because of you that we could become the state champion," said Mayna Sir, beaming with joy. "I could not realise this dream in my life as a player. But you have given me this joy today," he could not control himself as he said those words. For the first time, I saw this 6 ft-tall, strong man crying like a baby. "I am really proud of you all," he said, his lips trembling with emotion.

"Sir, Sushanta also played very well," I said while holding his hand.

"Yes, Sushanta played very well. Like you, Sushanta has a very bright future, too," Sir declared proudly.

When we were lifting the trophy, people were chanting only my name. I was adjudged man of the match. I didn't know what happened in the last 30 minutes or so. Everything seemed like a dream. I felt as if I were Maradona of the 1986 World Cup final when we lifted the trophy. I have never felt so jubilant before. I can't remember what was happening around me that evening as everything looked surreal.

To be honest, I have never felt so ecstatic in my life after that. That particular moment has still remained as the best moment of my life.

....

When I woke up the next morning, it was already 10.30 a.m. I had overslept and missed school. As it was raining in the morning, the weather had cooled down considerably and it was ideal for sound sleep. That's the typical Siliguri summer weather. If the temperature soared one day, you can rest assured that it would rain heavily the next day. I was tired. I was feeling very lazy too, and did not want to leave my bed. I realised that both my parents were already at their respective workplaces. In all likelihood, they were so upset with me that they deliberately did not bother to wake me up.

Like the night before, last night, too, I had slept very late. Some nights you can't sleep and some nights you don't want to. That's probably the difference between pain and pleasure. While the night before last I could not sleep because of agony, last night I did not want to sleep as I was revisiting and cherishing those moments of glory in the final match. It somehow compensated for my sadness of Argentina's defeat.

Last evening when I had returned home jubilant from the ground, with my 'Man of the Match' trophy, my parents did not talk to me. They saw me carrying the trophy but did not deign to ask me about it. Rather, the atmosphere at my home was as if they were in mourning!

I had entered my bedroom and kept revisiting the match as I could not come out of the hangover of the dramatic final match of that day. Ma indifferently called me for dinner around 10 p.m. At the dinner table too, my parents maintained their freezing silence. I had felt like sharing my joy with them, telling them about my extraordinary performance despite my injury, but had not been able to muster courage after seeing their apathetic and sullen faces.

I was very exhausted throughout the day, and the pain in my ankle was back. In the excitement of the match, I hadn't realised that the old injury had got aggravated. Although Mayna Sir had given us a break for the day, I wanted to go to the ground and meet Sir and all the players. But I didn't dare to, scared of parental wrath. If they didn't find me at home on their return from work, things might take a turn for the worse.

I dozed off again after my lunch. When I woke up, it was dark outside. It was still raining but the intensity had drastically weakened. It was, merely, a drizzle by then.

My fascination with mountains is perhaps equalled by a similar emotion for the rain. I found rainfall extremely charming when I was young. In fact, I still miss those days when we lived in a tin-roofed house, because I liked the sweet pattering sound of the raindrops falling on the tin roof. I liked to play football in the rain too. We had a lot of fun on the ground when it rained. The slippery ground made it ideal for us to slide, which was rather enjoyable during our practice sessions.

Sitting in my bedroom, I could understand that both my parents were back. When I was getting ready for my studies in the evening, I heard Baba welcoming someone into the house. I realised that Rathin Sir had come. Baba sat with him and started discussing about me. Ma came to my room after ten minutes or so and asked me to go to the drawing room where they were sitting. I went to the room and greeted Sir.

"What do you want to do in life?" Baba asked me in a disgusted voice.

I was fairly certain Rathin Sir must have told Baba about the class test by then.

"I want to be a footballer," I replied, showing some courage. Probably my confidence had gone up after the final match. Till then I had never disclosed my ambition in front of him or, rather, did not have the guts to declare my plans to him.

"Don't you want to become 'successful' in life? How much money will you earn by playing football?" Baba asked, as if money was the only yardstick to measure success.

"I don't know, but I like to play football and want to make a career out of it," I told Baba in a resolute voice.

"Siddhartha, you are too young to choose your career. When you grow up, you will regret your decision," Rathin Sir tried to convince me.

"Learn from Rathin's son, Amit. He is studying engineering at IIT, Kharagpur. He is planning to go to the USA for further studies and settle there," Baba told me, demonstrating how feeble my dream was in comparison with Amit da's.

I kept looking at the floor and did not say anything.

"I never have to tell anything to my son. He is very serious in his studies. He has set a goal for himself to settle in the US after completing his BE," Rathin Sir said proudly.

"And you? Look at your friends, Sushanta... his father runs a paan stall. These days I don't see you with Sourav, Rahul, Jayanta or Arka," my father said sarcastically.

Taking a cue from my father, Rathin Sir said, "That's very important in life. You should choose your friends according to your background and status."

"Sushanta is a very good footballer. Despite his poverty, he is playing football and continuing his studies," I tried to defend my friendship with Sushanta.

"And that man, what's his name? Mayna... he is a total failure in life. How would he teach you to be successful in life?" my father said mockingly.

My father knew Mayna Sir when we stayed in a rented house in the same locality as Mayna Sir.

"Please don't say bad things about Mayna Sir. He is my teacher. He loves me a lot," I protested firmly.

"Siddhartha, remember your background. Don't spoil your life. Subhash only wants you to succeed in life. He is saying these things for your betterment only," Rathin Sir tried to bring some sanity into the conversation.

"He won't understand, Rathin. He is totally spoilt by mixing with these lower-class children on the football ground."

I could not take it anymore. I rushed back to my room and bolted the door from inside. I could hear my father bellowing and Rathin Sir trying to pacify Baba.

Sometime later, I realised Rathin Sir had left. The intensity of the rain had picked up once again. I started studying. At night we had a quiet dinner. I was in no mood to talk to anyone. I was very upset with Baba for his harsh and demeaning words towards Sushanta and Mayna Sir and for making a mockery of my dream of becoming a footballer.

....

It was the 8th of July. I was very excited as I had been waiting for this particular day for a month. I would watch my favourite team and my hero in action tonight in the World Cup final, the biggest sporting extravaganza on earth.

On 8th of June, exactly thirty days ago, Cameroon's unexpected victory over Argentina in the opening match of this on-going World Cup had shaken – or roused – football fans across the world. Despite their ordinary performance, the Argentinean side led by the charismatic Diego Maradona had somehow struggled into the final.

My inter-district sub-junior final match had taken place the next day, on 9th of June. Even after 29 days, I was yet to come out of the hangover of that trophy-winning match. In the meantime, I had made a truce of sorts with Baba, who had allowed me to go to football practice every day in exchange of my assurance to study with an extra dose of seriousness. He had also let me watch the World Cup matches on TV – only those involving Argentina. I kept my promise and he did not disturb me either.

It was a re-match of the previous World Cup final. Defending champion Argentina were up against the erstwhile runner-up West Germany. To my utter surprise, Baba declared in the morning that he would watch the final match with me on TV.

He was also a football fan but, unlike me, he was a staunch Germany supporter. There was a time when he never missed a single World Cup match on TV. He once told me that when he was in Kolkata, he would go to watch the derbies between arch rivals East Bengal and Mohun Bagan. Baba was a Mohun Bagan fan.

In fact, he had even watched the last World Cup passionately. I was in Class V at that time. I would sit with Baba in front of our TV and we would watch the entire 1986 World Cup together. I was very close to him from my childhood. Ma would say that I got my height from Baba. My maternal grandfather would say that with my sharp nose and glowing eyes, Baba and I look very similar. But all this was before I fell in love with football. Ever since I got hooked on to this game, Baba stopped watching football; or, rather, he started hating football altogether. Our relationship had soured to such an extent that sometimes I thought he was my enemy at home.

Baba ensured that we had a special dinner that night as it was a special occasion – the World Cup final – where both our favourite teams would take on each other. We sat in front of the TV after dinner as the match started around 11.30 p.m. IST.

It was an ill-tempered and controversial match with two Argentinean players being shown the red card. Maradona looked off-colour as he was man-marked by Guido Buchwald of the erstwhile West Germany for almost the entire match. It was a very dull match as nobody could score till 84 minutes. But just 6 minutes from full time, West Germany plucked out a controversial penalty kick to seal the match in their favour. West Germany beat my favourite team 1-0.

My father was celebrating as well as teasing me after my team's defeat. I felt so upset that I broke down after seeing Maradona crying like a child after the defeat. After the match got over at around 2 a.m., I went to my room and cried myself to sleep.

Though I was very distraught over Argentina's defeat, I went to school the next day as usual. After returning home, when I was getting ready to go to the ground, I heard Sushanta calling me from outside my home. Despite my repeated requests, Sushanta never entered our house, perhaps due to an innate inferiority complex, as we did not belong to the same economic class. As I came to the balcony, Sushanta informed me that Mayna Sir had asked me to reach the ground as early as possible. The stadium, where we practised regularly, was just 5 minutes away from my home if I cycled there. As soon as Sushanta left, I hurriedly got ready and started cycling to the stadium.

Though it was a rainy season, on that particular day there was hardly any clouds in the sky. It was quite a bright sunny day with a clear blue sky. The world's third-highest mountain peak, Kanchenjunga, was clearly visible from Siliguri. In good weather conditions and a cloudless sky, the majestic Kangchenjunga was easily visible from Siliguri – and one can see it even today. From my childhood, I was fascinated by this majestic view of this mountain peak. It was so vivid that sometimes I would think it was just a few kilometres away from our house.

In fact, mountains have always attracted me. I was charmed by mountains from my childhood itself. Though I have been to Darjeeling, Kurseong, Kalimpong, Gangtok and many other places of Darjeeling and Sikkim countless times with my parents from my childhood, my thirst for the hills have never been satiated. It seems to me that they are simply waiting to embrace me with open arms.

I was so enchanted by the view of the Kangchenjunga that I just had to stop at the stadium's entrance for a few minutes to get a glimpse of this mesmerising sight before entering the stadium.

Mayna Sir saw me standing there, and shouted out to hurry up and meet him as fast as possible.

As soon as I stepped into the ground, Mayna Sir called me again.

"Hurry up, Siddhartha!"

Until then nothing had struck me as out of the ordinary, but his urgency suddenly got me thinking that perhaps something serious had happened. I saw Sushanta standing with him, looking anxious.

When I stood in front of him, he said, "Siddhartha and Sushanta, I have very good news to share with you boys. I have not yet revealed it to Sushanta as I thought I would share it when both of you are present together."

"What is the news, Sir?" I asked, concerned.

"Both you and Sushanta have been selected for the

state team," a beaming Mayna Sir broke the news to us. "I got this letter today from the state federation," he joyfully plucked out the letter from his pocket and showed it to us.

"Sir! I can't believe this!" I exclaimed, reading the letter again and again.

I hugged Sushanta who was also over the moon. But since Sushanta was less expressive by nature and less confident because of his background, he could not express himself that much, but it was evident from his face that he was just waiting for such a break that would change his life.

We touched Mayna Sir's feet, who seemed far more delighted than either of us.

"Sir, it's because of your guidance that we have been selected in the state team," I said while Sushanta nodded in agreement, smiling from ear to ear.

"I knew both of you would make us proud. I don't think two players from Siliguri have ever been selected for the state team together. You just can't imagine how happy I am today," he could not hold back his tears.

I had seen him cry for the first time after our final match, and again today, in front of us. I could understand this man's passion for the game and his unalloyed love for his students.

"Football is my life, Siddhartha. I dreamt of playing for my country. I represented the Bengal state team under the legendary Chuni Goswami, but I could not make a comeback to the team after injury forced me out. Moreover, I had no support system, either financially or mentally. But I dreamt that one day my students will represent India," Sir said while wiping away his tears with his left hand. "You know I still have financial issues at home, but I keep on training young boys like you with only one dream

– my students will represent India one day," he added emotionally.

Seeing him and listening to his words made me more determined. I think that day Sushanta had also vowed to realise Mayna Sir's dream.

"We won't let you down, Sir. We will give our best," I said, Sushanta vigorously nodding his head.

For a moment I forgot everything. I forgot the pain of seeing Maradona helplessly crying last night. I forgot my studies, my marks in my maths test, my parents, Rathin Sir and everything else. I even forgot the beautiful presence of the Kangchenjunga on that day.

I only dreamt of myself in my country's blue-coloured jersey, playing for India. I thought I had taken an important step towards achieving that dream. I was happy for Sushanta also. I wished and hoped that Sushanta would also become a national player and earn enough money for his family and make his parents and his four little siblings proud.

I read the letter again, which stated that we had to attend a one-month preparatory training camp in the Yuba Bharati Krirangan, which is also called Salt Lake Stadium, in Kolkata, for the entire month of August and then head to Goa in September for the national tournament.

While heading back home in the evening, I felt a strange fear amidst all this euphoria. After going home, I first shared the good news with my mother. Ma was initially happy, but as soon as she learnt that I needed to attend a training camp in Kolkata, she was taken aback. She expressed serious doubts whether Baba would allow me to stay away for such a long time. I tried to convince Ma that this was a big break and it came only after I had put in a lot of hard work. So many boys were giving everything to get selected in the state team.

"Let your Baba come and you discuss it with him," she suggested.

"You please talk to him," I insisted.

But she refused. Since we had had a great time watching the World Cup final together last night, I thought that Baba could somehow be persuaded. I decided to talk to Baba at dinner time.

As soon as I broke the news to Baba, he became furious.

"Are you mad or what!" he thundered. His face reddened; his eyes grew bigger. "These two years, you can't spoil a single day. I won't allow you to go to the training camp," he declared.

I tried to convince him how important this break was for me, but he refused to listen to anything. At night, I made several plans to make him agree. I even planned to run away from home in case he did not let me attend the camp. But I couldn't abandon my dream. Finally, I thought of asking Mayna Sir and other district football association members to convince Baba.

Next day, I told Mayna Sir of my plan. Since he also harboured the same dream as mine, of my playing for the country, he readily agreed to visit my house with the association people the day after and convince my father.

....

I was absolutely confident that Mayna Sir, along with the district football association people, would successfully persuade Baba. I was certain they would make him understand how big this opportunity was for me. As planned, Mayna Sir, Arun Sir and Bimal Sir came to our house in the evening. They were asked to sit in the drawing room. Baba joined them after a while.

I greeted them and went to my room where I was awaiting my fate with bated breath. This meeting would have special significance in my future career as a football player.

As I was waiting eagerly to hear the good news, I suddenly heard Baba talking in a very agitated voice. I came out of my room and stood just outside our living room, where the meeting was going on, to hear what Baba was saying.

"I can't allow that," I heard Baba telling them.

"Try to understand, this is a big opportunity for him," Arun Sir tried to convince Baba in a persuasive tone.

"But I want my son to do well in life. He is a brilliant student."

"But he has a very good future in football too. Our state federation officials are also very hopeful about his future. They are sure he will play for India in the future," Arun Sir told Baba.

"But we are educated people. I want my son to be a successful engineer like Rathin's son. I can't allow him to spoil his life by playing football," Baba was fuming with anger. "How much money will he earn by playing football?" Baba challenged Arun Sir.

"Money will come to Indian football very soon. Those who are still playing for the big clubs like East Bengal or Mohun Bagan are earning decent money," Bimal Sir said, but Baba remained unconvinced, his body language revealing as much.

Ma was also listening to this conversation standing near the door of the drawing room. I was standing behind her but I could still see all of them as I was much taller than Ma.

"But still I can't allow my son to attend the preparatory camp," Baba stood up; indicating that the discussion was over and there was no room for further deliberations. Baba looked adamant.

Till now Mayna Sir had not said a single word. He was listening to the conversation between Baba, Bimal Sir and Arun Sir, perhaps hoping that Arun Sir, a bank manager and at the same status as Baba, would be able to convince him. But when he found that Baba was unyielding, he sought Baba's permission to say something.

"Subhash da, Siddhartha is a very good footballer. Please allow him to attend the preparatory camp," Mayna Sir pleaded with Baba.

Though Baba had brushed aside Arun Sir's request, he had, at least, maintained a minimum level of decency and decorum because of Arun Sir's social status. But Baba lost his cool when Mayna Sir spoke up.

"Don't talk to me. You are a loser," Baba taunted Mayna Sir directly, his lips curling into a sneer. "What have you achieved in life? It's because of you that my son has become completely spoilt. You are responsible for all this!" Baba blasted Mayna Sir who was trying his best to convince my father despite being humiliated.

"I beg your permission, Subhash da. Please allow him," Mayna Sir told Baba with folded hands. "Siddhartha has all the potential to be a very good footballer. He will make you proud one day," Mayna Sir continued despite Baba's indignation.

"Just get out of my house," Baba spat the words at Mayna Sir in cold fury.

By then, I too had become angry. I strode into the room and confronted Baba, "You can't humiliate my coach like this."

I apologised to them on behalf of my father. Humiliated, they left our house in silence.

I had a heated argument with Baba that night. Ma tried to pacify both of us. Baba declared that come what may, he wouldn't sign the consent letter which was mandatory for attending the preparatory camp. That night I could not sleep. Mayna Sir's helpless, pitiful face haunted me again and again. But I was also beginning to realise that it would not be possible for me to continue football with so much resistance from my father. If I could not attend the training camp, it was no point playing football anymore.

Next day, I went to the ground to apologise to Mayna Sir again. Sir regretfully told me it would not be possible for me to attend the camp without my father's consent letter.

"It's very difficult to continue football without the support of your family," he lamented.

He gently advised me to instead concentrate on my studies and listen to my father. I knew these words were not coming from his heart, for deep down, he had nourished a different dream for me. But the previous day's shocking and shameful incident at my home made him realise that we both have to abandon our dreams, however painful it might be for us.

Since I had also realised last evening the same thing as Sir, I did not contest his words. I was, rather, trying to prepare myself to a life without my favourite sport. I could have thought otherwise had Mayna Sir provided me with some other option. But since he too had resigned himself to my fate, I had no choice left with me anymore.

I touched Sir's feet and asked for his blessings one final time.

"My good wishes are always with you, Siddhartha," Sir said, affectionately patting my back. "Just remember one thing: whatever you do in life, do it honestly and passionately like you did in the football field. Then no one can stop you from achieving anything in life."

I listened in silence as I had no mental strength left in me to say anything.

"You have learnt many things by playing football which will help you in future – the importance of team spirit, hard work, fellow-feeling, helping others in need. Football has already taught you that it's never too late to make a comeback in life. If you keep yourself mentally strong, you can always bounce back like you did in the inter-district final match a month ago."

Tears were rolling down my face as he said those parting words with a heavy heart. I felt my whole world crumble in front of me. I sensed a strange void in me – as if I had just lost someone very close to me. An unbearable pain engulfed my whole body and mind. I never thought my dream of playing football for my country would be nipped in the bud by my own father. But it became a reality from that day. I could not take it anymore. I just took my cycle, furiously peddled all the way home, to reach the loving comfort of my room, crying my heart out. I bolted the bedroom from inside and sobbed helplessly like an infant whose most favourite toy had been snatched away by a cruel giant.

****

3

I could easily see the hint of tears in his small eyes. I too had become a little emotional while narrating my break-up story with football. I don't know after how many years I had shared this story with someone.

I had started telling the story of my life about 45 minutes back. Ranjit had not spoken a single word in between. He had been listening to me with rapt attention.

"You did not play football after that?" Ranjit asked in a shocked voice.

"Do you think my father played football with me after that?" I replied jokingly as I wanted to make the situation a little lighter, as both of us had become a tad morose.

The mountains, which were covered with fog in the morning, were clearly visible as the sun rays had cut through and pushed away the mist. I sighed.

"How did you stay away from football? Did you not ever feel like playing again?" Ranjit asked me. The journalist in Ranjit probed as if trying to fathom the depth of my heartbreak and the impact of Baba's decision on me, a mere 15-year-old boy, who had earned an opportunity all by himself which only a few achieve. I simply smiled at him.

"Please have patience, Ranjit. There is a lot more to come," I told him mysteriously. Sensing his impatience to learn what happened next, I resumed my narration.

....

I was very depressed for a month or so after cutting-off all ties with football. I felt as if I were a child lost in a crowded place and frantically searching for my dear ones. To be honest, I lost my own identity altogether. Especially, the afternoons, when I would go for my football practice, hurt me most and I felt empty within. Sometimes, I would feel like running down to the ground to play again but somehow, I kept my emotions in check.

Before this experience, I had no idea how much heartache a break-up with your girlfriend, could trouble you. I thought the soreness of my heart was more than that. I was completely heartbroken and lost. I could not sleep at night. I could not eat properly. I kept only to myself, totally isolated from everyone. Apart from school and tuition classes, I stayed alone with a heavy heart. I almost stopped talking to Baba, though I had some formal routine talks regarding my studies, lunch, dinner or breakfast with Ma. Baba also did not bother to talk to me, perhaps because of my arguments with him when he had insulted Mayna Sir.

After 15 days or so, in school, Sushanta requested me to go to the ground again, but I refused. Sushanta told me he was sorely missing me in the football field.

"I will miss you in the state camp and the national tournament," Sushanta told me.

There was sadness in his voice and eyes as we were inseparable in the football field despite the differences in our social status. This separation hurt us both.

I felt bad for him. But I felt worse for myself. He was a poor boy, but that day I felt poorer. Despite his troubles at home, he could continue with football, whereas I was the one who had to quit. Still I did not say anything. Sometimes, in some situations in life, there is nothing to say. All you can do is to stay silent. It is probably the best way to express your feelings.

I just wished him luck for his future and we parted, each taking the road to a completely different journey.

Ma tried hard to convince me that Baba did not give the consent letter for my benefit.

"One day you will definitely realise the reason behind my action. I have saved your life," Baba told me after a couple of months.

He was talking as if I was a drug addict. By then Baba must have been very happy to see that I had quit football.

My parents and Rathin Sir were convinced that once I turn away from football, I would naturally concentrate on my studies. Being experienced men of the world, perhaps they were right in their assessment.

There cannot be any void in life for a long time. Maybe, that's the way nature works. Human beings are hardwired to adapt to new situations and embrace new people in their lives. I was not an exception.

As I stopped going to the ground, the vacuum created by the absence of Sushanta, Madhu, Sudhan, Atul, Binod – the sons of paan shop owners, daily wage labourers or rickshaw pullers –was filled up by Sourav, Rahul, Arka, Sayan, Jayanta – bright students who belonged to my social class. Sourav's father was a doctor; Rahul's father was an engineer; Sayan's, a professor; Arka's, a teacher; and Jayanta's, a bank manager. According to Baba and Rathin Sir, I was back to where I truly belonged before football had dragged me away.

A special bonding grew between Sourav and me; Sourav always stood first in our class. He started coming to my home sometimes for studying together, sometimes for adda. At times, I would go to his place. We solved maths problems together. During holidays, Rahul, Arka, Jayanta and Sayan came to my house for group study sessions.

By mingling with them, I had unknowingly developed a kind of competitive mind set in studies, which was earlier absent as my entire focus had been on the ethos of football—team work, helping each other and recognising the contribution of each one. I was, by nature, a serious boy. So, whatever I did, I did with passion. Earlier, it was football, which was my obsession. Now, without it, I concentrated fully on studies.

Though Baba was very pleased with me, I had deep down nursed and held on to a grudge against him for ending my football career prematurely. I never got along easily with him after that. I could not digest his offensive behaviour with Mayna Sir, even though many days had passed by. In fact, I could never face Mayna Sir again after that evening when I went to apologise to him.

Rathin Sir was also very happy as I hardly made any silly mistakes in maths and scored full marks. I was doing well in other subjects too. I gave my all to my studies just as I had given to football. I did very well in the Class X Board exams.

While Sourav topped the school and ranked third in the state, I came second in school and was among the top ten in the state. My parents were over the moon. I can still see their proud faces when they heard my results.

They celebrated my success with a grand party at our home, where all my friends and their parents were invited along with my relatives from my mother's side; my father was not in the best of terms with his own siblings. Since I was particularly good in science subjects, like all the brilliant students of our class, I opted for the science stream for the Higher Secondary Board Examinations.

After the success in Class X, my friendship with Sourav grew stronger. Sourav was a good-looking, charming boy and though he was slightly shorter than me, he was of above average height for a Bengali. He was not a typically diligent student who kept himself buried in textbooks. Rather, he was an all-rounder, who, along with studies, watched films and cricket matches, listened to music, partied with friends and was involved in many more fun activities. He would find time for his studies and would not sacrifice studies for anyone.

When we were in Class XI, he used to tell me about Hollywood movies and Western music. He had a very good collection of Western music. Since I had only lived, breathed and dreamt football, I had had no exposure to these interesting things of life. He made me listen to the Backstreet Boys, Metallica, R.E.M., etc.

His father was a very famous doctor of Siliguri, who had established his own nursing home. Naturally, they were very rich. In their house they had a DVD player. Since his mother was a schoolteacher, Sourav had the whole house to himself during the day. One day, he invited me to watch the blockbuster Hollywood movie, The Terminator.

"You will go crazy after watching the movie," he enticed me.

After watching it, I really went crazy about Arnold Schwarzenegger.

Earlier, I used to do physical training on the football ground, but after seeing the mighty man in this film, I joined a gym. I was so impressed with his massive biceps and muscular body that I wanted a figure like his.

Seeing my excitement for Schwarzenegger, Sourav asked me to come to his house again and showed me more movies.

"I will show you Predator, another hit movie of Schwarzenegger."

"I really like the man," I beamed while thanking him for introducing me to a completely new world.

"My favourite actor is Tom Cruise," Sourav told me as we watched more films together at his home.

Among the actresses, I found Catherine Zeta-Jones, who had just made her entry into Hollywood, very attractive. Influenced by Sourav, I not only started listening to Western music and watching Hollywood films, but also started adoring all things Western – lifestyle, mannerisms, behaviour and culture.

Sourav one day secretly bought two bottles of beer and took me to his house during the day. Initially, I was very reluctant to drink, as I had never seen anyone in my close circle consuming alcohol.

"Drink, Siddhartha, you will like it. We have grown up now," Sourav persisted, saying it's a common practice amongst Westerners once they reach high school.

This was the first time I drank beer and, to be very honest, I liked the feeling, although it had a bitter taste. Still, I could not finish the bottle. Sourav used to smoke from Class IX. I never thought of smoking as Mayna Sir told us never to smoke, since sportsmen were not allowed to.

Another day, Sourav offered me a cigarette which I unwillingly took and smoked for the first time in my life.

But I soon developed a strong liking for it. We would smoke in Sourav's house and in other places secretly when we returned from tuition in the evenings.

Since our school was an all-boys' school, there was not much possibility of getting a girlfriend in school. Sourav had a girlfriend who studied at Siliguri Girls' High School. He would go out on dates with her sometimes. I liked some girls of Siliguri Girls' High School whom I met at tuition, but I did not have the courage to open my heart to any of them, since my mother was a teacher there. Moreover, I had always been shy when it came to talking to girls. All my machismo would vanish the moment I came face-to-face with them.

But like Sourav, I did not ignore my studies because we had started dreaming many dreams of a rosy future. We dreamt of good jobs and all the material possessions which most people aspire for or we wished to enjoy all that most people of a generation hanker after.

I studied harder in the last three months before the Class XII Board exams. In fact, to utilise every moment for my preparation, I shaved off my hair so that I would not have to go to the saloon again and again. I gave every exam confidently and was sure that I would get very good marks in the Class XII Boards, as well as secure a very good rank at the Joint Entrance Exam (JEE).

"After the exams, all of us friends must go to Darjeeling and drink as much whisky as we can!" Sourav proposed before the exams.

Meanwhile, Baba informed me that Rathin Sir's son Amit was coming to Siliguri for a vacation. Amit da had shifted to the USA after completing his engineering and had now settled there with a well-paying job. I informed Sourav. A brilliant student, Amit da had performed extraordinarily well in both the Class X and XII Boards in West Bengal. I had met him a couple of times at family parties, but had not interacted much as I was many years younger to him. But this time, I was looking forward to meeting him and learning how he became a successful man within such a short span of time.

My parents were overjoyed when they saw my ranking in the engineering exam. I ranked 20th in the State JEE, which guaranteed my admission in the best engineering colleges in the state. I wanted to be a successful engineer like Amit da. Rahul, Sayan, Arka and some of my other friends also ranked within the top hundred in the JEE. Sourav wanted to be a doctor like his father. His ranking in medical was also as impressive and he was sure to get admission in any prestigious medical college.

My father, especially, was jubilant. I have never seen Baba so ecstatic. He had been very happy after my Class X Boards also, but the JEE result had more significance as it would open a new avenue for me in life.

However, a few days back Baba had been a little depressed with my Class XII Board results in which my marks were not up to his expectation, though I had ranked among the top ten in the school. Moreover, he was particularly upset that Rahul, whose father worked under him as a junior engineer, had got more marks than me.

After informing our parents about our JEE rankings, Sourav and I went straight to Rathin Sir's house to meet him and take his blessings for our future. But Sir was not at home. In his absence, we met his son, Amit. In his student days, Amit da was very good-looking. Although he was not tall, he had a good physic and his intelligent handsome face increased the heartbeat of many a young girl in Siliguri. But I was disappointed to see him that day – he had put on a lot of weight which spoilt his overall elegant look. Nonetheless, there was an added glamour about him which could be attributed to his settling down in the USA. He informed us that his parents were out of town for a day. We told him about our results. Congratulating us, he asked us to drop by in the evening for an adda.

We were looking forward to spending some time with him anyway, and were happy with his invitation. Back home when I told Baba about the upcoming adda with Amit da that very evening, he was pretty pleased as he told me that people like Amit da could show me the path to real success.

....

"I have been waiting for both of you," a smiling Amit da welcomed us when Sourav and I reached his home in the evening. I sat down on one of the two single sofas in their drawing room, and Sourav made himself comfortable on the other. Amit da plonked himself on the three-seater couch. Wearing a costly Polo T-shirt and a three-quarter trouser of some American brand, he looked every inch an NRI.

"Here, these rasogollas are for you, as you boys have done very well," he said cheerfully, serving us two rasogollas each.

Bengalis always celebrate good news or deeds with rasogollas.

"Congratulations once again! My father speaks highly of both of you," he told us in an American accent, as we picked up our plates.

I noticed that his way of talking had changed considerably, no doubt a side-effect of living in the USA.

"I have known Siddhartha from his childhood as our fathers are close friends," Amit da addressed Sourav. "We have met each other at different functions and family get-togethers. But I have never met you before."

"My father keeps speaking about you," Sourav told Amit da, his eyes bright with excitement.

"Yes, I know your father – Dr Chatterjee – very well. He is a great doctor," smiled Amit da.

Sourav's faced glowed at this praise from Amit da.

"I have a surprise gift for both of you which is perfect for today's celebration," Amit da said with an impish grin, as he stood up.

We looked at each other in surprise, wondering what it could be. We both tried to guess but we had no clue. The suspense ended when Amit da came back to the drawing room with a bottle of whisky in his hand.

"This is a very expensive, single malt imported whisky, which I have brought from the USA," he said patronisingly, looking at the bottle.

I felt embarrassed, while Sourav looked clearly thrilled.

"I hope you guys drink?" he asked us as we sat shyly looking at each other.

"Yes, we have drunk once," said Sourav, who could think on his feet, in an awkward tone. It was both a lie and a truth, as I have drunk only once, but Sourav many times.

"I can assure you, once you have this, you won't drink any other whisky," Amit da said smugly.

We kept quiet, but it might have been evident from our faces that we were eager to taste this expensive whisky from the US.

He kept the bottle on the centre table and went to get glasses.

He poured out a peg of whisky for each of us, and gestured us to pick up our glasses. I was feeling extremely shy and awkward about drinking alcohol in front of him. Seeing my hesitation, Amit da nodded egging me on to start.

Sourav was smarter than me, and he had picked up his glass as soon as Amit da gave us the green signal. But for some reason, I couldn't.

"Come on, Siddhartha!" said Amit da, "Cheers, boys!" raising his glass.

"This tastes really great. You will like it, Siddhartha," Amit da said, sipping the whisky, encouraging me to take a sip.

"Awesome taste! Thanks a lot, Amit da, for this wonderful gift," Sourav said, obviously trying to impress our host.

Amit da gave an 'I told you so' expression.

"You won't get this here in India," Amit da repeated with pride.

"I had beer once with Sourav, but I've never had whisky," I said bashfully, sipping a little at first. It tasted like raw spirit.

"How is it?" asked Amit da, eagerly waiting for my answer.

"Very good," I lied, surrendering to social codes of conduct, especially, since it had come from the USA.

Sourav looked at me, as if to convey how lucky we were to have got this opportunity to drink such an expensive whisky.

"I have met you after a long time, Siddhartha," Amit da remarked, while completing his first peg.

"I last met you in Bua Uncle's daughter's marriage, when you were about to leave for the USA," I reminded him.

Bua Uncle was a common friend of Baba and Rathin Sir.

"Yes, before I settled down in the US. You were in Class IX then. We had chatted a little bit. Subhash Uncle was very worried about you, as your whole concentration was on football at that time," he recalled.

After many days, someone had raised the topic of football in front of me. People in my close circle generally avoided this subject.

"He has quit it completely," Sourav informed him on my behalf, as if I had quit a bad habit like drinking or smoking.

Generally, I do not feel the pain anymore; it's been almost four years, but that evening I felt someone had again tugged at my heartstrings. I suddenly started to miss football and thoughts of Sushanta, Mayna Sir and everything connected with football surfaced from deep within, troubling me.

As I was lost in my thoughts, I came back to the present when Amit da said, "Good thing, Siddhartha that you quit. Otherwise, you would not have ranked so high in the JEE. It was a very good decision."

"Earlier, we used to call him for group studies or home parties, but he would never join us. He was totally obsessed with football," Sourav chipped in, as if he was my spokesman.

"Listen, you need to be very objective in your life. Never waste time on silly things," leaning forward, Amit da said in a matter-of-fact voice.

Sourav's company had made me forget football. But Amit da's words made a deeper effect on me. He was a 'successful man' after all, and everyone in Siliguri held him in high regard. Rathin Sir was also a proud father. Everyone in town would cite his example as a 'successful' father.

"When you go to a First World country like the US or the UK and enjoy life, you will understand how insignificant these things are," Amit da said, referring to football.

I kept quiet, and Amit da continued.

"There is no value of emotion in this world. You might love doing certain things, but if that does not help you earn money, it's worthless," he said, as though he was giving a lecture on the 'Philosophy of Life'.

"Yes, Amit da, you are right," agreed Sourav. "This is exactly what I told Siddhartha when he was depressed after quitting football," Sourav added. Clearly, he was bending backwards to please Amit da.

Though I had not been that impressed with Sourav's words, Amit da's words again struck a deep chord within me. There was something charismatic about Amit da's voice and personality. His voice had a touch of authority in it, just like Rathin Sir and all other talented people in the world have, I thought.

By that time, Sourav and I had finished our first peg. Amit da had finished his first too, a long time back, but was waiting for us to finish ours. I was impressed with his etiquette.

"I had many friends here, but I hardly keep in touch with them now. Last time when I came here from the States, Bishu, one of my friends, wanted to borrow money from me as his mother was hospitalised," Amit da shrugged, his tone indifferent. "This is the problem – unsuccessful people keep asking for financial help," he sounded annoyed.

"You are right," Sourav again agreed with him, as if it was his job that evening to say 'yes' to everything that Amit da said.

"People think that since I stay in a First World country, I have a lot of money. They don't understand that I have my own priorities in life. I have to pay EMIs for my house and for my BMW. I don't work to run a charity in India," Amit da added, irritated, shrugging his shoulder.

I had seen a BMW in a Hollywood movie that I watched with Sourav and was really impressed by the look of the car. The brand evokes an ambience. When he mentioned BMW, my admiration for this man, who had achieved so much at such a young age, went up by an extra notch or two.

"What is the BMW like, Amit da?" I asked.

"It is a fabulous car," Amit da replied, his face aglow. "You can't imagine the thrill when you get into the car. The finish, the plush interiors, the speed, it's simply awesome!"

"Amit da, I have told Siddhartha that one day I will buy a BMW. I have heard a lot about it from my London based cousin," Sourav added proudly.

Somehow, despite my sound economic background, I felt like a poor boy that evening.

"Don't you attend parties there? Or go to nightclubs?" Sourav asked Amit da, as those were not common in India in the mid-1990s.

"Yes, these are normal on weekends in the US. You work your ass off on weekdays and party hard on weekends," Amit da's tone was slightly condescending, I felt.

"May I ask you a question, Amit da?" Sourav asked hesitantly.

"Sure."

"Do you have a girlfriend there?"

"Yes, I have, but more than one," he said jokingly, and we laughed out loudly.

"I had one girlfriend in Calcutta during my IIT days, but it's very difficult to maintain a long-distance relationship. Moreover, she was not ready to shift to the USA and wanted to stay in India. So, I broke up," Amit da explained the rationale in a matter-of-fact way.

At that time in the 1990s, Kolkata was still known as Calcutta.

"Your current girlfriends are all from the US?" Sourav prodded on.

"Yes, yes," he said, bursting into a hearty laughter. He seemed rather amused at Sourav's inquisitiveness.

By that time, we had completed three pegs, and it was taking a toll on me. I was feeling dizzy and light-headed and felt like throwing up, but somehow controlled it. Images of the USA, BMWs, big bungalows, parties, nightclubbing, foreign girlfriends and all the fun stuff that I had heard and seen in Western movies floated in my mind.

I could still sense Amit da's and Sourav's conversation, but could not understand what exactly they were discussing. Unlike me, they both seemed far more stable. I wanted to go home as I was feeling queasy.

Unable to focus, I could hear Amit da's disembodied voice asking Sourav to carefully take me back home. Sourav pulled me up but my legs buckled. Leaning on Sourav, with one arm around his shoulder, I tottered out of Amit da's house.

Sourav had come to Amit da's house in his father's scooter that evening. I rode pillion with him, tightly holding on to his T-shirt somehow, my head spinning like a top. Depositing me at the doorstep of our house, Sourav zipped off after pressing the doorbell, but without waiting for Baba to open the door. Baba came out. I was so tipsy that I could hardly stand properly on my feet, and would have collapsed there itself had Baba not held on to me. I felt a strange unease inside my stomach and a burning sensation in my chest. I could not control it anymore and vomited on my father's arms.

"Are you drunk?"

I kept quiet.

"Are you drunk, Siddhartha?"

This time I somehow nodded my head in affirmation.

"With whom?"

"Amit da and Sourav," I mumbled.

He did not say a single word. He partly dragged, partly walked me to my room, staggering under my weight. I had pretty much lost my balance by then, and was unsteady. I was in no position to either sit properly or have dinner. I collapsed on my bed. I do not remember what happened after that. I would never know what Baba felt about me that night. I would never know whether he was sad or happy seeing me in that state. I guess he was happy to see me on the path of 'success' along with Amit da and Sourav.

....

The next few weeks saw me very busy. I was leaving Siliguri to pursue my higher studies in Calcutta. I had got admission in Jadavpur Engineering College, one of the most prestigious engineering colleges in West Bengal. I had joined the computer science course there. I was pretty excited as I was standing on the threshold of a new world in a bigger city. I was keenly waiting to have fun as a college student, away from home, as well as enjoy life in a metro city. Moreover, the excitement of staying out of my parents' scrutiny was also there.

Along with me, Rahul also got into Jadavpur Engineering College, but in a different stream and opted for the college hostel.

Though Ma was a bit sad to see me moving out of Siliguri, as I was their only child, Baba was super excited as I was leaving on a voyage for a successful life. Everything had changed after I got admission into the computer science course at Jadavpur. Baba's body language transformed overnight. Pride was evident in the way he spoke or walked. I heard Baba telling all our neighbours what a bright future awaited a student of computer science and how difficult it was to get admission in Jadavpur Engineering College. With immense satisfaction and pride, Baba would tell his friends what a brilliant fellow I was to achieve such a feet.

I had intended to stay in the hostel, but Baba decided, instead, that I would stay in his ancestral home in Maniktala, in Calcutta, where his siblings stayed. I did not like the idea, as I wanted to have complete freedom, but Baba was adamant as he thought that it was his right to enjoy his ancestral property – enjoyment by proxy!

As planned, Baba took me to his house in Maniktala, which was a two-storeyed, old, shabby house, overpopulated by family members of Baba's three siblings. From the discussions between my parents so far, I had garnered that Baba did not have good relations with his siblings. Sometimes, when we went to Calcutta and stayed in the rooftop single-room accommodation, which was kept for Baba, there was minimum interaction between Baba and his siblings and their family members. My father decided that I should stay in Baba's room.

I could sense from my uncles' conversations and their body language that they were not happy with Baba's decision to keep me in that house. However, Baba refused to reconsider his decision, and ignored my uncles' opinions and views. Baba returned to Siliguri after settling me in the house, totally unconcerned about the sentiments of the actual people involved: my uncles' and mine. As a result, I felt unwanted in that house from the very first day.

Sourav had, meanwhile, got a seat in Calcutta's Medical College Hospital to pursue his medical degree. As Sourav's father was very well off and had his own flat in Jodhpur Park, a posh locality in Calcutta, he had decided to stay there.

I somehow handled the ragging in college, which is a part and parcel of engineering colleges. I made some friends in college, and would go to Sourav's flat on Sundays.

As days passed, I became friends with some other classmates and among them, I was pallier with Rajarshi and

Shantanu. Though five girls were there in my department, I never got beyond the 'hello' stage, as I was always shy where girls were concerned. I spent my time with Rajarshi, Shantanu and some other boys.

Though I stayed with my uncles, Baba had arranged a cook for me before going back. I did not have much interaction with my uncles, aunts or even with my cousins, and neither did they take any initiative to talk to me, to get to know me. So basically, I had no guardian in Calcutta, which gave me the freedom to do as I pleased, to go out and come back home as I wished. I used to go out in the morning for college and come back late at night, sometimes drunk.

On weekends, my permanent place of fun was either Sourav's flat or Shantanu's PG (Paying Guest accommodation). By that time, Sourav's friends from medical college would also join us.

Among my college friends, Rajarshi was my drinking buddy, and we would have a couple of beers together, usually in the evenings after classes. Shantanu was addicted to weed, and sometimes, I would have weed, too. I liked the high of weed.

Shantanu was an easy-going and interesting boy who was a hard core communist and an atheist. He was an active member of our students' union, which was dominated by the SFI (Students' Federation of India), the students' wing of the CPI (M), and the ruling party of West Bengal at that time. I had no political orientation, but Shantanu would often tell me captivating stories of Che Guevera, the Cuban Revolution and the Vietnam wars. He would also tell me about the non-existence of God or the futility of religion.

"Do you know that religion was created to torture people?" Shantanu told me one day when we were sitting at Babu Ghat near the Hooghly. "That's why Karl Marx said 'Religion is the opium of the people'. In the country of reason, the existence of God cannot have any meaning."

Shantanu, who used to come to college wearing a Che Guevara T-shirt most days, had the power to impress people with his reasoning and oratorical skills. He was an avid reader. He would give me a lot of books to read. In fact, my reading had also improved under Shantanu's influence. I read fiction as well as non-fiction around this time. Some of the great books I read were: The Motorcycle Diaries by Che Guevara, How the Steel Was Tempered by Nikolai Ostrovsky, Naked Among Wolves by Bruno Apitz, The Communist Manifesto by Karl Marx and Friedrich Engels.

Shantanu told me about Che's major role in the Cuban Revolution and the fight against American imperialism and capitalism, which inspired many countries on the path of communism.

I had heard some of these things in Baba's discussions with his friends, though he had never discussed politics with me. As far as I remember, Baba once regretfully told me that he had lost an academic year in college when he had joined the Naxalite movement in Calcutta, in the Sixties.

Though I sometimes tried to argue with Shantanu, I would fall flat in the face of his counter-arguments. Influenced by his words, Che became an inspirational figure for me and I did not realise when I was converted into an atheist, though I could not become a communist in the true sense. Becoming a leftist was fashionable at that time. Though Marx's doctrine had made me a non-believer, I knew very well that in the coming days, I would have to work in some capitalist organisation or the other. Deep down, I wanted material possessions that were an epitome of opulence and prosperity — a great job, a beautiful house or an apartment, a luxury car and a very healthy bank balance – after completing my engineering degree.

That's the problem in following any particular doctrine. Romantically, all ideologies look very attractive at a superficial level, but implementing it at the personal level is very difficult. In fact, very few people can do it. And when you can't put it into practice in your own personal life, you are considered a hypocrite – as many communists of my generation were, in West Bengal.

I was so influenced by Shantanu and Marxism that I started disliking our own religion, our own ancient art and culture, literature, heritage, and religion, which, according to Shantanu, were 'full of superstitions and dogmatism'.

In those days, in West Bengal, no discussion would be complete without terms such as Marxism, communism, socialism, proletariat, bourgeoisie, class struggles, imperialism, etc. If you didn't know these terms, you were not an educated and progressive Bengali.

Sometimes, Shantanu, Rajarshi and other friends would come over to my place, much to the annoyance of my uncles. We would discuss politics, economics and religion over drink and weed.

I had spent two years in Kolkata by then. Despite my somewhat bohemian lifestyle, my results were not that bad. But I could gauge from my uncles' and aunts' behaviour that they did not like my friends coming to my room and the drinking that invariably followed. They had somehow tolerated me for almost two years now, but I could never have imagined that they, my own blood relatives, would get me into an ugly mess in the days to come.

....

One night, Rajarshi, Shantanu and I had a late-night drinking session in my room. We drank and smoked while arguing about Marxism, Indian culture and tradition, since Rajarshi was a traditionalist and had a tendency to take a contrarian stand to that of Shantanu.

We did not know when we fell asleep as we were totally zonked out. I heard a knock on the door of my room in the morning. I did not know what the time was, but I did know that I had difficulty in getting up. The knocking persisted, steadily growing louder, and I finally managed to open the door. My eldest uncle stood outside, his usual grumpy face replaced by one of fury, along with two policemen and the local councillor.

"It's because of your negligence that we have lost so many belongings! You did not lock the main door when you came back at night. I have told you repeatedly to shut the main door properly as you are always the last one to return home," he said angrily.

I tried to argue with him but one of the policemen under the garb of friendly advice, asked me to leave the locality. The local councillor demanded the same thing. I knew this was nothing but dirty politics played by my uncles, aunts and some of their neighbours.

People say blood relations are essential in life, but that day I realised that all relationships have to be nurtured. Probably my father did not take care of the ties between him and his siblings properly and I became a victim of it.

I updated Baba about the day's happenings over phone. To say that he was infuriated is to put it mildly. He immediately asked me not to leave the house, but I explained to him that it was unsafe for me to stay in that house any longer.

“If I stay here, they can come up with more conspiracies against me and get me into further trouble,” I told Baba.

Thankfully, Baba understood my point of view and with the help of a friend, he arranged a small rented apartment for me near my college in Jadavpur. I shifted there after a few days.

Though two years had passed since I entered college, my circle of friends was limited to only Rajarshi and Shantanu. Since Rahul was in the civil engineering department, we hardly got to meet each other. I would go to Sourav’s flat sometimes, but that too had become less frequent as he had his own circle of friends who were all from his medical college.

About a month or so passed by but, somehow, I could not get over the humiliating incident at my father’s ancestral house. Other than my ouster, one more thing was troubling me deeply. If my uncle’s allegations against my father - which he had made in the heated exchange of words that we had had that day — that my father did not bother to take care of his parents were true, my father had truly been an ungrateful son and elder brother. It’s true that ever since I was born, I had not seen Baba doing anything for my paternal relatives, nor his parents. In fact, nobody from his side of the family ever came to our Siliguri house, or stayed with us for even a single night - not even my paternal grandparents.

The incident at my uncle’s house left me with a bitter aftertaste. To tell the truth, I was happy to leave that house where I was always made to feel like an intruder. Moreover, I had my own rented apartment now, and could enjoy my freedom without any fear. But I was hardly aware of the surprises that were waiting for me in life.

....

One day, while I was sitting alone near our college canteen and smoking, Sushmita, one of my classmates, came to me and asked me what I was doing there, alone.

"Nothing," I replied brusquely.

I avoided girls as I still hadn't been able to overcome my awkwardness when it came to interacting with them.

"Is everything fine? You look down and out," she asked me in a caring tone.

"No… I am fine," I replied to show that everything was okay.

"But you are not telling me the truth," she persisted.

I did not say anything.

"Why are you smoking cigarettes one after the other?" she asked next.

Perhaps she had watched me for some time before approaching me.

"Don't you like smoking?" I asked her instead, not sure of what to say in this situation.

"Not like that, but you should not smoke so much," she said while I kept quiet.

On any other day, I would have been irritated by this disapproval, but that day I was still in a brooding zone.

"Have you eaten something?" she suddenly asked me in a tender voice.

I was touched by her question, and I could feel myself relaxing, a softness coming over me.

I did not know how she understood, but it was a fact that I had not had anything since morning. There had been many such days in Kolkata when I came to college without having eaten anything, but nobody had ever enquired after me.

"No, I have not had anything since the morning," I told her, looking at her for the first time, feeling grateful.

"Oh my god! It's already 2.30 p.m. and you are sitting here on an empty stomach!"

I again kept quiet, but it really felt good that someone was showing at least some concern for me.

"Let's go to the canteen and have something?" she suggested.

We went to the canteen and had our lunch together. Over lunch, we discussed our classes, favourite subject, projects, semester examinations, other classmates, about our professors and many other things.

I surreptitiously observed Sushmita closely that day, over lunch. She was a very simple-looking, short girl, but had a strange sweetness about her. She was not typically fair, and had a very soft and soothing voice, shy eyes and a lovely, innocent smile. When she smiled, dimples appeared on her cheeks and she looked rather pretty. I had not noticed all this even though we had been in the same class for the last two years. That day, I felt good that someone was taking care of me in Kolkata for the first time in two years.

After lunch, we had two more practical classes, and then she headed home.

Before leaving, she told me with a gentle smile, "Take care of your health and don't smoke so much."

In the evening I went to Shantanu's PG and had weed. At night when I was lying on my bed, I remembered

Sushmita's words, her soft and sweet voice, her caring demeanour, beautiful smile and the dimples in her face which made her so attractive. The incident in the afternoon had deeply touched me. I looked forward to meeting her again the next day.

Next day I went to college, expecting to see her. But she was absent. In those days, we did not have mobile phones, so I had no option but to wait for her to come to college the next day.

At night, she again came in my thoughts and I fervently hoped that she would be present the next day. I was very pleased to see her in class the next day, and once classes were over, I went to her and asked her to join me for tea in the canteen.

"Why didn't you come to college yesterday?" I asked her over a cup of tea, looking at her sweet face.

"Why are you asking? Did you miss me?" she asked me casually and laughed. Her dimples appeared once again, and my heart turned over! She looked so beautiful.

"Yes."

"What!"

"Yes. I missed you very much," I confessed, without thinking much of the consequences.

I did not know how I told her, but I told her anyway, and I was also surprised at my own courage. My emotions overpowered me at that moment and swept me away.

I have now realised that everything has a time and so does the beginning and ending of every relationship. When the time comes, it happens, irrespective of whether we want it or plan it.

It was an answer she had hardly expected from me. She was perhaps not ready for it. She was caught totally off guard, though I could easily see in her eyes that she liked what I had just told her.

It was winter in Kolkata, but I could see her face had turned reddish and a little bit of sweat glistened on her forehead. With some of her curly hair falling on her forehead, I could see the drops of sweat drenching those strands of hair. She kept touching her hair again and again. She was looking so attractive and charming at that time that I was unable to look away.

I have never experienced before what I felt that evening. I could feel my heart pounding in excitement. I have felt an adrenaline rush only before an important football match or during the Board exams. But this was a different feeling altogether, which I was experiencing for the first time in my life. It was uplifting, exalting, exhilarating; a feeling that can put you straight away on top of the world. It was a feeling that can transform you internally. The pain, the humiliation caused by the ouster from my father's ancestral house by my own uncles a few days back was completely overshadowed at that moment by the sudden rush of emotions that overwhelmed me. I felt that finally I had someone whom I could rely upon completely and spend the rest of my life with.

....

The entire third year we spent our off periods and evenings almost together, sitting with each other and planning our future days. We even did our final year practical project together. We made a demo office-management software, which earned a lot of praise from our professors. Once we were in the third year, the only discussion in college was about campus interviews and jobs. We also started to plan in a way so that we could stay together for the rest of our lives.

"We have to be in the same city after marriage," Sushmita told me one day.

"I want that too," I agreed with her, as we stepped into the canteen.

"We should select Delhi as our priority city in the interviews. I love Delhi very much. My elder Mama (maternal uncle) lives there. He is with the Customs' department."

"That will be very good for us. He must be an influential person," I said, thinking that if we ever get in trouble, he would bail us out. "I like Delhi too. I went with Baba when I was in Class VIII. Hmm, I liked it very much," I smiled, dreaming about our future in the capital city of India.

We carried our plates to a vacant table and sat down. We were both quite hungry, and fell upon our lunch eagerly.

"When did your parents reach yesterday?" Sushmita asked, after a while.

"Around 10 a.m. as the Darjeeling Mail was late," I told her, my mouth full.

"Have you informed your parents about our relationship?" she asked anxiously.

"Yes, I told them last night."

"What was their reaction?" a visibly tense Sushmita asked me.

"Ma did not say anything, but Baba has some issues, as you are not a Brahmin," I said nonchalantly, sipping water.

"But you told me that your father was an educated man!" she exclaimed, looking pretty dismayed and upset. "How can he have objections about these things?"

"I don't know, but don't worry. I'll handle it," I smiled at her, and changed the topic as I didn't want her to linger on the subject of my father's progressiveness.

It was already 9 p.m. I hurried back to my apartment as my parents would be waiting for me, so that we could have dinner together.

After dinner, despite Baba's objection, I somehow convinced him to at least meet Sushmita once and talk to her. I took Sushmita to meet my parents a few days later. When Sushmita left, my father told me that he wanted a better-looking girl for me.

"She is not the perfect match for you. She is so short. And you are such a handsome and tall boy. I am not in favour of this relationship," he declared, shaking his head dismissively. "Financially, too, they are no match for us. Her father is a mere clerk," Baba added.

"How does it matter?" I asked, agitatedly.

"It matters. You will realise it later," Baba said wisely.

"But she will be an engineer like me," I protested.

"But still, a family's social status and financial status matters a lot. The mentality of a person depends on those conditions," Baba proclaimed with authority.

"But I like her. She loves me! She takes care of me a lot," I argued, astounded by his obstinacy and narrow mindedness.

Ma was listening to our heated conversation silently, standing in a corner of the room. Sensing that it could escalate to a serious quarrel, she pleaded us to stop.

"I have told you my opinion. You decide what you will do now!" Baba cut short my words and went to the other room.

I knew that once Baba set his mind to something, it was very difficult to make him change that. At that instant, I revisited that fateful night seven years ago, when he had compelled me to quit football forever, and with it surfaced all the associated emotions that I had suppressed over the years. I felt as if he were that giant who was about to snatch another favourite toy away from me.

****

4

I stopped for a while. I looked at Ranjit's face. His expression told me that he was not at all happy that I had stopped the narration.

Actually, I had stopped because recalling my college days had brought back memories of Sushmita, the love of my life, after a long, long time. I loved her so much that there was a time when I could not think of staying away from her, living without her for even a single day.

As I allowed myself the luxury of a few moments to savour the images of Sushmita that had re-emerged in my mind, Ranjit shuffled restlessly in his chair. Seeing that he had caught my attention, he leaned forward, gathering his thoughts. He had a lot of questions, I realised, and I knew what he was about to ask.

"Your father did not allow you to continue your relationship with Sushmita? Why did you agree? You were a grown-up by then. Why did you listen to him?" Ranjit asked with an upset tone.

"Who said that I listened to him?" I countered him in a lighter vein to give him a breather.

He heaved a sigh of relief.

"I had already lost football, thanks to Baba. I did not want to lose anything else because of him. I did not want to lose Sushmita too," I told Ranjit in a serious tone.

"So... what did you do?"

Ranjit was now questioning as a friend, not as a journalist, because I could clearly see his concern for me.

I resumed my narration.

This time I was adamant. I made it clear to Ma that I could not and would not dump this innocent girl who loved me so much because of Baba's silly arguments and warped thinking. I told Ma bluntly that I will be marrying Sushmita whether Baba approved of her or not. If she could convince Baba to agree to this marriage, well and good. Otherwise, I would marry Sushmita 'without their blessings'. Ma talked to Baba, who probably thought as I was a grown up by then and about to get a job, it would be very difficult for him to impose such an important decision on me at that point in time. At Ma's persistence, he reluctantly agreed to the marriage.

Everything went according to our plan in the campus interviews. Both of us were selected in IT companies, and we were to be posted in the Delhi offices. While I got a job in BIM Infocom, she was selected by STC Software. Our respective companies informed us that before we joined the Delhi office, we would have to undergo a three months' training period in Kolkata.

"It's better to get married before going to Delhi," Sushmita proposed.

"So early?" I was surprised.

"It makes sense, na? I have already spoken with my parents. It's fine with them. You should tell your parents too," she suggested, rather firmly.

I talked to my parents regarding our marriage. Despite my father's unwillingness, both the families met and fixed a date for our wedding after two months. Much later, Sushmita told me that while her parents were initially reluctant to the marriage because of my father's snobbishness, Ma's gentle nature and charming behaviour had had a positive influence on them.

For the first time in my life, I took an important decision against my father's wishes. I felt I had finally avenged the end of my football career. It took a huge burden off my shoulders. And, it gave me a great sense of relief.

....

We shifted to Delhi in November 1998. Delhi has its own charm during the month of November, when the weather is very pleasant; this is the best time to visit Delhi, and attracts a lot of tourists from across the world. For a newly married couple like us, it was a perfect beginning to our eventful journey in Delhi.

My office was in Noida's Sector 63, but Sushmita was posted in Gurugram (formerly Gurgaon). Since Sushmita's maternal uncle or Mama also stayed in Noida, Sushmita insisted that we stay in Noida although she had to travel one and a half hours daily. She reasoned that we should stay near at least one close relative.

Though both are metro cities, there are huge differences between Kolkata and Delhi, or rather, to be very precise, the whole National Capital Region (NCR), which comprises Delhi, Noida, Gurugram and some parts of Ghaziabad. Delhi is far bigger in terms of area and far superior in terms of infrastructure. While the people of Kolkata mostly wear intellect on their sleeves and like to show off their brainpower, culture and heritage, Delhiites are mostly into material things, with conversations generally revolving around apartments, flashy cars, expensive clothes, shoes, watches, malls, foreign trips, etc. Another change happened after coming to Delhi. My name changed from Siddhartha to Sid, which I liked.

I used to read a lot of books in Kolkata and we discussed books, films, theatre or cinema, but in Delhi you would hardly find friends or colleagues, especially in the IT sector, who would be talking about these things. Moreover, I now rarely found time to read as the pressure of completing projects made it impossible to concentrate on the finer aspects of life. People get so stressed out or rather resentful during weekdays that on weekends, they let their hair down by going to parties, or clubbing, or dining out. Mall crawls and the like were the modern-day stress-busters.

I bought a small car just three months after coming to Delhi, as I felt that commuting in Delhi without a car will be tiresome. Moreover, almost everyone in my office had a car. It's a necessity as well as a status symbol in Delhi NCR.

We would have a blast on weekends, eat out in different restaurants and visit the glittering, dazzling malls. We would roam around and shop at malls as well as popular open-air shopping areas such as Sarojini Nagar Market, Kamala Nagar Market, Palika Bazar (at Connaught Place) and Janpath Market. Connaught Place was our most-preferred hang-out place, as some of the best restaurants of Delhi were located there. Pandara Road's food market was our favourite destination for weekend dinners.

Another reason I liked Delhi was because of its proximity to several hill stations. As mountains had always fascinated me, Sushmita and I would go to different places for long weekends, or sometimes on longer, planned trips to Mussoorie, Nainital, Chail, Kufri, Shimla, Kulu, Manali or Ranikhet.

After one year, Sourav also moved to Delhi for his MD degree at the AIIMS. He had always been an outstanding student, and his getting an opportunity to study at the AIIMS was not surprising, if one considered his brilliant academic performance throughout his life. Occasionally, he would come over on weekends and stay with us.

Sushmita's Mama would invite us for dinner at times, on a Saturday night or Sunday afternoon. Her Mami was a very good cook, and her home-made biryani was superb.

Some of my colleagues became good friends. Vaibhav, Vineet, Raj, Feroz, Shashank, Chayan and I would sometimes chill over a drink or two after work. At times, Sushmita and I would throw a party at our apartment, and invite our colleagues with their spouses, or we'd go over to a party thrown either by one of my office friends or Sushmita's. Or, we'd meet-up at one of the popular restro-bars of the city. Our stay in Delhi was so enjoyable that we didn't even realise how five years passed by – in a flash!

In the meantime, after staying in a rented house for two years, we had bought our own two-bedroom apartment in Noida. I had also exchanged my car for a hatchback after three years. We both got a promotion after five years and became team leads.

On the occasion of our fifth marriage anniversary, Sushmita arranged a surprise party. Vaibhav and Raj came with their wives, leaving their children at home, while Shashank, Vineet and Feroz, who were bachelors, came alone. Only Sourav, who was out of Delhi at that time, missed the occasion.

When they came with bouquets and all, I was pleasantly surprised to see them. Food was home-delivered by a reputed restaurant, and Sushmita had also arranged single malts and premium vodka.

"How did you arrange all this single-handedly?" I asked Sushmita.

"Don't underestimate your wife, Sid," Raj's quip drew laughter from everyone.

"Oh, he always does that! He thinks I won't be able to do anything on my own," Sushmita, who was dressed in a beautiful sari, said good-naturedly, smiling.

Sushmita was looking charming. And, of course, those dimples on her cheek made her even more attractive.

It was a fact that she was depended on me for everything, but that day I was taken aback by the way she had arranged everything, unassisted.

"Sushmita, your apartment is so beautifully done-up," commented Ankita, Vaibhav's wife, as Sushmita showed her around the house.

"But Sid still does not like this one as he thinks it's not that spacious," Sushmita told Ankita.

"Yes, it's a fact. See how everyone is sitting in the drawing room! Had it been a bigger living room, all of you would have been far more comfortable," I said, gesturing that there was not much space for our guests to sit comfortably.

"Don't worry, Sid. We are happy in your house," Vaibhav said courteously.

"But Sid has his own style. He does not like cheap things. Look at his watch," Raj teased, pointing to my Tag Heuer wristwatch.

"Please don't say these things in front of Sushmita. She will start her commentary on my expensive lifestyle!" I grinned as the others broke into laughter. "We have got one life. We should enjoy ourselves," I added when I saw everyone supporting me – everyone, except Sushmita.

"But I did not see any idols anywhere, Sushmita. Where do you do your daily puja?" Ankita asked.

"Siddhartha is an atheist. He does not believe in God. So, I can't do any puja at home," Sushmita said.

Sushmita was not an atheist and I knew that she would have liked to do her daily puja at home, but she was afraid to voice her wishes because of me.

"My parents also find it difficult when they come to stay with us. For them, puja is a part of life," Sushmita complained this time, tucking her hair behind her ear.

"It is their choice," I pointed out, unable to stop myself. "If they find it difficult, they should not come here. Even in my parents' house there is no worshipping. My father is also an atheist, so the idols didn't get a chance to enter our house, much to my mother's disappointment."

"What are you saying? My parents can't come to my house?" Sushmita looked as if she could hardly believe her ears.

"Yes, they can come, but on my terms," I replied curtly, gulping down the remaining whisky in my glass.

I could feel that Sushmita was miffed by my behaviour. Her face reddened, she touched her hair and kept quiet.

"You people should think about having a baby now," said Smita, Raj's wife, trying to change the topic and possibly suggesting that having a baby would solve all our problems.

Sushmita badly wanted a baby and we had had innumerable quarrels over this. But I was not ready. My logic was that since both of us were working, it would be tough to manage.

"We are thinking about it," Sushmita said.

"No. I am not thinking about it at all. Sushmita is the only one thinking about a baby," I said rudely. From their expressions, I could understand that the others were uncomfortable at the sudden change in my behaviour. "Let's be practical. She can't even manage the house and her office properly. How will she manage a kid?" I sneered.

Sushmita did not say a single word but it was evident from her face that she was hurt at the way I highlighted her inefficiency in front of the others.

Fearing that the situation may become worse, Raj changed the topic to a lighter one.

Sushmita was a very gentle girl. So, despite my shameful behaviour in front of our friends, she did not retaliate. She, rather, tried not to escalate our argument and kept quiet so as not to spoil the mood of the occasion.

Sushmita does not drink, but Ankita's and Smita's persistence paid off, and she drank a bit, albeit reluctantly, since it was a special occasion for us. We drank and ate to our heart's content till around 1 a.m. Though the party ended on a good note, the differences that had popped up between Sushmita and me, were far from over.

....

Three more years passed by. We had spent eight years in Delhi. Despite Sushmita's best efforts, she could not convince me about having a baby and this led to many fall-outs between us. By this time, Sushmita had changed her company. Her new office was now in Greater Noida, a little closer to our apartment compared to Gurugram. Since she was a sincere and focused girl, she was doing very well professionally. Her new company gave her a good hike and she was by then earning more than me. I had remained in the same organisation, though my life had become a little difficult as both my manager and delivery manager, who had liked me and exposed me to various opportunities, had left the company and moved on to better jobs. I was not able to get along well with the two people - Vivek Singh and Prem Kumar — who replaced Dubey and Arora, my ex managers, respectively.

Sourav, meanwhile, had made a name for himself as one of the reputed doctors of Delhi, and had joined Apollo Hospital. He had broken up with his school girlfriend as well as his medical college girlfriend. Eventually, he married his classmate from his MD days at AIIMS. His wife Mehar, a tall, fair and beautiful Punjabi girl, was a doctor at Delhi's Max Hospital. She hailed from a wealthy family; her father was a Chandigarh-based industrialist.

We invited both of them over for dinner on a weekend. They came late, for which they apologised.

"Such a hectic day! Actually, I planned to be free by 5 p.m., but then I got a call from the home ministry. The Home Secretary's relative wanted an urgent appointment. So, I had to wait for them. I am very sorry for being late," said Sourav apologetically.

Sourav had always been a very well-behaved person. That's why everyone liked him. My wife was not an exception. A very handsome boy, he had remained slim and trim even during his college days and that's the reason he had never been short of girlfriends. But of late, he had put on a lot of weight.

"It's okay. You were in an emergency service,"

Sushmita smiled at him, as we carried our drinks to the dining table. Since it was late, it was mutually decided to have dinner right away.

"Had it been from any other place, I would have cancelled it. But you know I can't avoid the Home Secretary," Sourav said. There was obvious pride in his voice.

"He has some very high-profile patients," as we sat down at the dining table, I told Sushmita about Sourav, who acknowledged this with a broad smile.

"As it happens I, too, am busy these days as the interior work for our new apartment is going on," Mehar informed us, as she took some rice to have with the chicken curry. We had kept the menu simple.

"You have bought another apartment?" I asked Sourav, who was helping himself to the prawn malai curry.

"Very recently. This is a 4-BHK apartment. We will shift there after the interiors are fully done," Mehar explained.

"I am also planning to shift to another apartment," I said, much to Sushmita's annoyance. "These days, we need at least a 3-BHK apartment. Otherwise, it is difficult to manage when our parents, friends or relatives visit us," I said, but my main objective was to get Sushmita's support to buy a posh, luxury 4-BHK apartment. Sushmita quietly continued with her dinner.

"Would this all have been possible through football?" Sourav asked mischievously.

"Not at all," I agreed, shaking with laughter.

"I keep telling the story of your comeback to many students who come to me for motivation," said Sourav over his drink.

"How is Amit da, by the way? You visited him when you went to the USA on work, didn't you?" asked Sourav.

"Yes, I went to his place. Amit da is incredible. What he has achieved at such a young age is amazing!" I proudly told Sourav.

Sourav reminded Mehar about Amit da, but she, however, could not place him.

After dinner, we trooped back to the drawing room, where our adda continued for a while on general topics, such as apartments vis-à-vis bungalows or kothis as they are called in Delhi, cars (Sourav drove a Honda City, while Mehar drove a Baleno), mobile phones, alcohol and the like.

Though Sushmita liked Sourav, she could not participate much in our discussions on material things. They left soon after, around midnight. Before leaving, Sourav gave us the news that Mehar was expecting. He also advised us to have a baby without delaying further, which probably made Sushmita happy.

"Now, I will book an upscale apartment next week – the one that I showed you in the newspaper – and sell this off. It's time to change my car too; I think I'll go for a glamorous sedan this time," I mused that night, lying on the bed, thinking about Sourav's new apartment and his gleaming white Honda City. "You saw how Sourav looked when he was driving the Honda City?" I asked Sushmita.

"But how is it possible? We will buy all this later," Sushmita brushed away my dreams.

"When? When will we enjoy? When we grow old and grey?" I sat up, annoyed.

"But it's not possible now," she said firmly.

"It's quite possible! I have calculated it. Whatever we

will get by selling this apartment, we will give as the down payment. Then you will take a home loan for the rest of the amount. Your salary has increased. You can very easily afford it. And I will take a car loan for the sedan," I outlined my idea.

But Sushmita held fast to her point of view. She wanted to stay in this 2-bedroom apartment as she did not want to burden herself with a significantly higher financial commitment. However, I was not the one to give up easily, either. I kept coaxing her, controlling my temper with difficulty.

Sushmita, rather, insisted that we follow Sourav and Mehar's example and get ready for a baby which I brushed aside, again.

From the day we got married, I had made sure that we both knew who would wear the pants in our house. I had always made Sushmita listen to me and do what I suggest, in every matter. Though she had become fed up with, what she called 'my controlling nature', she used to give in eventually. And so she did, in this matter as well. I booked a 4-bedroom apartment like Sourav and bought a Toyota Corolla, a very classy sedan, for us.

Honestly, I had thought that those things would make me happy. I thought the more I owned, the better I would feel. I thought those material objects would enhance our respect in the eyes of our friends, relatives and acquaintances.

....

"Go to the other room and talk," I told Sushmita as her constant chattering over the phone woke me up from my sleep.

"My mother is seriously ill. You get up now. It's already 8O' clock," said Sushmita irritably after disconnecting the phone call.

"But I don't feel like getting up now. I've got a headache. Don't I have the freedom to sleep a little longer on Sundays?" I asked in a sluggish voice. "Why don't you go to the other room and talk?" I requested her, politely.

"You didn't do anything fantastic last night. You just attended a party with your friends," she said, sounding more irritated.

"What's wrong with that?" I asked, getting irked. "Didn't I tell you just now about my headache?"

"I told you not to go to Raj's house. You don't have to party every weekend! You should cut down on your alcohol and change your lifestyle."

I understood that she was in a bad mood.

"What's wrong with you this morning?" I asked her, sighing.

"My mother is seriously ill. She needs to be operated up on immediately," Sushmita replied, in an anxious voice, sitting down on the bed, facing me.

"How is that related to my alcohol and lifestyle?"

"Of course it's related!" she snapped. "It's because of your extravagant, fancy lifestyle that I have to think twice before sending money to my parents."

"What extravagances?" I was by now fully awake, but still lying on my side of the bed. "Both of us are software engineers, working for more than eight years. We can enjoy this much."

"Yes, you can but there should be a limit to everything. I told you not to buy this costly apartment. Neither was there any urgency for the Corolla," she fumed.

"But we can afford these," I said in a matter-of-fact voice.

"It is still an unnecessary expenditure. We have to pay such huge EMIs," she said.

"We earn. Where's the problem?" I retorted.

"The problem is we don't have any savings, Siddhartha. Now I need money for my mother's treatment but I have to think twice before spending that extra amount. Moreover, if either of us suddenly loses our job, we will be in deep waters," she said, visibly concerned.

"You always think negatively. Why should I think about the future and spoil my present?" I propped myself up against the back rest of the bed, stifling a yawn.

"Enjoyment is the only word you know! Ever since we came to Delhi, you have been enjoying only," she grumbled. "You never took any responsibility. Your parents are well-settled, Siddhartha, but my parents are dependent on me. My father does not have much savings. Whatever he earned throughout his life, he spent on my education. I have to reconstruct our house in Kolkata. You know the dilapidated condition of the house... two elderly people stay there all alone. I have a responsibility towards them as I am their only child," she told me, pacing up and down the room, restlessly.

This was not the first time she was telling me all this. This has been Sushmita's regular 'speech' whenever we have argued over my lifestyle and expenses.

"You do your duty. But let me lead my life also," I said

without giving much importance to her words, and getting up from bed. "Why are you saying these things? Have I ever stopped you from doing anything for your parents?" I retorted as I headed towards the bathroom.

"You have stopped... not directly... but indirectly," she accused me while walking out of the room to prepare our breakfast.

I was about to say something but I restrained myself. I was not feeling particularly good, thanks to the hangover from the previous night's booze party at Raj's house. Sushmita had already spoilt my mood in the morning.

I sulked throughout the day. We neither went out that day nor did we talk to each other. I slept in the afternoon after lunch, which made me feel much better.

In the evening I felt like drinking again. Sushmita was sleeping in the bedroom. I sat down with a glass and a bottle of whisky in the drawing room.

Sushmita came into the room after half an hour or so and stopped short, seeing me drinking.

"You've started again?" Sushmita asked, exasperated.

These days I'm really surprised to find her in a perpetually sour mood. She had been a soft and sweet girl, but has been behaving very rudely and strangely these days.

"What else am I supposed to do on a Sunday evening?" I asked her, puzzled.

"Is this the only work you can do on a Sunday evening?"

"Yes. This is my only work! If you continue to behave like this, I will never listen to you. I don't even have the right to sleep late at my own house on Sundays!" I protested. "I have achieved a lot, and on my own, so far. Nobody gave me my job just by seeing my face, Sushmita! Nobody in our office has travelled to so many foreign countries like me within their first five years. I've been to Los Angeles, New York, Chicago, London, Frankfurt, Tokyo, Shanghai and so many other places. I was the best employee for three consecutive years!" I concluded triumphantly.

She kept quiet.

"But these days things in office are not going well, as you know. That's the reason I am stressed out and that's the reason I am drinking a bit more," I tried to justify my alcohol consumption.

"You just need an excuse to drink. Sometimes, you drink because you are unhappy; sometimes, you drink because you are happy and need to celebrate. Sometimes, it's cold so you need to drink rum; sometimes, it's hot so you need to drink beer. And it goes on," she said, unable to control her anger.

I did not speak for a few seconds as I really didn't have any excuses left. Yes, she was right; I needed an excuse to drink. But I couldn't stay without a couple of pegs these days.

"The work pressure is too much in the office. Sometimes it's unbearable," I put up the same argument again, sullenly.

"I am in the same profession, Siddhartha. I have work pressure too," she said, but in a gentler tone this time.

"Yes, I know. I am stressed out as I have to deal with two hostile bosses!" I was getting annoyed with all this back and forth.

"And you drink such expensive whiskies – Chivas Regal, Jack Daniel and all. When we go to any restro-bar, you always choose the costliest one. It's because of you that I can't send money for my mother's treatment," Sushmita had become furious that evening.

"What's your issue?" I asked angrily. Her constant pesky talks were now getting on my nerves - and it had started since the morning.

"I want you to stop drinking and stop this expensive lifestyle!" she said forthrightly.

"You send money for your mother's treatment, but don't ask me to sacrifice my life," I countered, obstinately.

"They have raised me. I just can't send money and stay here. Doctors in Kolkata have advised them to go to another city for better treatment immediately. I have decided to call them here," she explained, suddenly looking helpless.

"But next week my parents are coming," I said, taken aback.

"That's the problem. My parents don't want to come when your parents are here. They had a very bitter experience last time. Your parents, especially your father, insulted my father," she accused.

"Don't lie. They never insulted them," I said, raising my voice this time. "They just had an argument. That's not called an insult."

"No, that was an insult. Your father raised the issue of my father's social status and financial condition. He even accused my father of serving low-quality food at our wedding!" raising her voice, Sushmita came up close to where I was sitting.

I kept listening to her accusations against my father. But I could feel my temper soaring, my head throbbing.

"Your father has been interfering in our family matters for a long time. Anyway, ask them to cancel their tickets this time as my parents need to come here urgently," she said.

"I can't tell them. They are my parents. If they want to come, I can't tell them 'no'," I snapped, drinking a few sips of whisky in-between.

"You are a coward. You allow your father to torture your wife and her family. I have been facing this nonsense from the day I first met your father," she said, roughly.

The way Sushmita was accusing my father and me, caught me by surprise that day. This was a completely new Sushmita whom I did not know.

"Now you are hurting my self-respect. You know I fought with my father to marry you," I yelled at her.

"You did not do me any favour," she shouted back angrily.

I was already drunk. Her last sentence made me see red. Before I knew it, I slapped her hard.

"You have slapped me again?" she cried out, her hand against her cheek. "This is the second time you have hit me!" she screamed, as tears ran down her cheeks.

"Remember what you told me just now?" I was really angry and irritated.

"But that does not give you the license to slap me," she said, still crying. "I have tolerated a lot. This time I will inform Mama," she threatened, wiping her eyes.

"Do whatever you want," I mumbled. By that time, I was pretty drunk; I really had no sense of what was going on, what I had said or done.

"My biggest mistake was to marry you. I have been suffering for that. It was my decision, so I can't even tell anyone. But now I will tell at least Mama; he must know your true colour," she said, stomping off to the bedroom.

I had two more pegs after she left. That night, neither of us had dinner. I did not go to the room either. I slept off on the drawing room sofa.

....

Next day, Sushmita did not talk to me. I tried to talk to her, but she did not reply. I went to great lengths to convince her that it was she who had provoked me and these things happen between husband and wife. I did my utmost to make her understand how much I loved her, and that I just hadn't been able to control myself in that inebriated condition.

The following weekend, her Mama and Mami came over to our apartment and explained that we have to stay peacefully together. Her Mama warned me that if I beat Sushmita one more time, he wouldn't tolerate it again.

I knew that I had made a mistake by slapping her, but I loved her too. I was pretty upset with her that she had told her Mama about it. Why should she tell any outsider? She hurt my pride that day.

In the meantime, I had managed to convince my parents, who by then had retired, to cancel their tickets. As usual, my father was very upset with me and even accused me of being a henpecked husband.

Sushmita's parents came to Delhi the week after. Although everything seemed normal between us, Sushmita's behaviour was still far from cordial when we two were alone.

Anyway, we admitted Sushmita's mother at the Ganga Ram Hospital for her surgery. After the operation, her parents stayed with us for a month. Sushmita and I ensured that we did not fight in front of her recuperating mother.

Before leaving for Kolkata, her mother told me, "Now, you should have a baby immediately."

In the meantime, our relationship had started to become normal again. I finally agreed to have a child. But six months passed by and Sushmita did not conceive. We then decided to consult an infertility specialist. The doctor prescribed some tests for both of us. The test reports revealed that my semen count was far less than normal and this was the reason behind Sushmita's not conceiving. The doctor prescribed some medicines for both of us.

"You need to quit smoking and cut down on your alcohol intake," the doctor told me categorically, when we showed her the test reports. "You need to lose weight, too, as you have high cholesterol," the doctor looked at me, as she handed the reports back to us.

I kept quiet and came out of the chamber assuring her that I would abide by her suggestions.

"I have told you many a time in the past to stop smoking, but you never bothered to listen! Your father thinks that the problem is with me," Sushmita told me bitterly, as we drove back home from the hospital. "The doctor also told you to lose weight. If you stop drinking, you will automatically lose weight," she added. "Siddhartha, please start exercising! You were so slim and handsome when we came to Delhi. But now you are more than 100kg. Have you seen yourself in the mirror?" she asked, her mouth a straight sulky line.

I did not know whether she was accusing me or trying to motivate me.

"I don't like to impress any other girl apart from you," I replied, wanting to make the situation a little lighter, but she was clearly not in the mood. "Stop talking rubbish!" she said angrily.

"But these are not the only things the doctor said," I retorted, stopping the car as the traffic signal changed.

"But these are the main things she pointed out."

"She spoke about stress also. You know how stressed I am because of work and office politics," I reminded her, trying to justify my position. "Plus, in the metro cities with so much traffic and pollution, anyone will be stressed out in my position," I said, gently accelerating as the signal changed to green.

"Then do yoga and meditation if you can't manage your stress," she suggested.

I laughed and said, "You very well know that I don't like yoga and all. I can read a book or listen to music to reduce my stress, but I can't behave like those sadhu babas with long flowing beard, doing yoga and giving lectures. These are all unscientific."

"For god's sake, Siddhartha, yoga is a science," Sushmita stared at me incredulously. "Don't have any preconceived notion about India's culture and ancient past. Now even Westerners are adopting yoga as a stress reliever," she said.

"Let them," I shrugged. "Only the idiots in the First World countries are doing yoga, not sane people," I countered, overtaking the car in front of us. "I've told you the situation at work, haven't I? Even after nine years, I have to prove myself again. We could not deliver two projects to our US clients on time. Kumar was livid with me. He thought that I was responsible. But the fact is that it was due to his own incompetence. He openly promotes my juniors. He is encouraging my juniors to bypass me!"

Really, I was almost at my wit's end, devising ways and means to tackle my manager Prem Kumar.

"I know he doesn't like you, but these days you are not giving your hundred per cent to anything, Siddhartha, are you? Be honest. I am your wife. I can see your attitude has changed drastically. For you, fun and enjoyment have become the most important things in life," she pointed out.

"I am stressed out. I need a break. I can't take the pressure anymore," I said, getting exasperated with all this lecture, accusations, and gyan.

"But how will you take a break? Who will pay the EMIs for you? The EMIs for our house and car are so much that we both must work," Sushmita sneered. "That's why I told you not to buy such a costly apartment and car together."

"But these are necessities," I countered.

"No... unnecessary! We needed an apartment and a car, but not the high-end ones. Then you also spent so much in decorating the apartment," she complained.

"Oh no, don't start again!" I groaned, driving the car up the gentle slope and inside the society complex, and then slowly turning right and straight into the basement parking lot.

"Okay, I won't say anything. But that won't end your troubles," she said as I parked the car in our dedicated parking box. We both entered our apartment without speaking to each other.

In the evening, I got a call from Kumar who unnecessarily blamed me for a mistake when I wasn't even at fault. I tried to defend myself but he insulted me and disconnected the phone without giving me an opportunity to speak. It was becoming difficult for me to take it anymore. I felt like quitting my job the very next day. But then I remembered the EMIs too.

I took out a bottle of Chivas Regal from the gleaming mini-bar that I had personally designed with great care and interest. Everyone who came to my new house praised the design of the mini-bar in the drawing room.

Sushmita was in some other room when I was talking to Kumar. I had already made myself comfortable with my drink when she entered the drawing room.

"What on earth...?" she asked astounded. "Have you already forgotten what the doctor told you today?" To say she was livid would be putting it mildly. "That means you don't want a baby?"

"I want a baby, but do you know what Kumar told me just now?" I said in a tired voice.

"That's part of our job. I also face these. But I want a baby anyhow and you have to quit alcohol and smoking," she warned me.

"I won't be able to quit it. Do whatever you want," I responded rudely, probably because of her behaviour.

"But you have to quit!" she demanded, trying to snatch my bottle and glass away.

This was getting too much. I pushed her back and she fell on the floor. I hurried to pull her up, but she did not allow me to touch her. She got up on her own. She did not tell me a single word. She went into her room and started sobbing, lying on the bed.

....

Though the push was not a deliberate one and it was not to hurt her, I hardly realised that on that night I had unknowingly pushed myself out of Sushmita's heart completely. That was probably the end of her feelings for me. After that incident, Sushmita never behaved normally with me. Things never got back to the same again.

Apart from some routine stuff, she had stopped talking to me completely. We lived in the same apartment, but it seemed we were living in two different houses. She would make breakfast and we would have it together but we did not talk to each other. She would go to work in her office cab, while I would drive down to my office. In the evenings, after returning from work, she would call up her parents, relatives or friends and colleagues or resume some office work on her laptop. When dinner was ready, she would call me for dinner and we would have a silent meal.

After three months or so, on a Sunday, she went for a bath just before lunch, her mobile phone was lying on the dining table. I heard the ping of a text message on her mobile. I casually checked it, thinking there might be an important message from her boss. But I got the shock of my life when I read the message.

It was from Himanshu, Sushmita's colleague. The message read 'Miss you'. Sushmita used to talk about Himanshu, but I never had any doubts that he was anything more than a colleague to her. Likewise, since the day we met in the afternoon at the Jadavpur Engineering College campus, I had never doubted Sushmita's integrity and character; I knew she was not, and never would be, interested in any other man in her life. But that day, I was stunned by that message. I felt insulted, as though she had struck me across my face. In the evening, I asked her about it.

"You saw the message? Actually, I was also surprised to see the message from Himanshu. I messaged him back.

He replied it was meant for his girlfriend," she said.

But she did not sound convincing. Her expression suggested that she was lying and trying to hide the matter from me.

"Show me his replies," I challenged her.

"I have deleted the messages. If anyone sees it by chance, what will they think?"

Though I could not catch her red-handed, my doubts remained. And as my doubts grew stronger, I became more restless. I could sense that our distance had grown wider, because these days she did not ask me to stop drinking or smoking. She did not ask me to go out. She did not plan a vacation or a weekend trip.

I became more of an alcoholic as days passed. I started to drink like a fish and smoke like a chimney. For the first time in my life, I felt detached from Sushmita. I felt that she was not totally with me, that she was drifting away.

It started taking a toll on me. I could not concentrate on my work at office as I kept thinking about her secret affair even though I had no proof of it. Unintentionally, I handed Kumar – who was already displeased with me – one opportunity after the other to further humiliate me at office.

My suspicions grew stronger when I saw Sushmita keeping her phone with herself all the time. Earlier, I would use her phone sometimes for banking transactions and for some other work. But these days, she was reluctant to let me use her phone. One other thing that struck me as odd was that she returned rather late from her office. Earlier, she would return by 8 p.m., but nowadays, 9.30 p.m. became her regular time.

Six months went by. Sushmita's behaviour and attitude further fuelled my apprehensions. In the meantime, one of my colleagues, Prateek, had joined her company. After giving the matter some thought, I met him one day at a bar and confided to him about my suspicions on Sushmita and Himanshu having an affair. Though he was in another division, I requested him to keep an eye on her in the office.

"Please inform me. It's about my life," I pleaded.

"I'll do that. Don't worry," Prateek assured me.

After seven days or so, Prateek called me up and said that although nobody was sure about Sushmita and Himanshu's relationship, they could be seen taking lunch or breaks together.

One day, it was around 10.30 p.m. but Sushmita hadn't yet come back from work. I kept calling her from about 9.45 p.m. or thereabouts, but she didn't take my calls. I was sitting in the drawing room having my usual whisky, when she finally strolled in at 11 p.m.

"Why are you so late? I have been calling you for so long. Why didn't you answer the phone?" I asked her agitatedly.

"I had an important meeting at office. I had kept the phone on silent mode," she replied coolly.

"Why are you adding to my worries?" I asked her quietly.

"No need to be worried about me. I can see you were having a good time," she told me as an obvious reference to my drinking.

"But I was worried!" I protested.

"Really? You care about me?"

"What do you think?"

"No, you don't. You only care for yourself."

"So, who cares for you then? Your colleague Himanshu?"

"Don't talk rubbish! All this alcohol has addled your brain," she said, going to the bedroom to change.

I was getting angry, but since I didn't have any evidence that Sushmita was involved with Himanshu, I held my tongue. I decided to not rush things.

After sometime she called me for dinner. We were having our dinner quietly. Suddenly, she broke the silence by saying,

"I am going for a one-month tour to the USA to meet a client."

"You are going alone?"

"No. Two of my colleagues are also going."

"Who are they?"

"Himanshu and Tanvir."

"You can't go with Himanshu."

"What?"

"You can't go with Himanshu," I said firmly.

"It's official work. I need to go," she insisted.

"I said 'no'. You can't go."

"Don't be silly. I have to go," she said, finishing her dinner.

I was sure by then that she was having an affair with

Himanshu. If they would go together, their bonding would become stronger. I would not be able to prevent her from drifting away from me further. I wanted her back. But I did not know how.

....

Despite my resistance, Sushmita went for that office tour to the US. I can still remember the day when she was leaving. I begged her not to go till the last moment. I didn't want to lose her.

I was so upset that I did not go to office that day, and started drinking from the morning itself. Sushmita's flight was at night but she remained indifferent to me despite seeing me drinking like a fish.

When she was finally leaving, I felt my heart would burst, and, although I knew it sounded silly, I again pleaded one last time, "Is it that necessary to go? Can't you cancel the tour?"

While putting on her shoes, she told me coldly, "I'm getting late."

As she went out of the apartment, I felt I had lost her completely, that nothing was left between us. I felt all alone again, after so many years. I felt like crying out aloud. I felt like running down to the taxi and pulling her out. I felt like begging her 'to forgive me one last time, but please don't leave me, I don't want to be alone'. As these thoughts and emotions kept running through my mind, I saw from the balcony her taxi pulling out of our gated society.

I never thought Sushmita would ever change like that. I can still remember our Ranikhet trip, just after a year of our marriage. It is a perfect destination for romance for any newly married couple. My love for mountains added an extra flavour to our love. It is a picturesque, tranquil hill station in Uttarakhand, maintained beautifully by regiments of the Indian army. It was a sunny day when we reached Ranikhet. After lunch, we went sightseeing. Just before sunset, we lay down side by side on the vast green meadow of the golf course and pledged not to leave each other.

In the evening it got really chilly. We visited the bar of Ranikhet Club, a British army club still patronised by the local cantonment officers, where Sushmita first tasted alcohol in a cocktail, and felt a little dizzy. We had a sumptuous Continental dinner, since she loved Continental food. After dinner, when we were walking back to our resort in the dark hilly roads, amidst a stinging chilly wind, she clung to me and whispered 'I love you' several times.

Next morning, when we were walking on the winding roads surrounded by the beautiful pine and oak forests, holding each other's hands, she told me, 'Please don't leave me for even a single day!' The beautiful Kumaon Hills were witness to our love and pledges of love. We were inseparable.

We visited so many places together. But whenever I think about some of our happy memories, the Ranikhet trip comes to mind first and foremost. We enjoyed the whole tour in each other's company amidst beautiful natural surroundings.

Next morning when I woke up, it was already 11 a.m. I did not remember for how long did I continue to drink after Sushmita had left for the USA the previous night. I did not feel like going to office anymore. I felt distraught throughout the day. In the evening, Sushmita messaged me that she had reached Los Angeles safely. Relieved that she had landed safely, and yet depressed that she had gone, I sat down with my bottle of whisky that evening.

Next day when I reached office, Kumar called me and wanted to know the reason behind my absence for two consecutive days. I replied that I had been unwell, but he blasted me in front of my juniors for neglecting my work.

"You know we have to complete this on-going project within seven days. How can you bunk office at this time? How irresponsible of you, Sid!" he reprimanded me severely. "If you don't feel like working here anymore, I suggest you resign," he told me in front of my juniors, giving me a final warning.

Two days later, Prateek called up to say that he had come to know from someone close to Sushmita that she had confessed to her friend that she was in a serious relationship with Himanshu.

So, my apprehension was correct! At night, I had a terrifying dream: Sushmita was roaming around in Los Angeles with Himanshu, enjoying herself. They were holding each other's hands, and staying together in a hotel room. I woke up at around 4 a.m., sweating profusely. I was very disturbed. I went to the drawing room, where I had kept the half-finished bottle of whisky and the glass on the centre table. I poured out some whisky for myself.

I'm not fully certain, but I think I drank till about 8 a.m. I was feeling drowsy; totally out of my senses. But I could not miss office that day as it was a very important day; we were supposed to be assessing the nitty-gritties of that prestigious 'on going' project before handing it over to the client.

I somehow got ready for office and plodded to the parking slot, even forgetting to lock the main door of the apartment. As I sat in the car, I felt tipsy and befuddled. Still, I had no option but to reach office on time, and so I drove to work. I could not understand what was happening around me on the road. Everything was looking distorted: pedestrians, cars, buses, buildings all were hazy and blurred. I may have driven recklessly but I still made it to office in one piece!

I tried very hard to look normal and behave normally, but I was completely drunk. I was sitting at my work station, when Kumar called me for the meeting with him and our delivery manager, Vivek Singh. I stumbled and tottered into the conference room. Soon after I started speaking, I began fumbling. I felt I was stammering and could not express myself clearly.

Kumar asked me, taken aback, "Sid, have you been drinking? Are you drunk?"

I did not say anything, but he understood by then that I was in an inebriated condition.

"This is not done! You can't come to office like this," he said.

I suddenly lost my cool and started shouting.

"I know… but youuuuuu… have forced me… me... to come like this!" I steadied myself, holding onto a chair, and proceeded, "Despite working… soooo… hard, you insulted me in front of my juuu… juniors. You son of a… bitchhh," I yelled at Kumar, who was by then probably a bit scared.

He took a few steps back.

"Sid, behave yourself. Whatever problems you have with Kumar, we can solve it by discussing amicably, but this is not ethical. Today is such an important day and you have come in this state!" Singh spoke up sternly.

"But he is a buuuuustard. Our problem… my prob… belm cannot be re… rectified by simply talking," I continued incoherently.

“Enough is enough, you go home now,” Singh said in a firm voice.

I was about to say something but Singh asked me to get out of the meeting room and leave the office then and there.

I did not know what to do. I thought of punching Kumar on his face. But I didn’t. When I unsteadily walked out of the office, it seemed to me that everyone on our floor was standing up, staring at me. I somehow drove back to my apartment and drank till I lost all awareness of sense and perception.

Under the influence of alcohol, I could not understand what had exactly happened or how much damage I had inflicted on my professional career. My personal life was already in jeopardy. Now, my professional life was hanging in balance too.

****

5

Vivek Singh, the delivery manager in my office, told me not to come to office till our Ethics Committee completed its investigation. I was served a show cause notice by the Ethics Committee by email after three days of the incident. I wrote my side of the story, holding Prem Kumar responsible for the fiasco while, simultaneously, requesting pardon for going to office in an intoxicated state.

After 15 days or so, I got a mail from my office, stating that I have been terminated from my employment due to 'unethical practices and working contrary to the policies laid down by the company.'

I had worked really hard in the initial five years, which saw me becoming a team lead. After becoming the team lead, my performance increased manifold mainly because of my rapport, professional relationship and deep understanding with Arora and Dubey. When they resigned three years ago, they both offered me a position in their respective companies in Bengaluru, but I did not accept as Sushmita's job was in Delhi, NCR. Moreover, my office was 10-15 minutes' drive from my apartment, which was another attraction for me. I did not like driving through heavy traffic. To tell the truth, my current job had become like a cocoon which gave me both security and comfort. Admittedly, working in the same company had made me complacent too. That day, I understood that in the private sector no one remembers your past performance. Only the present matters here.

A call on my mobile from an unknown number broke my reverie.

I ignored it as I wasn't in the mood to talk to anyone at that moment.

The phone rang again.

And this time, I reluctantly answered the phone.

"Is that Siddhartha Lahiri?"

"Yes, speaking."

"This is Sushanta. Do you remember me?"

"Which Sushanta?"

"Arre, Sushanta, your football teammate from Siliguri. We used to play in the same team... remember?" he said excitedly.

"Ohhh... footballer Sushanta?"

"Yes, yes. How are you?" he asked cheerfully.

I really did not know how I was, so, I evaded his question.

Instead, I asked, "How did you get my number?"

"I got your number from Arka. He told me that you were in Delhi."

"Yes, I am in Delhi, but where are you these days?"

"I stay in Kolkata most of the time."

"In Kolkata? You are posted there?"

"I play for the Mohun Bagan team and also for the

Indian team."

"Oh! That's great, Sushanta," I said.

"Our national camp is currently being held in Delhi. That's why I have come to Delhi. I was thinking of meeting you," the eagerness in Sushanta's voice was unmistakable.

Though I was feeling down and out only a few minutes back, I suddenly felt better hearing Sushanta's voice. I had not met him since I quit football almost 18 years ago, nor did I have any clue about what he had been doing all these years.

I didn't know he was in the national team. After I left football, Sushanta had continued playing, and I had concentrated solely on my studies. Though sometimes we would bump into each other in class, I never met him after he failed in Class IX. Moreover, I had become so self-centred and busy in my own life that I never really bothered to enquire about him.

"You are in the Indian team!"

"Yes. I've been playing for India for the last five years."

"I am so happy for you," I said, genuinely pleased for him, as I had seen him struggling a lot during our schooldays.

"Siddhartha, you could have also played for the country had you continued," he said.

"Leave it. That's over and done with."

Suddenly, my football memories flooded my mind.

"Tell me your story. How did you make it to the Indian team?" this time it was I who was excited.

"I'll tell you when we meet. When do I get to see you?"

"I'll... I'll let you know," I said.

"I can hardly wait to see you, Siddhartha!"

"I too want to meet you," I told him cheerfully.

We spoke for a few more minutes and then hung up, promising to meet soon. Once our conversation ended, all my memories associated with football returned to agonise me. Sushanta had reignited those images of the past. My formidable combination with Sushanta on the football ground, my friendship with him, the excitement around the matches, Mayna Sir's training, Baba's insult to Mayna Sir - even, how heartbroken I had been with Argentina's performance in the World Cup finals! Despite my situation, I couldn't help smiling. I had so many memories with football.

Sushmita called me in the evening. I told her I had lost my job, but managed to restrain myself from talking about her relationship with Himanshu. I had decided that I would tackle that when she returned to India. She asked me many more questions, specifically, on office politics, but I didn't feel like discussing anything with her.

"You are responsible for this day. I had warned you. Alcohol will spoil your life," she began. "If you had—"

I cut her short, "You needn't worry. You enjoy your holiday."

"I have come here for work," she retorted, "not to enjoy."

"You know better," I said and disconnected; I didn't feel like talking to her anymore.

In the meantime, I contacted my former bosses, my former colleagues, my classmates, but they all said they would get back to me if there was any vacancy. I applied to several other companies as well.

When my parents learnt that I had lost my job, they booked train tickets through the tatkal scheme and came to Delhi within a couple of days to be with me. Since Sushmita was not here, my parents did not want to take the risk of leaving me alone in such a mental state.

Sushmita came back from the US, but the chord in our relationship was broken permanently. Sushmita hardly spoke with me. If she ever talked to me regarding any family matters, her relationship with Himanshu would invariably pop up in my mind and I could not be normal with her. I thought of asking her about her relationship, but I felt that I should first get some evidence.

Moreover, those days, whenever she spoke with me, she didn't look at me directly. She was either avoiding me or, perhaps, her relationship with Himanshu, so preoccupied her that she forgot my existence altogether.

I was staying at home most of the time after I lost my job, and had become so volatile that I could not maintain any shred of decency. I would drink in front of my parents, which was deeply disliked by my parents and Sushmita. My favourite drinking spot was the drawing room, as my mini-bar took the place of pride there. Baba and I often argued over this. I told him I could not live without alcohol; if he did not like my way of living, he was welcome to go back to Siliguri.

I had no clue why I was getting furious with Baba. He was not responsible for my dismissal from work, nor for Sushmita's affair, yet my resentment towards him grew day by day. Maybe, deep down, subconsciously, I held Baba responsible for every single thing that went sideways in my life at that time.

....

It was our tenth marriage anniversary. Every year, Sushmita and I celebrated this day with our friends and colleagues with dinner. The previous year too we had had a decent celebration. Sushmita had promised me that we would celebrate our tenth anniversary in a grand style.

But given the circumstances, I did not expect a grand party, but I still harboured a slight hope that Sushmita would make at least some suitable arrangements to mark the occasion. Ever since she had thrown that surprise party for me on our fifth anniversary, she had taken the onus of organising everything, from A to Z, down to the last detail. To my utter surprise, I saw Sushmita getting ready for her office, her expressionless face revealing nothing.

Still in bed, thinking about our wedding anniversary celebrations all these years, I sighed wistfully. I was fully awake, but did not feel like getting up.

"Isn't today your marriage anniversary?" I heard Baba asking Sushmita, as she ate her breakfast.

Sushmita kept quiet.

"Have you invited people for dinner?" Baba asked her.

Sushmita didn't respond.

"Should I go to the market to buy fish or chicken for today?" Baba enquired again.

"I have some very important work in office today. I will be late in the evening. You people do what you want to do," she replied coldly.

"You will be late today?" Baba told her disapprovingly, after a pause. "You should have taken a day off."

"I have already told you; I have an important meeting at office today," Sushmita repeated.

"Siddhartha has been suffering so much. He would have felt better if you had arranged something for the evening," Ma told Sushmita politely.

"You arrange. I have not stopped you. I will be late," Sushmita said in a clipped tone.

Ma kept quiet.

"Really, Sushmita, you are not giving enough attention to Siddhartha! This is the time he needs you the most. He has been drinking throughout the day… you are not even trying to stop him," Baba said in a reprimanding manner.

"Do you think it is possible to control your son? I have tried many a time in the past, but he is beyond control. So, I have stopped," she said in a voice devoid of any sympathy.

Her voice clearly reflected her complete disgust and indifference towards me. She was saying those words as if she was talking not about her husband but about someone else in our family.

"Haven't you got any responsibility towards him?" Baba asked her, annoyed.

"No. I've tried my best, but I have given up," Sushmita said firmly, with a hint of arrogance.

"Then you are a complete failure as a wife!" Baba accused her blatantly.

"If I am a failure as a wife, you are a failure as a father!" Sushmita retorted in an even harsher tone.

"Do whatever you want to do," Baba said, disgusted, and stomped back to their room.

Sushmita completed her breakfast, picked up her bag and left the house without saying anything, either to me or my parents.

I sighed; life can be very cruel sometimes. When you have everything, you don't value those things. You understand the value of things once they are gone. That day, though I was upset with Sushmita, I was more saddened at my predicament. Even a year back, I would never have imagined that I would be ignored in such a way on our tenth marriage anniversary.

I kept lying on my bed even after Sushmita left.

I got up eventually; I just did not feel like getting out of bed that day. After some time, Ma served me breakfast, but I didn't have any appetite. That day, everything looked dull and every dish tasted bland and unpalatable to me.

Everything seemed tasteless, soundless and emotionless. I knew I had lost my job, but I would get another job. But would I ever get Sushmita back in my life?

....

We had a quiet and simple lunch, as I had told Baba during our breakfast not to arrange anything special for that day. I hardly talked to my parents for the rest of the day, as I was irritated after Baba's conversation with Sushmita in the morning. I did not like it when Baba insulted her or spoke badly of her, because I still loved her. She might have drifted away from me, but I still wanted to shield her from Baba.

Yes, I did have a lot of grudges against Sushmita, but when Baba said something negative about her, I would get angry with him. I was probably protective towards Sushmita from the day Baba met her at our rented apartment in Kolkata for the first time - and I continued to shield her from Baba. But the moment I would think of her relationship with Himanshu, I would lose all sense of propriety, as jealousy and rage would cloud my mind.

I started to drink from the afternoon. My parents did not talk with me either, probably fearing my cranky temper. I knew they were also upset, but I was in no mood to talk to them.

As I drank, beautiful memories of our days together came drifting back – our first meeting, the wonderful time we spent at the college campus, the evenings at the restaurants, our wedding, the initial days in Delhi, and our vacations at different locations and many more good things.

I continued drinking throughout the evening; I had never felt so lonely before.

When Sushmita finally came back from office, it was around 10 p.m.

I was hoping that she would talk to me, but she ignored me despite seeing me drinking. She went to the bedroom to change and did not come out.

I went to the room where Baba and Ma were discussing something. I asked them to have dinner without waiting for us and then go to sleep.

"You two won't have dinner now?" Ma asked.

"I will have it later, with Sushmita. You and Baba have your dinner now."

As I was too drunk, they did not argue with me. They had their dinner and quietly went back to their room.

Sushmita did not come out of the bedroom for even a moment. Once my parents retired for the night, I entered our room where Sushmita was lying in bed, on her stomach, chatting on her phone. Seeing me, she disconnected the call, promising to call again later.

Making herself comfortable on the bed, she said, looking at me, "Please have your dinner. I don't feel like having dinner today."

"What's... happened... Sush... mita? To... you..." I asked in a strangely rasping voice.

Drowning in whisky, day in and day out, was obviously taking a toll on me, both physically and mentally – the words came out jumbled, and I was swaying unsteadily.

"I hate seeing you like this," Sushmita said peevishly, sitting up on the bed.

"Wh... whom... do you want... to see then?" I asked her, grimly, but she avoided my question.

"Tell me – the truth," I said menacingly, clenching my fist. "I... I have got... all my information... from your office."

"What? What are you talking about?" Sushmita asked, acting as if she didn't know what I was talking about.

"Yes, you... youuuuu... are having an aff... affair with Hi...manshu! You went to the USA... with him... to have fun... with him," I said, trembling with rage, jabbing the air with a finger.

As it is, l was already under the influence of alcohol and, now, seeing Sushmita's fake behaviour, I was on the verge of losing my senses.

"Mind your language, Siddhartha," she yelled at me.

"You are... are a... bloooody bitch!" I was hysterical by now.

"You are crossing all limits now, Siddhartha. Back-off or I'll call the police," she threatened.

"Call – call who... ever you want. I'm... no...nottt scared," I retorted, teetering unsteadily towards her. I had lost control over my faculties by then.

"You have already spoilt my life. You can only torture your wife," she shouted at the top of her voice, and then spat, "You are impotent!"

Her face was red with fury, her eyes filled with hatred.

The word 'impotent' hit me so hard that I caught her by the hand, and struck her with all my might. And again, and again. I really did not have the capacity to understand the consequences of this fight. When I landed a good, solid blow on her nose, her scream rent the air.

My parents came rushing from the other room.

Blood oozed out from her nose.

Ma rushed up to Sushmita, and gently took her to the wash basin in the bathroom and kept pouring small quantities of water on her nose. Baba looked on, dazed.

"Just leave me alone," she whimpered in-between sobs and pushed Ma away.

Sushmita's scream, the blood, and the look on my parents' face suddenly brought me back to my senses. Mechanically, I picked up some cloth or something and went to her to wipe away the blood, but she snarled, "Don't touch me! You've ruined my life. I'm calling the police."

Her face was all puffed up, stained with tears and blood, nose swollen, eyes wild, Sushmita called her Mama. Sobbing and sniffling, she described what had happened and begged him to come immediately.

As I sat stunned in the drawing room, still unable to fully grasp the gravity of what I had done, Sushmita, weeping all the while, packed her suitcase. My parents were taken aback by this sudden turn of events.

"What have you done? You hit your wife!" that was Ma, despairing.

"How could you do this? You should not have beaten her! What's got into you?" that was Baba.

Hearing their words, Sushmita came out of the bedroom and said wearily, "This is not the first time that he has done this. I've never told you, but he has been doing this for a while. Whenever we had any arguments and he was drunk, he would hit me."

By this time, she had washed away the blood from her face, and had almost regained her composure. I was still sitting on the sofa, bent forward, my head pounding, resting on my hands; my parents, completely bewildered by the events of the night, stood in front of me.

"You also mentally tortured me and my parents," Sushmita said bitterly, directly accusing Baba. "We may be poor, but we know how to behave with people. You don't even know that. I've had enough in this house. I'm going for good, today," Sushmita finished, her lips trembling, tears rolling down her cheeks.

Still in a stupor, we all were startled when our doorbell rang suddenly, sounding unnaturally loud. Sushmita rushed to open the door.

Sushmita broke down completely when her Mama strode in through the door.

"Oh my God! How is this possible?" Sushmita's Mama said in utter disbelief, when he saw her.

Baba tried to say something, but her Mama was in no mood to listen.

"I had warned Siddhartha the last time, Mr Lahiri," he said severely, "if he physically assaulted Sushmita again, I will take action. Sushmita, come, let's go."

She readily went to him; her Mama took the suitcase from her hand.

"All of you... now get ready to face the music," her mama threatened as they stepped out of the apartment.

While she was leaving, I wanted to tell her, 'I've made a mistake, please don't leave me', 'please give me one last chance', 'please comeback' – but I could not say anything. Or, rather, I had lost the right to say anything to her.

....

"Siddhartha, get up! The police have come," Baba told me nervously, shaking me.

It was around 10 a.m. and I was sleeping.

I sprang up from bed.

I could hear Ma asking the policemen to sit in the drawing room. I noticed the frightened look on Ma's face, seeing those two policemen at home.

I hurriedly splashed some water on my face and entered the drawing room to meet the two policemen, very afraid, but trying not to show it. I have never faced any policeman in my life before.

"Mr Siddhartha Lahiri, your wife has lodged a formal complaint against you and your father for domestic violence. You two have to come with us right now to the Sector 24 police station," one of the two policemen announced formally and stiffly.

Ma had already started to sob. Giving her a weak smile, I told her not to worry.

We were taken to the SHO's (Station House Officer) chamber, which was a shabby and cluttered room, with worn-out chairs and a table. An old, faded photograph of Mahatma Gandhi smiled genially at us from the wall. Cobwebby and dusty, with noisily whirring ceiling fans, the room looked quite like the police stations that I had seen in movies. The SHO gestured us to sit; fearfully, Baba and I sat down on those rickety chairs.

"Your wife, Mrs Sushmita, has lodged some serious complaints against the two of you, Mr Lahiri," said the SHO, glancing at Baba and me as he spoke.

A heavy-set Jat, he was probably around 45 years old with a rounded, thick moustache that covered his upper lips. From his appearance it looked like he had been a wrestler in his younger days. His authoritative voice and wrestler-like physique was enough to instil fear in anyone. In any case, we were already pretty scared. A shiver ran down my spine when he said those words.

"You seem to be from a good family. But her charges are serious against you and your father," he continued. "She has registered complaints against you both, under Sections 498 A and 325 of IPC."

"What are you going to do with us now?" Baba asked him apprehensively.

"We have to take you into custody. The man who accompanied your wife is an influential person. We have got orders that we have to arrest you for at least a day," the SHO's words struck panic in our hearts. My shirt was damp with sweat; my throat, dry as a bone.

I could see Baba was terrified as well.

There was no emotion on the SHO's face, or in his voice, as they were accustomed to dealing with cases like this. But his words created enough anxiety in us. My heart had begun to pound hard in fear of my imminent arrest.

"Sir," I implored the SHO, "is there any option to avoid arrest?"

"No, no. We have pressure from higher authorities to arrest you. You can talk to a lawyer - but he has to be skilful — who will get bail for you as soon as possible," he suggested sympathetically, which was uncharacteristic of his overall physical appearance.

I have never faced any such situation before. Despite living in Noida for almost ten years, I did not have any connection whatsoever with anyone who could bail me out of this situation. I did not even know any lawyers here. I called Raj and Vaibhav from the SHO's chamber, but they said they did not know any lawyer and assured me that they would come to the police station soon.

I then called Sourav. Since he was a high-profile doctor and had many high-profile patients, I was sure he could help me in this situation. Sourav listened to everything and asked me to wait a bit till he managed a good lawyer through his patients' network.

Both Baba and I were very hopeful that Sourav would be able to bail us out in this situation. I waited for half an hour or so, but I could not get the call through to him. Then I called him without waiting much longer, as we were running out of time. But he did not pick up my call. I called him again, but again there was no response. I called Sourav almost ten times, hoping every time that he would answer the call. But when he did not take any of my calls, I felt terribly let-down and dejected. Never in my life had I felt so betrayed and disillusioned.

"What happened? No one responded?" asked the SHO, chuckling.

Though I was feeling panicky as well as betrayed, I felt some respite seeing him smile for the first time. His amused expression suggested that he was anticipating it.

"No," I said, unable to keep the disappointment from my voice.

"It happens," he shrugged. "I have seen this several times. When you need your friends the most, they show you their back," he said with a smirk.

At that moment, I could not agree with him more. I was getting tense. Baba was looking helpless and frustrated. He kept asking me to call Sourav again, as he could not believe that Sourav would betray us at that moment. I asked him to stop talking, as I knew Sourav was trying to avoid me deliberately.

"Ranjit, that day I realised you can't call anyone a 'friend'. They are simply 'fair-weather friends' - they will laugh with you, spend time with you, they are with you in your good times; but they will vanish into thin air the moment you desperately need them. You will not realise who is your friend, until you land in trouble. I have used the term 'friendship' often with so many people that I hanged out with. I thought I had many friends in my life. But no one stood by me when I needed them the most."

I was at my wit's end, wondering whom to call, who was that one person who would stand by me now - and then, yes! Sushanta. He would surely help me! But then, I hesitated; all my other 'friends' had turned their back on me. I was supposed to meet him but with things going from bad to worse after our chat over the phone, I hadn't been able to; besides, I had actually forgotten about him. However, when you have no hope left, the unthinkable comes to your mind. I decided to take a chance as I had exhausted all other options.

"Hullo? Sushanta? Siddhartha here," I began nervously, but Sushanta sounded happy at my phone call.

"When are we meeting, Siddhartha?" he asked me eagerly.

"I will meet you, but I am in deep soup right now," and told him all that had happened.

He told me not to worry as he had a lawyer friend in Delhi. He told me to give him 5 minutes. Since Sourav had also told me the same thing, I was a bit doubtful, initially.

But after a while, Sushanta called me back and gave me the number of a Mr Chatterjee, saying that he was a renowned lawyer with the Supreme Court.

I then spoke with Mr Chatterjee, who assured me that he would send his junior to the police station in an hour or so to take the details of the case. Also, that he would personally appear in the court the next day to plead for our bail.

As promised by Mr Chatterjee, a lawyer came to meet us and noted down all the information.

After some time, following due procedure, we were formally arrested and kept in the police lock-up. Fortunately, there was no one in the lock-up that day except the two of us.

The cell was very small, dark and dirty, with the foul smell of stale urine and full of cobwebs. The bathroom in the police station was equally appalling. We were given two filthy, sticky blankets and asked to sleep on the floor.

Baba kept asking me who was this friend, who 'rescued' us, helped us get the lawyer. I deliberately did not tell him about Sushanta. Instead, I told him he was an office colleague.

The whole day passed in the police lock-up. Baba and I were sitting side by side, but I was in no mood to talk to Baba; he wanted to discuss something with me, but I was not interested. For both lunch and dinner, we were given four pieces of chapatti, a small amount of daal and some kind of a mixed vegetable preparation, but the food was very ordinary and tasteless. Of course, food was the last thing on our mind.

After dinner, we laid down the blankets on the floor, to use as a mattress. Although we were mentally exhausted, there were enough mosquitoes to keep us awake. I could see Baba was also finding it difficult to sleep.

I have never slept on the floor or inside such a dirty room. There was a fan, but it was moving very slowly. I had grown accustomed to a top-notch lifestyle. Without AC or at least a proper fan, it was almost impossible for me to fall asleep.

I stayed awake most of the night, thinking about the previous night, when I had hit Sushmita repeatedly. I thought about her injured nose. I thought of enquiring about her health. I kept thinking about her only.

I was sure that it was her Mama who had forced Sushmita to press charges against us. Otherwise, she would not have gone to such an extent. I still believed that while she might not be in love with me anymore, she would not cause me any harm.

But one part of me did not accept this logic. It told me that it was Sushmita who wanted to land me in trouble and get married to Himanshu. Once this thought came, I found myself again seething with rage. It was because of her that we were here in this filthy, stinky, dingy place, sleeping on the floor in police custody that night. One part of me also wanted to take revenge on her.

But despite all this trouble, I had a soft corner for her. How could I forget the good times we had spent together? I hoped one day she would remember it all and come back to me. Yes, I yearned for her; I wanted to tell her how badly I was missing her. My face suddenly felt wet - tears were rolling down.

Through the tiny slit in the lock-up, I saw the darkness of night gradually disappear. Baba, who had been tossing and turning, restless through the night, had finally fallen asleep sometime in the course of the night.

We were produced in the Noida court at around 10 a.m. As expected, Mr Chatterjee, a sharp, handsome lawyer in his fifties, argued our case and we were granted bail without much trouble.

I thanked Mr Chatterjee. After the due procedure of getting bail, as we, along with Mr Chatterjee, were coming out of the court, I saw Sushanta waiting for us outside. I was surprised to see Sushanta wearing a three-quarter stylish pair of trousers, a branded T-shirt, Ray-Ban sunglasses perched on his nose. We hadn't met each other for so many years. His physique and facial structure hadn't changed much, and yes, by God, did he look glamorous!

I became very emotional seeing him after so many years and hugged him spontaneously. Admittedly, I did not believe in God, but at that moment, after the 24-hour ordeal, he appeared as nothing but an angel to me.

"What the hell have you become, Siddhartha?" the disbelief in Sushanta's eyes and voice was apparent, as he looked me up and down. "You have put on so much weight. I wouldn't have recognised you if had I seen you in a crowded place!"

I glanced away, feeling awkward and ashamed.

"I'm really thankful to you, Sushanta," I said, gripping his hands. "You are the only one who responded when my other friends turned their back," I could feel my voice quivering with emotion.

I was about to burst into tears, when he put his right hand on my shoulder.

"Siddhartha, I was eager to meet you ever since I learnt you were in Delhi," Sushanta's eyes crinkled as he smiled warmly. "You don't know how much I have missed you since you stopped coming to the ground."

"I was also looking forward to meeting you since the day you had called me, but I got very busy after that. A lot of things happened in my life... I never wanted to meet you this way, my friend," I told him, shaking my head, my eyes downcast.

"But, finally, we met! That's the main thing," he said excitedly, thumping my back. "By the way, let me 'formally' introduce you to Mr Chatterjee, your lawyer, and my friend and a loyal supporter of Mohun Bagan. Whenever I come to Delhi, I remain in his custody," Sushanta's laughter rang out, free and loud.

I thanked Mr Chatterjee once again, shaking his hand.

Baba, who was standing clueless next to me, was listening to our conversation. Did he recognise Sushanta?

"Baba, do you remember Sushanta? He used to play football with me in Siliguri," I turned to Baba, gesturing at Sushanta.

Sushanta bent down to touch Baba's feet. Baba's body language had changed by then, shock and disbelief etched in his face. He was completely dumbfounded.

"What do you do?" Baba asked Sushanta hesitantly.

"I play for Mohun Bagan, as well as in the Indian national football team," Sushanta smiled at Baba.

"You play for Mohun Bagan and India! I had read in the newspaper that one boy from Siliguri is playing for India. I never thought it was you, my son's childhood friend! I was once a hard core Mohun Bagan fan. I am so proud of you." Both disbelief and admiration were evident in Baba's face.

"Yes, Uncle," Sushanta answered with humility.

"We are indebted to you. You have saved us today," Baba said, his voice suddenly heavy. "I don't know how all this happened," Baba began, lamenting.

"How is Mayna Sir?" I asked Sushanta, swiftly cutting off whatever Baba was about to say.

"Mayna Sir is fine and still very fit," Sushanta's eyes sparkled, a big smile on his face now. "You know, Siddhartha, he was recently bestowed the Dronacharya Award! He is very happy and proud that I am playing for India. Despite his age, now, he regularly goes to the field and still guides the youngsters," Sushanta told me in the same breath, and then, added wistfully, "he still talks about you, Siddhartha. He thinks you would have definitely played for India, had you continued with football."

I was extremely happy to learn about Mayna Sir. He has served football loyally for more than fifty years. In fact, he had given his all for the development of football in Siliguri. He had dedicated his entire life for his countless students. I was overjoyed to see that Sushanta had fulfilled Sir's dream of playing for the country.

By then I could intuitively sense Baba was feeling ashamed of himself – seeing Sushanta's achievement and hearing about Mayna Sir's success had perhaps reminded him of his distasteful behaviour towards them all those years ago.

I felt deep down that Baba must be regretting it all now.

I have seen this in my life. Life can sometimes be harsh and tricky. It can give you the biggest of surprises. The king becomes a pauper and a pauper becomes the king. Sometimes, the very same person whom you had ignored or insulted in the past, selflessly bails you out. That's how life teaches us its lessons. But how many of us learn from life?

Things had taken a 360-degree turn for all of us. I didn't know why I was so damn pleased that Baba was feeling embarrassed, awkward and ashamed that day. Probably, I never forgave him for insulting Mayna Sir in our Siliguri house.

I requested Sushanta to come to my apartment, but since he had come with Mr Chatterjee, he had to leave with him.

"I will see you soon," Sushanta promised, as we hugged again.

Ma was waiting for us, anxiously. We hired a cab to go back home. But where was I heading to? Did I have any answers?

****

6

Sushmita didn't contact me after walking out of our apartment. I did feel like calling her once or twice, asking her how could she be so cruel. But then, my ego would tell me that since she had left me in a lurch and landed me in such serious trouble, I should never call her again.

The worst part was that all these incidents were taking a huge toll on my parents, who were fairly aged by then. Especially my mother, who had high blood sugar and high BP, and was getting worse day by day. My father had already crossed seventy, while my mother was around 67.

I was mentally devastated. I was in no position to restart my professional career. I badly needed a break. I sold my Toyota Corolla and decided to go back to my hometown Siliguri for the time being, until I found myself a job in a different city. I had made up my mind not to return to Delhi again.

After a month, I, along with my parents, returned to Siliguri. I hadn't gone back home - not for a long vacation - once I'd left it after my Class XII Boards. I was always in a hurry to either return to Kolkata or to Delhi. But this time I wanted to stay there for a longer period until I regained some mental stability, and could focus on how to restart my professional career.

After I came back to our house in Siliguri, I stayed in my newly built room on the first floor while my parents stayed on the ground floor. I would go down only for my meals and that was the only time when I would interact with Ma and argue with Baba. Ma would invariably side with Baba to tell me how I was spoiling my life by drinking and not looking for a job.

The whole day I would remain in my room, drinking and smoking. I would go out of the house only to buy some bottles of whisky and packets of cigarettes. I would get up late and start drinking mostly from the afternoon. It would continue till I would pass out, completely sozzled at night. My smoking had also gone up; I smoked 30/40 cigarettes a day.

After returning to Siliguri, I felt a strange vacuum within me. Somehow, I could not forget Sushmita. I still found it difficult to believe that she had undergone such a dramatic transformation - from a soft, gentle and well-behaved girl she had completely turned into a rude and arrogant person. At the same time, neither could I accept her absence from my life. The more I tried to forget her, the more I kept thinking of her and, subsequently, I was deeply troubled and disturbed. Since I did not know how to get rid of my pain, I continued to take refuge in alcohol and smoking.

While I was always taught how to become successful, I hardly knew how to deal with failure. I was flying high when I was leading a 'so-called' successful life. But once I faced roadblocks, I had no clue about where to go, what to do. I was like a rudderless boat in a rough sea. I simply tried to run away from my problems by just taking a dip in a glass full of alcohol. I did not know of any positive power, or a source of inspiration, or a way to make a comeback.

Baba stopped going out except to buy some daily essentials. I figured that some of his and my friends had heard about our troubles in Delhi. So he avoided meeting them, lest he faced uncomfortable questions about his son's 'failures' in life. It was he who used to brag about me. He wanted to show-off to all and sundry what a 'successful father' he was.

"You know, Ranjit, there is a subtle difference between bragging and inspiring others. We tell our success stories humbly to inspire people. People get motivated by these and act accordingly to become successful by taking away some positive lessons from our inspiring experiences. But in bragging, you shame others, make them feel how poor they are, how unfortunate they are. It causes them pain; it humiliates them. And when you deliberately hurt people, it is bound to boomerang one day."

....

One evening when I was drinking, Ma called me downstairs to the ground floor. I found Rathin Sir sitting in our drawing room with Baba. I was surprised to see how unwell and sickly he looked. Once a handsome and well-built man, today, he looked fragile and frail, with wrinkles all over his face. Age had taken a heavy toll on him. Despite being of the same age, Sir looked older than Baba.

I greeted Sir who, in a weak, soft voice, asked me to sit beside him on the sofa. His confident voice, which used to inspire awe, was very much absent. Since I was drunk, I deliberately sat on a chair slightly away from him.

"I was thinking of coming over to see you ever since I heard of your return from Delhi. How did all this happen? So suddenly? I was horrified to hear all that you have gone through, Siddhartha," Rathin Sir expressed his anguish and sympathy in a feeble voice.

Sir was so weak that he was speaking with difficulty.

"I didn't want to trouble you with our problems, Rathin, when I heard about your bypass surgery," Baba told Sir, and then turning to me, "Rathin had the operation when we were in Delhi," since I was out of the loop about everyone in Siliguri.

"I understood that. But why did Sushmita decide to leave? Whatever I saw of her, she seemed to be a nice girl. She also took very good care of Siddhartha," Sir said, puzzled.

"She was never a good girl. I never agreed to the marriage, you know. Nor did I like her family background," Baba said grumpily, which again angered me.

From Ma's expression, I could understand that she was getting tense at the possibility of another quarrel between us.

"Baba, please stop. Stop blaming Sushmita for everything," I said, roughly, much to the discomfort of Rathin Sir.

"No, you stop. You could not even guess that your wife was having an affair, because you are blind to her faults. You are suffering for believing in her blindly," Baba told me harshly.

"Will you please stop?" I pleaded with Baba, despite feeling annoyed.

"Please, both of you, cool down," Sir's request somehow reminded me of his earlier commanding voice. "Siddhartha, have you applied for a job anywhere?" Sir asked me softly.

"Sir, I am not in a mental state to work right now. I will start working once I am mentally fit to work," I told him.

"How will he work? He has been mourning for his wife by drinking throughout the day," Baba said in a chagrined voice, much to my discomfort and irritation.

Sir tried to intervene and begged us to stop fighting. Ma also supported Rathin Sir.

"Subhash, you are lucky that at least your son is with you. You can see him whenever you want, you can talk to him, fight with him. I'm not even that lucky," Sir despaired.

It was evident from Sir's face that he was feeling miserable and depressed. We were all surprised to see him in that state.

"I did not tell you, Subhash, because this is not something that you tell even to the closest of your friends. When I had this bypass surgery, I wanted my son to be with me. Prior to the operation, my doctor had cautioned me that chances of my recovery were slim," it was difficult to say whether Sir's voice was feeble because of his poor health or because of his anguish. "Naturally, I wanted to see Amit once because I could have died. My wife requested him to come for a few days, but he refused, citing work and family commitments. These days Amit is so busy that he hardly calls us. Earlier, he used to at least call us, but he has almost stopped that nowadays. I can't recall when he last visited us," he sighed, and after a pause continued, "My only child, my Amit... he doesn't have time for us anymore, Subhash." Sir took off his glasses to wipe his tears.

"What are you saying, Rathin!" my father asked in disbelief; Ma stared at him stunned, her eyes moist.

"Yes, Subhash. This is my fate, my destiny," Rathin Sir said philosophically, crying openly now.

After gathering himself, Sir continued with his philosophical observations on life.

"Subhash, we wanted our sons to make it big in life. That's why we taught them how to get a good job and become successful in life. We were only concerned about their grades and marks when they were students, when they were in the formative stage of their life. We wanted them to study hard, become brilliant students, but we never thought of or encouraged them to develop a sympathetic, loving heart, which would help them understand the needs of others. We cited examples of people who gained only material success in life. But we did not talk about their responsibilities towards their parents, the society or country. We did not tell them that their parents matter, the society matters, their country matters. We did not teach them to stand beside their friends when their friends are in trouble. We did not encourage them to help the needy, the poor. That's why I don't blame Amit; I blame myself. I blame our education system or the faulty collective thinking of our society. My son is simply a product of this system, which produces selfish people whose only goal is to accumulate more for themselves and lead a selfish life."

By now, Sir was weeping like a child.

I don't know what my father was exactly feeling after listening to Sir's painful experience, but I felt terrible for Rathin Sir. I had seen how Amit da's life had changed in the US. When I met him in the States, I had realised that his priorities in life had completely changed. In trying to achieve more success, more wealth, more affluence, his parents had slid far down his priority list. When we met in the USA, I appreciated his hard work, dedication, commitment, his single-minded focus on his job and all that he had achieved in a foreign land, but that evening, sitting in front of Rathin Sir, I thought of Amit da as a 'failure' in life.

Losing your son is heart-breaking, but when you lose your son despite him being alive, is more agonising. I saw that particular agony in Rathin Sir that day.

That evening none of us was in any mood to talk anymore.

When Sir was slowly leaving our house, his fragile, gaunt body needed the support of his walking stick. I felt hollow within me. I felt pity not only for him, but I felt sorry for every one of us – Baba, Rathin Sir, Amit da, Sourav, my 'so-called successful' friends and acquaintances and, also myself – who were totally cut-off from our roots and were unaware of what they were missing in life. I felt that whatever I had done so far in my life was utterly meaningless.

"Ranjit, can you imagine my situation? I was asked to grow up idolising Amit da – someone who showed no concern and care for his dying father. I was encouraged to make friendship with Sourav, who let his best friend down in the time of crisis. Baba had made a mockery of Sushanta, the son of a paan shop owner, for being my best friend in my childhood. But it was Sushanta who bailed us out in the darkest hours of our life. That evening, I finally felt pity for myself for making all the wrong choices in life. That night, I could not sleep properly, even after having quite a few glasses. I felt restless during the night. No matter how hard I tried, I couldn't erase the image of Rathin Sir's helpless, crying face from the slate of my mind."

....

Almost eight months had passed since Sushmita had left me, but her memory would linger on still. In the meantime, Sushmita had filed for divorce. Her lawyer informed me that if I did not contest, she would drop all the criminal charges against me. I decided to give her the divorce without contesting it. I had to go to Noida to complete the divorce formalities. Sushmita came to the court with her Mama. We had no dispute over anything. Our apartment was in her name and she was paying the EMIs of the home loan. Since I had not taken a single thing apart from some of my clothes and my laptop from the apartment, and handed over the keys of the apartment to her, there was nothing to be said. She wanted freedom from me, which I gave her without any fuss.

"Ranjit, I realised in the months after my arrest that everything has an expiry date. And so does every relationship. Dragging it beyond a certain point is futile. That's why I agreed to the divorce. Once someone decides to leave you, it's very difficult to get them back. I learnt the hard way that we must nurture all our relationships – every day, every moment. Sometimes, we take our close relationships for granted. And the obvious fall-out is the pain and heartache."

"You are absolutely right, Sir. I think whatever you did was right," Ranjit agreed.

I drank a glass of water before resuming my story.

One night, when I was drunk as usual, and had staggered downstairs for dinner, Baba suddenly said, "Now you get yourself a job. How long will you stay at home like this and keep drinking?"

"Give me some time. I will... soon," I mumbled vaguely, not looking at him directly.

"Siddhartha, I have a problem with your attitude towards life. Now stop thinking about your wife and focus on your life. Will you spoil the rest of your life for that girl? " Baba said gingerly.

"Who says I'm not trying?" I said wearily, fed up with him, my situation, everything, "but somehow, I just can't forget her."

"You have destroyed my life and my reputation. Because of you I had to stay in police lock-up and was charged with harassing her. Despite that I'm tolerating you under my roof," Baba shouted. "I had told you not to give away the apartment to her so easily. But you didn't listen to me. I wish you weren't my son!" Baba ended bitterly.

Ma protested, "Please don't say that! Don't say anything now. Let him have his dinner peacefully."

But Baba did not listen to her.

"You have brought dishonour to our family. You are nothing but a 'failure'," Baba ranted on.

I pushed away my plate and got up. Ma's eyes were beseeching me to finish my dinner, but I had had enough of Baba.

"Just see how I spoil my life," I said while going upstairs.

Ma came rushing behind me, probably thinking that I would commit suicide. I assured her that I would not do anything like that and told her to bring my food to my room, so that I would be spared from seeing Baba's face thrice a day.

I needed a strong support system to make a comeback, but when I did not get it from anywhere, I lost all hopes. I was drinking a lot anyway, but from that night onwards, I started drinking and smoking round-the-clock. There was not a single moment that I spent without alcohol. I wanted to spoil myself, as I was in a hopeless state of mind. I had no capacity to comeback, because I had no one who would hold my hand and help me usher in a new life.

After my arrest I had stopped calling my friends, as I had understood by then that most of them were fair-weather friends. I did not have any contact with my childhood friends living in Siliguri, as I hadn't bothered to keep in touch when I had left my home town. Only Sushanta would call me up sometimes. But he was away and very busy. Moreover, we had just met for 10 minutes or so, and that too, after 18 years. I could not share all my feelings with him over the phone.

Whenever I found that I had run out of whisky or cigarettes, I would go out to buy 'my essentials'. Generally, I would take a rickshaw right from the gate of my house. That same rickshaw would take me to the wine shop and back to my house. I would buy two to three bottles of whisky and many packets of cigarettes. While going on the rickshaw, I could not recognise my own town, my own people. I could hardly identify Venus More, Hill Cart Road, and the roads which led me to that wine shop. Sometimes, I felt someone was waving at me – maybe some of my old friends or acquaintances – but I could not recognise them. I could not place anyone.

Though Ma, in spite of her on going ailments, served my food in my room, I stopped eating regularly as most of the time I would be knocked out of my senses. I lost touch with reality. I couldn't differentiate between different periods of the day anymore, whether it was morning or evening, day or night. Nor was I able to understand where I was. The more I became frustrated, the more I drank. Sometimes, the thought of Sushmita and all those memories of Delhi would come to haunt me like dark clouds. Sometimes, I would vaguely remember some names, some places or some occasions, but everything was blurred and hazy, and with no link with the other. CR Park, Ranikhet, Jadavpur, Sourav, Himanshu, Sushanta, Vaibhav, football, Rajarshi, my father, my uncles, Raj, Himachal Pradesh,

Kanchenjunga Stadium, Noida court, Kumar, my office, movie scenes, police lock-up, etc., would come to my mind like fragments of stale memories. Some more things would drift into my mind at other times... Rathin Sir's crying face, Amit da's US home, Sourav's betrayal, my mother's illness, that final match where I won the man of the match trophy; Mayna Sir's parting words to me, Saibal Sir caning Sushanta, Maradona crying... I don't know how many incidents, how many characters or places surfaced in my mind, but neither did they have any meaning nor made any sense. They were all jumbled up, the puzzles of my life, which I could not re-arrange despite trying my best. I could not even realise whether I was dead or alive.

One evening, I faintly heard voices while I was lying wasted on my bed. I could very vaguely make out that three to four shadowy figures had entered my room. I was not sure who they were and what they were talking about. I was not sure what they wanted to do, either. I could feel myself being lifted, then put into some sort of vehicle. And after sometime, they threw me into an unknown place. I don't know what happened after that.

....

When I woke up, I found myself sleeping on a bed in a worn-out room. I realised I was not in my room. There was a single bed in the room which was unoccupied at that time. I couldn't understand where I was.

At that time, I felt like a warrior who had just come back to his senses after lying injured and senseless in a battlefield for days with no one around. I tried to get up, but there was acute pain in my body. With great difficulty, I sat on the edge of the bed, put my feet on the ground. I was feeling wobbly. I felt hungry too. I could see some marks of injuries on my hands and legs. My clothes were old and shabby. I was puzzled. Where was I? From where did the injury marks come?

I touched my face. I felt the fuzz of a beard on my face. 'Seriously, where was I?' In a hospital? Or, had I been abducted by terrorists who had hidden me in a secret place? I could not see anyone. I was beginning to panic. I tried to stand up, to walk out of the room and find someone, but I immediately trashed that plan: I found out that I couldn't stand up properly, forget walking. I sat down again on the bed.

Suddenly, I saw a young boy peering into my room.

"Don't move from here. Just sit. I'll call the doctor," said the boy — he was around 18 or so - and disappeared.

I was still sitting clueless where I was. Within 5 minutes, a man with a stethoscope around his neck came in to see me. He checked my blood pressure, my pulse, took my temperature and checked my eyes. He applied some ointments on my injuries.

I asked the doctor where I was.

"This is a rehab centre in Siliguri, for alcoholics and drug addicts."

I was shocked to know that I was in rehab. I never thought I would land up in a rehab centre one day. For that matter, neither had I thought I would spend a night in a police lock-up. But everything unthinkable was happening with me.

"Go to the washroom and freshen up," that same young boy told me, once the doctor left, after giving him some instructions.

When I came back from the common washroom, I saw a barber was waiting outside my room. He shaved my beard and cut my hair which somehow made me feel better. After bathing, I was taken to the doctor's chamber. I was given some medicines. I came back to my room after lunch and slept till evening.

Later in the evening, I was taken to a prayer hall, where I was asked to join the other patients of the rehab centre in what seemed like a group prayer activity. I was an atheist. I had never attended a religious service before. Some mantras were being chanted by a man and we had to repeat those after him. I just sat there, silently.

That day, there was no alcohol for me. I found it very difficult to stay without alcohol. My craving started evening onwards, once the prayers were over, and the hankering worsened as time passed. I felt like running away from the rehab centre and get a bottle of whisky from somewhere. I don't know what happened within me at that time that I started screaming in frustration. The owner and all the staff came rushing to my room. I felt so frustrated that I started hitting the wall of the room with my fist. I was sure they brought me here under Baba's orders. I was getting terribly angry with Baba. I felt that I would die without alcohol. I started hitting my head against the wall of the room.

They were, of course, accustomed to seeing such things with newcomers like me. As soon as I started hitting my head against the wall, 3-4 people came along with the doctor and got hold of me. They forced me to lie on the bed. I wanted to get rid of them but finally, I gave in. The doctor administered an injection. I do not remember when did I sleep after that.

Next day, the doctor prescribed me some more medicines as I was going through the withdrawal syndrome, but my craving for alcohol did not abate. During the day, the head of the rehab centre came to talk to me; he was around fifty. Our meeting lasted for about 15-20 minutes or so, in which he told me the rules and regulations of the centre; that I could not leave the centre, nor use my mobile phone; explained how excessive alcohol affects the human brain and body; the importance of quitting alcohol and said he needed my cooperation and support in this respect. He also informed me that my father wanted me to stay here until I was completely addiction-free. I was then put under the wing of a senior inmate who had recovered by then.

The rehab centre was a one-storey, cemented L-shaped building with around twenty twin-sharing rooms. Fortunately, there was no one else in my room. The entire area was surrounded by a high boundary wall, like we see in jails, making it impossible for anyone to run away. When I was there, around 25 people were there in the centre. There was a lawn in front of the building where the inmates played volley ball in the evening. The prayer hall and the beautiful garden were taken care of by the inmates. Apart from that, there was a small library with some Bengali books, a dining hall, a community hall, where they would all congregate for group activities, or classes. There was a doctor's room near the prayer hall where regular check-ups of the inmates was done.

But living without alcohol was very, very tough for me – as it must have been for the other inmates too. Every alcoholic faces this when they try to, or are forced to, quit alcohol. Mentally, it was really tough. Initially, I could not sleep. I had spent sleepless nights for seven days straight. My severe hankering for alcohol was there for a month or so. I would sometimes reach such a level that I would try to run away. For the last one year, I had lived on alcohol. I was totally dependent on it. I would feel depressed and lonely sometimes.

Gradually, I was made a part of the routine which consisted of prayers twice a day; motivational classes during daytime, gardening and some other routine work to maintain the centre. We had some classes on how to change our mind set, so that we could stay away from alcohol and the advantages of quitting alcohol. But in my early days at the rehab, I could hardly understand those words, as my craving for alcohol remained very strong. I generally kept to myself. I did not feel like talking to anyone. But gradually, I started interacting with other inmates and listened to their stories.

One day, a swami from Ramakrishna Mission came to the centre and gave us a lecture on the meaning of life. I sat there trying to concentrate hard, but my mind would skip on from one thing to another. I would think of Sushmita, my days in Delhi, my previous company, my parents and many more things.

Sometimes, I would wonder about the life Sushmita must be leading, now that we were divorced. Where was she? How was she doing? Had she married Himanshu? It would not be difficult for me to ferret out all this information about her, since I had known many people in the IT sector. In moments of dejection and loneliness, I would tell myself that once I'm out of this place, I must find out about her. But then, I would tell myself that I mustn't do anything of this sort; I had caused her enough unhappiness as it is. I felt that just like she had – must have – moved on in her life, I too must move on. Why upset myself by thinking negatively about her? I only wanted to keep my good memories with Sushmita.

My craving for alcohol had lessened drastically after two months. Deep down, I wanted to make a comeback in my life. I wanted to lead a better life – a peaceful and happy one. When the other inmates would play in the evening, I would sit in the library and read the books. Despite being an atheist, I started leafing through some books on spirituality which were there. I hardly understood what they meant.

After three months or so, one morning, when I had just about woken up, our head of the rehab centre informed me that my father had called up to say that my mother was seriously ill and had been hospitalised. I was permitted to go to the hospital. There, Baba informed me that Ma's blood sugar level had dropped drastically the night before and she was in the ICU since then. However, Ma's condition had worsened considerably from the morning. I peeped into the ICU to see Ma; she was lying senseless. Oxygen and saline were being administered to her, and tubes from various machines were monitoring her vitals. It felt strange to see Ma like this.

From what I could make out, Ma looked even skinnier than before. She had never been plump, but to my eyes that day, she appeared emaciated. I was deeply saddened to see how bony she had become in these three months, while I was in the rehab. Before that, I had actually never seen her as closely as I did that day. I rued the fact that I, being the only child, her son, had never taken care of my soft-spoken mother. For the last one year or so, I was so caught up with my own problems that I had ignored her and her health issues completely. The issues in my life had taken a toll on her health. She was never an extrovert. She never discussed her worries, fears, aches and pains with anyone. At that moment, I realised that I had failed as a son. It was because of me that Ma's health had deteriorated severely in the last 8 to 9 months. I broke down, crying softly. I couldn't bear to see her like this, and returned to where Baba and my mamas were standing, some distance away from the ICU.

I stood beside them, silently. A nursing staff came and informed us that the doctor tending to her wanted to talk to us. Baba and I went to his chamber.

"The patient is in a very critical condition... We have done all that we could - perhaps a bigger hospital would be better equipped..." the doctor informed us gravely.

"What should we do now?" Baba asked him.

"You can take her to Kolkata, Delhi or Hyderabad for better treatment. But whatever you do, do it as soon as possible," he advised.

Coming out of his chamber, Baba and I discussed the options we had, to shift Ma to Kolkata as soon as possible. After some deliberations in which my mamas also pitched in, we decided on getting the air ambulance. As we were preparing to arrange her transfer to Kolkata, the doctor came to us, looking anxious.

"She is in a very critical state. Anything can happen..." he prepared us, gently.

I didn't know how to react. Baba was also looking puzzled. My maternal uncles and other relatives - who had gathered by now — were also looking helpless. What were we supposed to do? Standing in front of the ICU where Ma was admitted, I could sense a sudden rush of doctors and nurses — they were frantically coming out and going in. I could sense things were going wrong.

One nursing staff asked Baba and me to come into the ICU. When we entered the ICU, I could see Ma gasping for breath. It was terrifying. I've never seen anyone in such a state; in fact, I've never seen death closely. I could see Ma's body becoming passive, then gradually still, and eventually limp. Within 5 minutes, I had lost my mother in front of my own eyes. Time had stopped for me for a few minutes. I stood there motionless. My head was spinning.

Through the haze that had enveloped me, I could hear Baba sobbing loudly; I saw him leaning towards Ma and gently touching her face.

Before that, I had never thought about death. For me life was important. In enjoying life, I had forgotten that death was the only reality.

……………………

Though I was supposed to stay at the rehab centre for some time more, I did not go back there after my mother's death. I did not need to, as I had already quit both alcohol and smoking. I wanted to pick up my professional career but this time I decided that I would not join the corporate sector. Instead, I started sending my CV to different IT colleges for a teaching assignment.

After Ma's death, I confined myself to my room. I tried to gather myself, but a deep sense of emptiness had started to swallow me up. I needed something to cling on to, in order to make a comeback in life. After quitting alcohol, I needed something which would fill the void and pull me out of the distressing circumstances I found myself in. In those moments, I could only think of taking refuge in books – an ideal companion for me, as in my college days I used to read a lot.

One day, after lunch I stood in front of the bookshelves in our house. It was Ma's home library as she was an avid reader and collector. So many books! I took out one book after another. The fragrance of the books filled me up with a new hope. As I ran my hands over the books, I could feel Ma in them. It was Ma who read those books. I could feel her touch in every book I took out. So many fond memories of her filled me.

Finally, I took out Paulo Coelho's The Alchemist, Rabindranath Tagore's Gora and some other books written by Satyajit Ray. I started with The Alchemist. As I read, I found solace in this book, and in the others. I hoped these books would show me the path to restore and revive myself.

After coming back from the rehab centre and losing my mother, my routine, my behaviour, and my relationship with Baba changed considerably. I would go downstairs in the morning and prepare tea for both of us. We had our meals – prepared by our cook – silently together. I'm pretty sure Baba was heartbroken and lonely without Ma. But I never knew his innermost feelings as we did not have that kind of relationship where we would sit together and openly talk about feelings and be each other's support in this difficult time. Nor did I make any such attempts.

Though we did not argue and quarrel with each other anymore, we communicated only when necessary. Baba was more than seventy years old and had become frail. I would sometimes enquire about his health. Though he would never say anything to me, I could understand he was mentally devastated after Ma's death. On top of that, he was traumatised once again when he heard of Rathin Sir's death from a common friend. Sir had passed away some days after my mother's death. Moreover, Baba was crushed to learn that Amit da did not even come from the USA despite hearing about his father's death. After that, Baba became more subdued. He lost his earlier dearly held views on life.

One morning, I went downstairs to make tea for Baba. He had always been an early riser and these days, he would wake up before me, and wait for me to come downstairs and make tea for him. But to my surprise, I did not find Baba in the drawing room. I called him but there was no answer. I went to his bedroom. I saw him sleeping. I was surprised to see him sleeping as he never slept beyond 6 a.m. I called him again. When he didn't respond, I shook him. But I got no response from him. My heart in my mouth, I shouted, "Baba… Baba!" Again, no response! I turned him towards me so that I could see his face. I saw something oozing from his mouth. His head was stiff, face pale, body cold to the touch, eyes closed. I hysterically cried out, "Baba… Baba," as loudly as possible, trying to wake him up. But there was no reply. I had by then understood he would never respond again. He would never criticise me again. He would never fight with me again. He had gone beyond my reach. He had gone beyond everyone's reach and to a different place altogether. And with him went all his pride, snobbishness, anger and ego.

When his body was going inside that electric crematorium pyre, it finally struck me that I had lost everything. There was no one close left for me in this world. I felt terribly lonely. I felt like crying out loud, expressing my anguish, my torment, my wretchedness. But somehow, I could not bring myself to do so. Not a single word came out of my mouth. Not a single tear fell from my eyes. My maternal relatives were telling me something. People were discussing about Baba, about me, my future. But not a single word or phrase registered.

I did all the rituals that I had performed just a month ago for my mother. But this time, I hardly understood what I was doing; I simply followed the instructions like a robot. I did not know who they were and what they were telling me. I stopped talking to everyone. I was in a state of senselessness, but different from intoxication. I was in a trance. I did not have any feelings or understanding or reasoning left. For the next 15 days or so, till all the rituals were completed, I remained nonplussed.

When I finally got out of the trance, I experienced severe depression. It had taken me years to earn and accumulate so many things in my life, but I had lost everything within a year. Just when I was trying to focus again, I was hit hard by destiny. I had become totally forlorn. Everything seemed meaningless. Who should I blame? I was responsible for the back-to-back deaths of my parents. That's why I was not able to forgive myself. I felt guilty. I felt as if I had murdered my parents with my own hands.

At night, I saw their dead faces staring at me. I would see them when I was awake. I would see them in my dreams. A kind of hallucination gripped me. I could hear my mother calling me for dinner or my father's annoying words to me. They seemed everywhere. They would not let me sleep anymore.

Guilt enveloped me completely. I would suddenly wake up at night, drenched in sweat, scared. I could hear my heart pounding. I sometimes feared that I would have a heart attack anytime. Sleep eluded me. If I fell asleep by chance, I would wake up shivering after some time, feeling suffocated. My whole existence became so painful that I started seriously considering taking my own life. Life had very little to offer me.

****

7

The Buxa river flowed past, flanked by the mountains, and was glittering at this moment; the sun's rays reflecting on the crystal-clear water, sand and numerous pebbles lying on its enormous bed. Though the river had turned quieter in winter – just as it always did in the colder months — I loved listening to the fury of this wild river when it overflowed with water during the rainy season.

The winter sun, after gracefully dispersing the morning mist, had finally come out with full force, making the day warm. Ranjit had already taken off his sweater. I also removed the jacket of my tracksuit, which I had worn over a sports T-shirt to keep myself warm in the morning cold.

There was absolute quietude near my cottage and in the vast meadow surrounding it. The school was closed for the winter vacation, turning this area into a perfect 'silent zone'. Apart from the high school and the primary school, there was nothing in this part of the village. The school was on the left side of my room, near the jungle.

While watching the beautiful Buxa and the mountains, my mind drifted back to those gloomy days of the past, which I had been describing to Ranjit just a few minutes back.

As I was lost in my thoughts, Ranjit's sudden comment pulled me out of the reverie.

"Sir, I did not expect your story to be so tragic," Ranjit said, realising that I hadn't heard him the first time.

It was evident that Ranjit had become very distressed after listening to the tumultuous journey of my life. The fact is that I had also become very nostalgic. My heart had become heavier recalling those dreadful days and events of my past, which I had been narrating to Ranjit since morning.

Still, I managed to keep a grip on my emotions and asked Ranjit if he would like some water. As I asked him, I saw Ganesh coming with my lunch, which he served me sharp at 12.30 p.m. every day. I requested Ganesh to give us some more water. He returned with two glasses of water.

While handing over the glasses, Ganesh asked, not too happily, "Haven't you had your breakfast?"

"We forgot to eat, Ganesh," I told him apologetically. "Ranjit and I will have lunch together."

"Shall I bring some more rice?" Ganesh asked.

"That you may; we will share the rest," I told Ganesh.

"Okay, Sir," Ganesh said.

"Ranjit, please take a few deep breaths and relax," I told him smilingly, so that he could shake off the sombre mood that he had slid into after hearing the tragic path my life had taken till that point.

"Sir, I was not at all prepared for such a story," Ranjit told me, a sense of disbelief apparent in his voice.

"To tell you the truth, to get the best in life, Ranjit, sometimes you need to face the worst. Unless you go to the brink, you don't realise the value of life. I have seen everything in life. I have faced every possible trouble a man could face. That's why I could discover my true self," I said reassuringly.

Ranjit looked at me in bewilderment. I understood that he still had many questions because so far he had only learnt the problems of my life, but not how I had bounced back.

"What did you do after that?" Ranjit asked, since I had been at the brink of ending my life - yet had got out of that pit.

"Please, have lunch first and then, we could resume."

"No, Sir. I can't wait to listen to your full story. Please complete the story first. We will have lunch after that — I can't have lunch now!"

"Okay. As you wish," I complied to his anxiousness. From time to time, I can't help but wonder how things shaped up in my life. Sometimes, when I look back, I feel as if I'm watching an incredible transformational movie or reading a motivational novel.

Do miracles happen by chance? Can we control our destiny? Or, is everything pre-determined? Can we become what we want to become? Can we get what we want to get? Is there divine intervention or connection in all these?

Does anyone have answers to these questions?

....

As I was going through a very bad patch of depression and contemplating suicide after my parents had passed away, I needed a miracle to happen and change my life. And that miracle happened after a few days. I got a mail that actually worked as a catalyst to turn around my life and the many lives of this beautiful scenic village.

I've already mentioned that after I came out of the rehab centre, I had applied for a teaching job in some colleges, which had advertised vacancies. A newly established government IT College in Bhutan considered my candidature, took a telephone interview and sent me an appointment letter. I read their appointment letter written by Lhato Jamba, the president (head) of the college. Apart from some formal words, there were a few lines which tugged at my heartstring immediately.

Some of the lines of that life-changing letter were:

"We may not give you the best of salaries, but we can provide you that which no one in this world can offer. We will give you a very clean and calm environment to live in, where you can get peace and happiness, which you won't find in any other place. I hope you will have a nice time detoxifying your lungs which must have been exposed to pollution during your stay in Kolkata and Delhi. Here, amidst nature, you will witness no pollution as we are a carbon-negative nation, the only such country in the world. And the hospitality of the Bhutanese people will never allow you to feel that you are in a foreign country, away from your close ones."

After reading this mail, I did not give the job a second thought. I had always loved mountains. Not surprisingly, therefore, I felt strongly drawn to the Himalayas to make a complete turnaround of my life. I was already looking for a place where I would get mental peace and there was not a better place in this world than this tiny Himalayan nation, known for its 'happiness quotient'. Though I had never been to Bhutan, that country was all about peace, serenity and happiness, which I found reverberating in the deep recesses of my mind. That letter filled me up with new hope and a meaningful purpose in my life. It ushered in the optimism of a better tomorrow. It lifted me from inertness to a new life. It swiftly dispersed all the darkness in my mind.

I did not delay in replying that I would be happy to join.

Since that was a new college, they had asked me to join as early as possible, mentioning a date of joining, which was only ten days later.

As I was going about my preparations to go to the tiny Himalayan nation, I got a call a couple of days after receiving the mail.

"Hello, Dada, kemon ache (how are you)?" a man asked me in broken Bengali.

"I am fine but who is this?" I asked politely.

"This is Lhato Jamba, President of Gyalpozhing College of Information Technology, Bhutan," said the man in a typical Bhutanese tone.

Though I had guessed this as the college I was about to join, I could not recollect its name.

"Yes, Sir. I am fine. How are you?"

"Welcome to Bhutan, Dada. We are eagerly waiting to host you," Lhato Jamba said.

I was surprised, as I had not expected the head of an institution to call me and welcome me in such an informal way.

"Thank you, Sir. I am also looking forward to go to Bhutan and join your college."

"I am in Siliguri. I will return on Sunday. Since you will be joining on Tuesday, you can accompany me to Bhutan if you wish," he said.

"Sir, I will definitely join you," I said, as I thought it was an ideal situation for me. I would not have to take the trouble of going on a public transport or finding the college on my own.

"I will call you in the evening on Saturday. See you then," he said and hung up.

I hardly knew anything about Bhutan and the Bhutanese, but that email and phone call gave me a very good impression about the country where I will be staying at such a crucial juncture of my life.

Among the many things that I had learnt till then, the crucial one was that your intentions matter a lot. When your intention is good and honest, you will meet benevolent people who will help you out in life or sometimes, they will help you in rediscovering yourself. Everything around you will be good as well. And, the reverse is equally true.

Over the next few days, I packed my bag with some summer clothes, some warm clothes and some books that I took out from Ma's library. I informed my mamas about my job in Bhutan. They were initially worried and asked me to find a job in India, but I allayed their fear and told them that I had already confirmed the college people that I was joining.

As promised, I got a call from Mr Jamba that Saturday evening. He asked me to get ready by 5 a.m. the next morning. We decided to meet at a mutually convenient place.

I could not sleep the whole night, partly because of depression and partly from excitement. I finally got out of bed at 4 a.m. and began getting ready. Boro Mama (elder maternal uncle) came in the morning to see me off. I gave him the keys to my house and set out for a voyage to the

'Land of the Thunder Dragon' to rediscover myself.

I spotted a white Toyota Hilux truck. I could easily identify a Bhutanese man of around fifty years of age waiting for me, standing outside his vehicle. He was wearing a pair of Bermudas and a T-shirt. I was not sure whether he was the head of the college or not. I went near him and said, "Good morning, Sir. I'm Siddhartha Lahiri."

"Welcome, Dada, welcome. I'm Lhato Jamba. Please sit in the car," breaking into a smile, Jamba said warmly, gesturing with his hand.

He received me as if we were old friends. I took the back seat while he sat in the front, beside the driver.

"Sorry to disturb you so – by spoiling your sleep," chuckled Jamba, but I was still not sure whether he was the president of the college, as neither his appearance nor his way of talking was in tune with his post or position.

Of average height, with a fair complexion and an oval-shaped face, Mr Jamba's small eyes reflected a jovial nature.

"Don't worry, Dada. I will give you a chance to compensate your sleep when you reach Bhutan. You can sleep as long as you want in Bhutan. No one will be there to disturb you," he said cheerfully.

"It's okay, Sir," I replied, "I'm fine."

"If you want, you can sleep now as Barma is a good driver. He will drive so smoothly that you won't have any problem in sleeping. But I can't guarantee about the holes on the road, which may give you some trouble," he said in a lighter vein while introducing his driver Barma, whose face wasn't fully visible from where I was sitting in the back seat.

But I was surprised by Mr Jamba's dry humour. Although he had told me on the phone that he was the head of the college, his friendly and youthful behaviour left me perplexed. By that time, our truck had moved out of Siliguri town and was moving towards the Dooars through a very scenic landscape.

The mornings in this part of West Bengal are beautiful, but it becomes even more beautiful during autumn. As we were heading towards Bhutan, leaving behind my city of birth, Siliguri, I felt as though I was leaving behind all my problems and worries. It seemed I was moving to a new land, full of hopes and new promises.

Mr Jamba was talking in his usual humorous way while we were crossing the military camps on one side of the road and a forest on the other side. From my childhood, I have enjoyed travelling on this 25-km stretch from Siliguri to Sevoke, a small hilly place in Darjeeling district. It is basically a junction from where one road goes straight to Sikkim, and another road turns right and crosses over the famous century-old Coronation Bridge, built in the British era, over River Teesta and goes towards Bhutan, Assam and all the north-eastern states of India. We took the right-hand road as we would enter the eastern part of Bhutan through Assam.

The whole stretch was picturesque; the entire left side was guarded by hills, with tea gardens at the foothills, and the right side was equally charming with forests and green paddy fields. Another striking part of north Bengal and the lower Assam region was its vast area of tea gardens. Tea gardens are everywhere in the entire Darjeeling hills and Dooars area, as well as in Assam. The huge tea gardens in the valleys and at the foothills added to the splendour of the blue sky and green mountains.

I did not know after how many years had I opened my eyes as well as my heart to the beauty of nature. In the last five years or so, I had been so engrossed with myself and the life in a metropolitan city that I had forgotten that there was a life outside of city life. I had forgotten to enjoy the little joys of life. I had forgotten how, by simply looking at Mother Nature, we can become joyful and blessed. I had forgotten that we did not need so many things to be happy in life. Actually, I was trying to find happiness where it actually did not exist, and that's the reason I had struggled so much in life.

As I was deep in my thoughts, our Toyota Hilux had gathered speed and was zipping past the hills, tea gardens and forests like a cheetah trying to catch its prey. Through the open windows, the sound of our vehicle swooshing past the wind filled me with thrill and excitement. Barma switched on the music system, and the Bhutanese music that floated through the stereo complemented the soothing natural scenery outside.

I saw Mr Jamba sleeping (and snoring) on the front seat, his head nodding this way and that. Sometimes, his nodding head would cause him to wake up with a start, but a few seconds later he would snooze again, his head on the backrest of the seat. Since the traffic was considerably less at that time of the morning, our vehicle zipped passed the border of West Bengal into Assam in just three hours. The beauty outside, the wind and the previous night's lack of sleep made an ideal setting for me to feel drowsy, but I did not want to sleep as the natural beauty captivated me like a lissom lass. But Jamba's uninterrupted sleep was so contagious that I did not realise when I snoozed for a few seconds.

"Dada, chaye khabe (will you have tea)?" Jamba asked me in broken Bengali, breaking the silence, as well as my nap.

I had understood by that time that Jamba knew two or three Bengali words like "Kemon ache" which will be basically "Kyamon achen or acho or achis", meaning "How are you?"; "Chaye khabe" or "Bhat khabe", meaning "Will you drink tea or eat rice?"

"I think you are feeling sleepy," he added, without giving me any time to say anything.

He told Barma something in Bhutanese language. After 5 minutes or so, Barma stopped the truck at a roadside rural village market. Only 2-3 tea shops were there, bamboo structured and tin shaded with all sides open.

"Dada, you won't feel sleepy after having tea here. I drink tea here, so that I can remain awake. I like to be awake you know. So much to see in this world," he said with his typical dry humour.

After having tea, we started again and took the National Highway 27, which goes straight to Guwahati. Barma, chewing paan and soft betel nuts, picked up speed on the main road.

I saw Barma clearly for the first time while we were having tea. A rather short man of around 35 years, with typical Bhutanese features in a round-shaped face. His small eyes reflected an innocence that is not to be seen much now-a-days. He was so affable that I liked Barma from the very first look.

"The tea was fine?" asked Jamba, without looking back towards me.

"Yes, Sir," I replied.

"It seems you think too much," Jamba said suddenly, breaking silence.

"No, Sir. I'm just looking outside, at this stunning view of nature."

"Have you not seen nature before?" he asked in a lighter vein.

Jamba's question threw me into confusion, and before I could reply, he posed another question, "Aren't you feeling hungry?"

"Not that much, Sir," I replied, even though I was.

I somehow could not bring myself to admit to my supposed head of the college that I was indeed feeling hungry. From my childhood, I could not open up instantly to someone I had just met.

"You had food at 4 a.m. at home or you don't like to eat?" he asked in his typical manner which would confuse you about whether he was serious or just joking.

I found his questions difficult to answer, to give him an appropriate reply. I could, but I thought it was better not to speak much, at least initially, with my next boss, even if he was an interesting person with a dry sense of humour, which he frequently resorted to for some mirth.

"No, Sir. I will eat when you people feel like eating," I said softly.

"Eat this till then."

He took out a packet of cornflakes, opened it and offered me.

I took some from it.

Taking some himself, he told me, "This is from Bhutan, very fresh and organic. Eat this till we get to a good place for breakfast."

By then we had crossed Bongaigaon, the first major town in Assam. After eating the cornflakes, he fell asleep again. Hearing him snore, I laughed to myself that Jamba had said some time ago that he liked to be awake as there was so much to see. But I could not sleep as waves of memories swept over me, especially, the passing of my parents.

It was around 10.30 a.m. when Jamba asked Barma to stop near a roadside dhaba. We went inside the dhaba. The eatery looked like a very popular place, as it was full of people having their breakfast.

After placing our order for samosas, puris and some sweets, Jamba turned to me, "These are popular items here, and this restaurant offers the best quality food. We always eat our breakfast here. I like the food here so much that I got our college canteen cook to come here and get trained under the chef.

"We should have hands-on education, yes? What's the point of reading all those books if you can't apply it in your life? Most of our problems come from the fact that we don't have practical skills to solve those."

I nodded in affirmation. From the very beginning, Jamba seemed to be an interesting person. But his ideas made me feel that this man thought differently and had a unique way of dealing with things. By this time, I was beginning to feel a little bit sure that this man might be the head of the institute. While leaving the dhaba, Jamba made his customary jokes and exchanged a few words with the owner in broken Hindi.

After breakfast, Barma hit the accelerator, chewing away on the paan and betel nuts that he bought from a stall next to the dhaba. He offered me, but I declined politely.

"Did you like the breakfast?" Jamba asked.

"Yes, Sir. Very much," the food was really good, in terms of taste, freshness and ingredients.

After half an hour or so, I could feel we were entering a town.

"Have you come to Barpeta Road before?" Jamba asked me, although I had already told him that I had never come to this area before.

"Can't this man remember? Or does he like to have fun all the time?" I thought.

"No, Sir," I told him politely, though I was feeling a little irritated; still, I successfully hid my annoyance.

"You know, there is a railway station here; Barpeta Road station. You can catch the train from here and go back to Siliguri now," Jamba gave an impish smile.

"Why on earth should I go back now?" I kept quiet.

Jamba said something to Barma in Bhutanese, which I didn't understand. Soon after, our vehicle left the national highway and took a left turn, towards Barpeta town. I couldn't understand where we were heading to. When I had searched the internet for the direction to the college, the route that was suggested to go to Samdrup Jongkhar was from Rangiya. But this route was completely different from what I had found on the internet. I was rather surprised.

"By the way, are you scared of animals?" Jamba asked.

"Why is he suddenly talking of animals now?" I thought, frowning slightly.

But Jamba had this habit of coming up with unpredictable questions every now and then. Though some of his questions might be annoying, he did have a knack of coming up with funny comments in his own typical humorous way with a straight face. Despite my initial mild annoyance, I couldn't help but like him and his dry sense of humour.

"Yes, if it is a wild animal," I replied.

"Are you not scared of domestic animals?" he asked me in his typical style.

I could not find the right answer. So, I kept quiet and smiled.

"But, where are we heading for, Sir?" I asked him, trying to avoid his questions on animals.

"Dada, please enjoy the journey. Looking for a destination will make you tense. Is it not so?" he again came up with something that I did not have a reply to.

I thought how easily and with such simplicity did Jamba express such a deep philosophical idea. It is true that all our worries emanate from wanting to achieve something or our concern about reaching a target.

Meanwhile, Barma was driving slowly and carefully when we were going through the busy lanes of Barpeta town. Once we crossed the town, we found that the road conditions were not good – bumpy at some places, broken and potholed at others.

"How do you feel, when the journey becomes bumpy like this? Will you still feel good?" he said in serious tone this time.

"No, Sir," I replied.

"That's the problem with most people. They only want to enjoy good roads like we had on the national highway.

Once they are on the difficult roads of life, they keep complaining," he said solemnly.

Listening to him made me think about my own life. When the going was good in my life, I flew high and never did prepare for the rough weathers ahead. That's why I could not handle it properly. It made me depressed and frustrated. And suicidal.

I had so far seen his funny side, but his last observation touched my heart. The more time I spent with him, the more fascinating I found him. "Yes, at this hour of crisis, I need a man like this," I thought.

"Life is so unpredictable. Whoever you are, you have to eventually face tough times. What do you think?"

"Yes, Sir," I said softly.

"That's the rule of nature. Good and bad come to us in cyclical order. That's the sign that nothing is permanent in life. So, we should enjoy our journey without fussing much about how the journey is," he said in a philosophical way, and then, chuckling, "so, you should not be scared of animals!"

I could not stop laughing the way he turned a philosophical topic into a funny one. "I had never met a man like this before," I thought, amused. He could switch on and off so easily that you would fail to realise if he was in a serious mood or otherwise.

"You know, Buddhist monks go for deep meditation in jungles amidst the wildest of animals. But animals never disturb those monks," Jamba said in a serious voice.

"Why?" I was astonished.

"Because, monks don't eat good food. So the animals think their flesh won't be tasty," he said and laughed out loud this time.

Jamba could make your mood change instantaneously, like the English weather!

Amidst this merriment, I saw we were standing in front of a big gate. 'Manas National Park' said the signage over it.

I understood then why he had asked about wild animals.

"Sir, are we going inside the Manas National Park?" I was excited.

"Don't be scared if you see any wild animal inside," he grinned, turning towards me.

He asked Barma something in their language, who said something to the gateman in Hindi, which I could not hear properly. The gatekeeper opened the gate and Barma drove the vehicle inside the national park.

I was visiting a forest sanctuary after a long time. The last time I had visited a sanctuary was several years ago with Sushmita. We had gone to Jim Corbett National Park - or Corbett, as it is popularly called — in Uttarakhand, from Delhi. We had seen elephants, deer and some other animals - and, we were very lucky to have spotted a tiger. I still remember how terrified Sushmita had become on seeing the tiger.

My reverie was broken when Jamba suddenly told me, "If you are not scared of elephants, look to your left."

I turned to see a herd of wild elephants, standing, some gently swaying their trunks. Some other vehicles, most of them jungle safari jeeps, had also stopped there, like us, to get a glimpse of these giant, magnificent animals.

"These are wild elephants and very dangerous. Would you like to get out of the car and click selfies with them?" Jamba asked me.

"No, Sir. I'm fine where I am," I said softly.

By then, I had got some courage to say something more than 'yes' or 'no' to his questions.

Barma started the car, and as we cruised along the forest road, we also saw some deer, bison and a lot of peacocks. Barma drove for almost 45 minutes into the forest and we reached deep inside the national park near the Manas river. We took a right upward turn from a junction. Barma's skill as a driver came to the fore as he drove the truck upwards to a hill where a board said, 'Welcome to Bhutan'.

I was rather thrilled and happy to see that we were just about to enter Bhutan.

I asked Jamba, "How far is our college from here? How much time will it take to reach our college from here?"

"Two days," he replied very calmly.

"Two days!" I stared at him in disbelieve.

"Do you have any problem in travelling for two days?" this time with an impish grin on his face.

"No... not that... but two days?" I really could not understand what Jamba was up to.

"I told you earlier, be ready to face the unexpected every time, because life is full of unforeseen events."

This time I really couldn't understand if he was serious or joking.

After a stiff uphill drive, the beautiful but narrow road went a little downhill. There were hills on the right-hand side, adjacent to the road, while far lower on the left-hand side flowed the mesmerising Manas river, through Bhutan to Assam, amidst picturesque mountains and forests. The water looked so green and pure that I could not take my eyes off the river and the forest on the other side of the river.

It was around 2 p.m. I was feeling hungry, but was still very shy to ask about lunch. Nor did I see any eatery in the vicinity. After 20 minutes or so into Bhutan, we reached a small habitat where I spotted some shops and small eateries. Jamba spoke to Barma who stopped the car near a small wooden restaurant. I was relieved; lunch at last.

Sir asked me to come out. I followed him and Barma into the semi-dark eatery where some young men in their mid-twenties were drinking beer. They got up and greeted Jamba, and they exchanged pleasantries in their language.

This small eatery was stacked with a variety of things, from almost all grocery items, to vegetables, like potatoes, chillies, tomatoes, etc., and also beer and breezers. I was intrigued and amused, never having seen such a unique dhaba or restaurant. When I asked Jamba how he knew these boys, he told me that they were his former students. Jamba asked me if I needed to buy any drinks.

"You can have beer, if you feel like drinking," Jamba said with a smile.

"No, Sir."

"You don't like?"

"No, Sir."

"You should have sometimes." The same wicked smile on his face.

"I have quit, Sir."

"I've made up my mind. I made a mistake once in my life by not following my heart. I don't want to make that mistake again. You just give me your support, Sushanta," I said earnestly and humbly.

"I'm always with you, Siddhartha. Don't worry," Sushanta told me, his lips trembling, and his eyes bright with tears.

"Just be with me," I said, putting my right hand forward.

He also extended his. We held each other's hands, overcome with emotion and the ties that we shared from our childhood.

We remained like that for some time, felt the warmth and profound bonding of our friendship and silently pledged to work together for the needy without saying a single word.

I felt as though a huge burden had finally been lifted off my chest. I did not know what kind of burden it was, but I finally felt fully free and blissful.

If my sessions with Jennings kick-started the process of my liberation, I was finally able to liberate myself that evening, as I sat face-to-face with my friend Sushanta.

After returning to Bhutan, I told Jamba Sir about my plans, two days later.

"Follow your heart. Do whatever that makes you happy because at the end of the day we are all working for our happiness," Jamba Sir told me with a joyous smile on his face.

Then I went to meet Jennings.

"I knew it was about to happen. That is the only path for you now," Jennings told me happily, as if he was expecting the turn of events and my decision.

Jennings suddenly chanted a Sanskrit sloka from Katha Upanishad and said: *"उत्तिष्ठ जाग्रत प्राप्य वरान्निबोधत / क्षुरस्य धारा निशिता दुरत्यया दुर्गं पथस्तत्कवयो वदन्ति"* which, in English, means: 'Rise, wake up, seek the wise and realise. The path is difficult to cross like the sharpened edge of the razor (knife), so say the wise'."

The title of Maugham's book, The Razor's Edge, was inspired by this sloka. Even Vivekananda often repeated this sloka in various places to inspire people.

I was surprised to hear the Sanskrit sloka from this monk from London – and was impressed by his Sanskrit pronunciation and enunciation.

Then Jennings added, "Yes you have chosen probably the right path, but remember one thing: This path is not easy to follow."

Jennings kept looking at me, his beatific smile on.

"Look Siddhartha, we are what we think, act and behave as. Buddha became the enlightened one through meditation, by reflecting on his experience of life and determining to penetrate its truth. So, anyone who does these things, can become a Buddha."

"Can 'anyone' become a Buddha?" I asked in wonder.

"Yes, Buddha never claimed that he was a god. He was like an enlightened friend, who could guide people out of their miseries and suffering. So, anyone who can take people out of their pain can become an 'enlightened' one, just like Buddha. That's why I can see that this Siddhartha, who is sitting in front of me, is already on the path of becoming a Buddha," Jennings said, gently raising and stretching his hand towards me, a mild smile hovering on his face.

"You have achieved your enlightenment. Your blissful life starts now," Jennings said, his eyes closed – as if he was looking at me with his third eye.

A shiver ran up my spine as I listened to his concluding words. He gave me all the strength that I needed to undertake the difficult journey to the world of selflessness. It was my time to go back to my country and to serve my people.

....

It was around 3 p.m. Ranjit had put on his sweater again. The temperature had suddenly dipped. I realised Ranjit was staring at me with awe. I could see disbelieve as well as ecstasy in his eyes. I guess he hadn't expected such a turbulent as well as transforming story of my life.

"Sir, you are lucky. God was with you. Despite having gone to the brink, you could come back to serve people," Ranjit summed up my life's story.

"Ranjit, the best comes out from the worst only. Whenever you see something very bad happening, you can expect a great turnaround. That turnaround happens not only to the individual but to the society also."

Ranjit nodded in agreement.

I suddenly remembered that Ranjit had not eaten anything since morning.

"You must be very hungry, Ranjit. It's already late. Hurry up! Now we must eat our lunch."

"Sir, I was so engrossed in your story, I forgot everything, including my hunger," Ranjit said, getting up.

After lunch, Ranjit asked me, "But, I still have a query. How did you come to Buxa?"

"Yes. I forgot to tell you that. Actually, I had nothing in my mind about the place except for a tribal region when I was leaving my job. I called Sushanta. One of his fans, who stayed nearby, arranged my stay at Buxa. He asked me to stay at Ganesh's place, initially. Then, after a couple of months he got me this room."

"That means Sushanta is still in touch with you and this academy?"

"Yes, he is. Sushanta helps the boys get into different clubs and sends them to trials organised by big clubs. It's all due to his efforts that so many children play in the different academies and the big clubs. He also sends money for the academy regularly. So, we owe a lot to him for the success of our football academy."

"But why did you people not reveal your identities?" Ranjit asked in a surprised voice.

"Sushanta and I wanted the villagers to shoulder the responsibility of their lives. Until these people understand that what they need to do to grow in their life; until they go through the process of changing themselves, long-term success is not possible. Otherwise, it will end once we die. We did not want that."

"Ranjit, I believe that everyone has potential. There is a Sanskrit sloka, *'अमंत्रमक्षरं नास्ति नास्ति मूलमनौषधम् । अयोग्यः पुरुषो नास्ति योजकस्तत्र दुर्लभः'* which, in English, means, 'There is no sound that is not a mantra, no plant that is not medicinal; there is no person unworthy, what is lacking is an 'enabler'.

Everything will decay, everyone will die.

The good news is that we are alive; the reality is that we don't know for how long. So, we should wisely use this life as an opportunity to serve others and do some good before we breathe our last.

****

"Accordingly, I think every villager is worthy of attaining success. What they require is an enabler. I just act as an enabler, or you can say, as a catalyst. I only instil the belief in them that if they try, they can achieve anything in life.

"After my spiritual training under Jennings, my objective in life completely changed. I wanted to work for these villagers and help them succeed in life.

"It has never been about me and my name, Ranjit. It's about the others, because you get real happiness and peace when you put others before yourself.

"Giving and expecting nothing in return gives an enormous satisfaction. It's a beautiful way of living your life. It's just a joy to live. That's why a monk, who has given everything away, is so rich.

"We all have come to the world empty-handed and will leave this world the same way. So, how long you live is not important, but how fruitful your life is, is what matters. At the end of the day, a successful life is not about how much money you earned or what you have achieved in your own life, but how many lives you have touched."

It was around 4 p.m. The winter sun had started dipping in the western front and subsequently, the temperature had gone down further. It was time for Ranjit to leave.

After Ranjit's departure, I sat quietly and watched the magnificent mountains and the sparkling river.

I know the life I have chosen is a very difficult path to pursue, but it gives me enormous peace and happiness each time a village girl or boy accomplishes something. And that peace and happiness is far more valuable than cars, apartments, bank balance and other material possessions.

"Why did you quit? Look at my students. They were drinking and enjoying it so much," Jamba said, smiling.

Fascinating man, Jamba! Was he seriously telling me to drink or not? To tell you the truth, I was surprised that Jamba's students were drinking alcohol in front of him. It was, and still is, unthinkable in India.

"Sir, you didn't mind that your students were drinking in front of you?"

"Not at all. They are all grown-ups now. They have learnt to take care of themselves. We have taught them that also. I am sure, by now, they know how to balance it in their lives."

I kept quiet, thinking that we were never trained how to take care of ourselves. We were just taught how to earn money. Jamba's way of thinking was simply amazing.

Barma bought rice, potatoes, chillies, tomatoes and onions from the shop.

It was around 2.30 p.m. My hunger had become unbearable by then. I thought we would be eating there but Jamba asked me to get back into the vehicle again, once Barma had finished buying those essentials.

Barma took a U-turn and the vehicle turned towards the way we had just come from. I was cursing Jamba in my mind thinking that it would take more than an hour to get out of the national park and find a restaurant outside.

After about 5 minutes or so, Barma, on Jamba's instructions, parked the car near a waterfall, adjacent to the hills. They got out of the car and gestured to me to come out. It was a wonderful place with a beautiful cascade flowing down through the hills and down to the road on the left, with River Manas on the right-hand side. I cupped my

hands and, taking some water from the waterfall, drank. It was an amazing experience. This place was so idyllic and charming that I forgot about my hunger for some time. I saw Barma opening the boot of the vehicle.

"You like the place?" Jamba asked me.

"Yes... very much, Sir."

"How will you feel if we cook our lunch here with water from this waterfall?" Jamba asked me, though I was not sure whether he was teasing me or not.

"That will be wonderful, Sir," I replied joyfully.

I was so hungry that the word lunch gave me a huge relief. But I became more excited at the prospect of having lunch cooked with the water of these falls in this beautiful place. It would be a unique experience.

Jamba helped Barma to take out a portable cooking gas cylinder attached with burner, utensils, pressure cooker and the rice and vegetables that Barma had just picked up from that shop. I also offered my two cents in cooking.

Jamba broke some big leaves from a nearby tree, washed those and handed them over to me. It was really a wonderful experience for me. Soon, the food was almost ready. It was around 3.30 p.m. by then. My hunger had reached its zenith.

Just when I thought we were ready to eat finally, I saw three unknown Bhutanese boys passing by. Jamba called them and offered them our food. I felt really anxious, as we could not feed three more people with the amount of food we had prepared. I thought that if they agreed to have food with us, what would we eat? I was so hungry that I was in no mood to share my food with anyone. The thought of them eating our food took me momentarily to the level

of insanity. But Jamba was adamant to give them food; the boys patiently convinced Jamba that they had just had lunch and could not eat at that time.

I heaved a sigh of relief when the boys finally left the place.

"We should offer food to everyone we meet. What do you think?" Jamba asked me.

If I were honest, I would have said 'not when you are that hungry', but I did agree with him.

"Yes, Sir," I said reluctantly.

"When you feed someone, you do good karma, which in turn, comes back to you and helps you in the future," Jamba explained.

But I was so hungry that I was in no mood to wait even a bit.

Barma served me and Jamba rice and potato curry on the leaf; I fell upon it eagerly.

"How is the food?" Jamba asked.

"Very tasty," I said.

In fact, I was so hungry that the simple rice and potato curry tasted like Hyderabadi Biryani!

"You know why I was offering food to those boys despite being hungry?" Jamba asked me.

Actually, that question had crossed my mind.

"No idea, Sir."

"Because we all can give when we have something extra, but when you have very little and still you give, it helps you become stronger mentally. Real happiness comes

when you give unconditionally. Only mentally tough people can sacrifice for others," Jamba elaborated, adding, "sometimes, we need to test ourselves if we can sacrifice our own comfort when someone else needs it more."

All my pre-conceived notions about giving or donating got shattered in a second. I had never thought of it this way. I felt a little guilty just to think about my hunger. Normal people like us are only concerned about our own hunger; we often forget that others' hunger is equally important. We all take credit for giving away something to others when we have more, but how many of us can give everything we have?

As we were eating and talking, I looked at the beautiful Manas river calmly flowing through the forests and mountains, without drawing anyone's attention, or seeking appreciation or approval. I thought that there were so many parts of this river and forest which no one had ever seen and known. I looked up at the enormous clear and bright sky; there were some white clouds that drifted lazily on the blue sky. The sky had been the only witness to the many unravelled and unseen and unknown parts of this world. I felt myself to be so tiny in front of this enormity of nature. Suddenly, I found my problems were nothing in comparison to the myriads of problems faced by my fellow human beings.

"Are you planning to stay here?" Jamba asked me smilingly.

I saw Barma had put everything back inside the truck, cleaned the area and was ready to move on.

"Let's go. We have to reach Samdrup Jongkhar before 8 p.m." Jamba informed me, wiping his hands on his handkerchief. I hastily washed my hands and mouth.

Barma started the vehicle after having his usual paan. We again took the previous route and exited Bhutan within 20 minutes. I could neither understand anything about our route nor about our plan, destination or anything. We were supposed to reach my new college at Gyalpozhing, but somehow, we were still wandering around Manas National Park! I could not make head or tail of it.

One more thing that had struck me about Jamba was that he would not reveal much before we actually reached a particular place. He liked to keep everything in suspense. That's his style. That's his way of living.

Soon, within 10 minutes, Jamba fell asleep. So much for his claiming that he liked to be awake as there is so much to see in this world! Still, despite feeling a bit exasperated at this habit of Jamba's, I had to admit to myself that if one can sleep easily and anywhere, he or she is surely a happy person. Sleep is a sign of a happy and uncluttered mind. I have just met two people from the land of happiness, and whatever I had seen of them so far, they looked happy, content and satisfied. I had already started liking Bhutan without actually having reached the country.

In the meantime, our vehicle reached Rangiya, via Barpeta Road. It was almost evening when we reached Rangiya. Jamba told me that from Rangiya we would go to Samdrup Jongkhar, which is a one and a half hours' drive. Around 8.30 p.m., we reached Samdrup Jongkhar, an important city of Bhutan, adjoining India. I came to know this after Jamba informed me that this was the place of our night stay.

We had to do some formalities at the entrance. After entering Samdrup Jongkhar, Barma stopped his vehicle in front of the Indian military office. It was written BRO – Border Road Organisation. It was an Indian Military Guest House, which was very neat and clean. It seemed that

Jamba was a frequent visitor here, as he seemed to know each and every one of the staff.

It was already quite late. Soon we had our dinner and came back to our room. It was around 10 p.m. I was feeling a little cold as the temperature here was slightly less than that in India, but the difference was not that much as this town was at the foothills of Bhutan.

"Would you like to go for a walk?" Jamba asked me in his typical mischievous way.

"No, Sir," I replied, smiling too.

"You don't like walking?"

"I do, but not now," I replied, still smiling.

"Then sleep. We will get up at 5 a.m. tomorrow," he told me, gesturing towards the bedroom. "You sleep there on the bed and enjoy your sleep," he said.

"Where will you sleep?" I asked.

"I will sleep on the sofa."

"Why, Sir! The bed can easily accommodate even three people. We both can sleep quite comfortably," I said.

"No, no… I will sleep on the sofa."

"But, why?"

"I like to sleep on the sofa. And what's the difference? We need to have a place to sleep, nothing else. If you are happy you can sleep anywhere, no?"

"But still…"

"Can you sleep with your enemy even if it were a 5-star hotel room?" Jamba asked me.

I kept quiet.

"That's it. Quality of bed or room is not important; what's important is happiness. If you are happy, you can sleep anywhere. That's what we have been taught from our childhood," he said, as he walked towards the sofa.

I thought this was his style of practising mental toughness, which had helped him become kind, empathetic and generous.

I crawled into the bed thinking about Jamba and the day that had just gone by with him. This was one of the most amazing days of my life.

"Ranjit, I had never met a man like him. He had already taught me so many important life lessons in a single day. He held such a high position, but he lived like a very ordinary man. Probably, this was the key to his happiness and contentment.

"When you can live like a poor man despite being rich, when you can shed your ego and vanity despite holding a high post, when you care for people despite being very powerful, you are bound to be happy. Peace and happiness are bound to come your way. You don't have to chase these things anymore.

"Most importantly, Jamba's presence and his words had already started the process of healing the inner wounds that I was carrying to this 'country of happiness'."

I was extremely tired because of travelling throughout the day and of the previous night's lack of sleep. But that night my nerves felt soothed and I slept without any trouble.

....

The alarm clock in my mobile phone woke me up at 5 a.m. the next morning. I saw Jamba sleeping on the floor on the cushions of the sofa. God knows when at night he had shifted himself from the sofa to the floor.

As I was getting ready for a morning walk, Jamba got up.

"Good morning, Sir," I greeted him.

"Good morning, Dada. Hope you had a good sleep. Give me 5 minutes to get ready," he said.

I opened the door and stepped out of the room. The sun had just come out but I felt a little cold.

"Let's go for a walk," Jamba said, coming out of the room.

As we walked in Samdrup Jongkhar town, I could see the morning sun gradually peeking out from between the mountains. We walked for almost an hour through this small town. There was a monastery in the heart of the town, where a flock of hundreds of pigeons were sitting, sometimes waddling and sometimes flying like they were doing their morning exercise. People were giving them food, which they were pecking at happily.

The sight of people feeding the pigeons and the sound of their cooing and the flapping of their wings in ecstasy started my day with positive vibes.

Jamba wished and greeted almost each and every one that we came across. We met the local SP (Superintendent of Police) who was Jamba's friend and some of his other friends in higher echelon of the bureaucracy. I found there was a large number of Marwaris and Biharis in the town. Jamba told me that they were the main trading community in this town. But what struck me was that Jamba greeted

everyone on our way – known or unknown, rich or poor, young or old. When he met any Bhutanese, he greeted in their language, but when he met any Indian, he said 'Namaste' with folded hands, even to the sweepers.

I initially thought that he knew everyone in this town.

"You know everyone here?" I asked in surprise. "No."

"But you are greeting almost everyone you are coming across!"

"We should greet everyone we meet. What's wrong in greeting an unknown person? In the worst-case scenario, he or she may not greet you back. That's his or her problem. That's their karma. I do my own karma – that's to love each and every animal on this earth. That's the only secret to happiness," Jamba explained with a hint of smile in his eyes.

I was beginning to understand that this man had shed his ego to an extent that he did not think of what anyone thought of him or whether anyone ignored him. I thought I could have done better in life, had I understood and controlled my ego better. After getting a good job and enjoying all material pleasures, I had started thinking of myself as someone very important and successful. Sometimes, I had not cared for the feelings of my close ones. My ego had got better of me till then.

While returning to our BRO guest house, Jamba told me, "We need to get ready by 8.30 a.m. as we have to reach the Immigrations Centre sharp at 9 a.m."

After completing the formalities at the Immigration Centre, we started from Samdrup Jongkhar at around 10 a.m. After leaving the town behind, we went uphill, entering deep into the wonderful mountains of Bhutan, where I could see only mountains and forests.

"How far is our college, Sir?"

"Not far," Jamba replied.

"How long will it take?" I asked again.

"Just 12 hours," he said with a chuckle. "Will it be difficult for you?"

"No, Sir."

I really didn't know how far it was as Jamba's style was not to reveal much before reaching a certain place. Anyway, I concentrated on the beautiful hills and forests of Bhutan outside, as Jamba went into deep slumber after some time— 'there is so much to see in this world'. My mood got better once we were in the mountainous region.

We were crossing mountain and after mountain, and valley after valley, and many more rivers in-between. The shades of green of the nearby mountains and the deep blue of the distant sky fascinated me so much that I could hardly take my eyes off. There was absolute tranquility everywhere. Only the chirping of the insects and some birds was the constant soothing sound I heard in those mountains and forests. I saw beautiful flowers like junipers, magnolias, orchids and blue poppies (the national flower of Bhutan). The mountains were covered with daphne, giant rhubarb, pine and oak trees.

When Jamba woke up after two hours, he revealed the real reason for our one-night stay at Samdrup Jongkhar. The Immigration Centre was closed on Sundays. That's why he took me to Manas National Park on Sunday, so that I could start my journey to Bhutan on a positive note.

It was around 1 p.m. I saw a big machine was removing some debris of landslides from the road. Barma stopped the vehicle and informed us that the road would be closed

for 30 minutes due to the construction work. Jamba came out of the vehicle and asked me to come down and follow him. Under his guidance, I somehow crossed the debris and started walking with him.

"Whenever I face roadblocks, I start walking amidst nature. I don't waste my time in sitting and waiting in the vehicle. Barma will catch up with us when the road opens," Jamba said.

He informed me that landslides and roadblocks were very common in these hilly areas and Bhutan was no exception.

"Just enjoy the nature," Jamba gestured at the green and blue forests of Bhutan.

"In our country, we have over 70 per cent of green cover," Jamba said, justifiably proud. "See those trees on the mountains? They are consuming all the carbon dioxide released by us. If we sell all our trees, we will get a lot of money. But that will be harmful for us and our future generations. If we cut these trees and build houses or factories, we can increase our GDP, but we will lose our abundant oxygen supply. Sustainable and equitable socio-economic development, as well as environmental conservation are an important part of Bhutan's gross national happiness (GNH) programme."

I have been to many other hilly places in India and outside of India, but I have never witnessed such a vast green cover and so little pollution. The difference between the mountains in Bhutan and the mountains of the other countries, including India, was that these are completely virgin, mostly unexplored by people. There were no guest houses, no restaurants, and no houses on most of them. It was not yet spoilt by the 'materialist' world. It was a different feeling altogether. It was full of oxygen; it was

natural detoxification. I felt as if I needed that booster dose of oxygen badly at that critical time of my life.

"At a time when most nations are finding it difficult to reduce their carbon emissions, our country is already carbon negative. The vast woodland of the country takes more greenhouse gasses from the atmosphere than it emits. Forests cover almost 70 per cent of the country, which absorbs carbon dioxide naturally, leaving only pure oxygen for the citizens of Bhutan. When we will lose this quality of oxygen, we will feel stressed out, which in turn, will make us angry and frustrated." Jamba paused to look at me, and suggested, "Stop breathing for a minute. See how you feel. Will it be possible to feel good or happy if we don't have quality oxygen to breath?"

Jamba continued to talk as we kept walking amidst pristine nature. "People outside our country keep asking me, how is it that the people of Bhutan are so happy? I tell them one thing: we respect nature. It's in our Constitution that we have to preserve at least 60 per cent of forest cover in our country. We have successfully maintained a natural co-existence with nature. We have realised the fulfilling relationship with nature. Our existence on earth depends on our co-existence with nature. If we live this way, our lives will be happier and more joyous. We, as human beings, should recognise this first. Our body requires nourishment. Nature is producing fresh oxygen or rather giving us oxygen for free. There is no distinction when nature gives us oxygen. Suppose you are a Brahmin. Will nature give you more oxygen than it will to the shudras?" Jamba asked me solemnly.

When Jamba mentioned the caste system, I asked him, "Is there any caste system in Bhutan?"

"No. Because even nature does not recognise the caste system. Fresh air is available for every one of us," Jamba

said smilingly.

We had walked for almost 45 minutes before Barma came from behind and caught up with us; we got inside the truck.

It was around 2.30 in the afternoon. Jamba said something to Barma, who, in turn, kept looking at the hills as if searching for something. After about 10 minutes, Barma stopped the vehicle in front of a dilapidated wooden house. From the look of it, I could understand that this was not an affluent house. Jamba told me that since we could not locate any waterfalls here, we would have our lunch in this house.

"You know them?" I asked, a little taken aback.

"No."

He gave some instructions to Barma, who went up to the house. An old lady opened the door. Barma talked to her and then started unloading some vegetables and rice from the vehicle. I was observing all this from inside the vehicle.

"We will cook in their kitchen," said Jamba, getting down from the vehicle.

I was rather surprised, as I had no such experience of going into an unknown person's house and cooking in their kitchen. But here everything was so different, so unique. I would not have known that such compassionate people existed on earth, had I not been to Bhutan.

For the next one hour, we stayed at this unknown house where I could see only an old couple. They did not let us cook. Jamba offered some vegetables and rice, but they did not accept that either. As Barma helped them in cooking, they asked us to sit in the open yard of their home.

We had rice with Kewa datshi, a curry made with potato and cheese, and Ema datshi, a curry made of big chillies and cheese, sitting on the wooden bench in their yard. These two are the common curries in Bhutan which they eat with rice. They had also given us a home-made local alcoholic soup, which I did not have. Later, Barma told me that it's a custom in Bhutan to offer the local drink to guests. I was pretty touched by the hospitality and warmth of this unknown old couple. While bidding adieu, I expressed my sincere gratitude to them.

As we went on our way, I felt what a wonderful place this world could have become if we harboured feelings and concern for one another's needs. I had gone to so many big cities in my life and visited so many houses, but I have never experienced this kind of hospitality. They would probably neither meet us again, nor would they get any benefit from us in the future. Yet, they did everything for us without any expectations. Who in this world could be happier than them?

After an hour or so, we crossed Trashigang town, one of the important towns of eastern Bhutan. Then we passed Kanglung, a town where the famous and the oldest college in Bhutan – Sherubstse College – was located. Jamba told me that he had studied in this college and later taught here too. So, he had some fond memories here. He also informed me that his ancestral village was near this college and after retirement, he would come back and serve the poor people of his village.

"We need to give back to our roots," he said. While talking about his childhood he told me that he had to walk almost 10km daily to reach his school and college.

After crossing the town, Jamba asked Barma to stop. I saw a schoolboy standing beside the road with his bag. Jamba spoke with him and then, asked him to get into our truck.

The boy sat beside me. I asked him his name and which class he was in. He informed me that he was waiting for a bus and would get down soon. After 20-25 minutes, he got down at his village.

While getting down, he thanked us. Jamba just told him in English, "Give people lift when you have a car, too. It's very important to help people."

We crossed a few more small places before reaching Gyalphozing at around 9 p.m. It was very dark, so I could not see much of the town and the college. I did not know what was in store for me in the coming days. On that dark night, I only wished that there should be enough light for me in my coming days in Bhutan.

****

8

I had been allotted a beautiful wooden cottage as my accommodation in the college campus. Next morning when I woke up, I shivered a bit. At the end of September, Gyalpozhing was definitely a little colder than Samdrup Jongkhar. But when I opened the windows of my bedroom, I was delighted to see the mountains standing majestically behind my cottage and a river – the Kuri Chu – flowing past my cottage. It was a childhood fantasy to gaze at mountains immediately after waking up in the morning. And here I was, lucky to get a river in addition to the mountains! It was something beyond my dreams. I could see the river passing in-between my college and the mountains. I immediately fell in love with the place. It was my 'meet cute moment' with Gyalpozhing.

The previous night, Jamba had asked me to reach his office by 8.30 a.m. to complete the joining formalities. Jamba had also told me that till I find and hire a permanent cook, Barma would cook for me.

As promised, Barma appeared at 7.30 a.m. He greeted me with a smile showing his paan-stained front teeth and politely asked me about my first night here, and what would I like for breakfast that morning.

"What do people eat here generally?" I asked.

"Rice, Sir, la. But Sir you want, you eat bread-butter

toast, la," Barma replied in broken English.

Using 'la' at the end of each sentence was a mark of respect in Bhutan. Generally, people who are junior or in lower posts, use it while talking to their seniors or elders.

I had already noticed that morning that the college authorities had stocked up my kitchen with some basic foodstuff like rice, potatoes, chillies, tomatoes, onions, eggs, bread, butter, tea, sugar and milk, so that I would not face any difficulties in the initial days.

I asked him to prepare tea and butter toast for breakfast and went to get ready.

"Breakfast ready Sir, la," Barma smilingly said once I came out of my room after getting ready.

Barma's unique smile can make your day.

When I finished my breakfast, it was around 8 a.m. Though Barma told me that it would be a 10-minute walk to reach President Sir's office, I wanted to have a good look at the college before I met Jamba.

Gyalpozhing College of Information Technology (GCIT) was started just two years back. I could see a total of eight buildings in a vast campus apart from nine cottages – including one for the president, Jamba, and one for myself – and some more small houses made of bamboo and bamboo boards with tin sheds for the support staff of the college.

Gyalpozhing is a town in the Mongar district of Bhutan, which is not at a very high altitude. It was basically a valley surrounded by two massive mountains, the Pongtua la and the Yongko la.

Our college was located between Pongtua la and Yongko la, both, standing on either side of it, seemed to be

protecting it from any external challenges. On the western side was the main road adjacent to Pongtua la, while on the eastern side flowed River Kuri Chu, downhill, along with Yongko la. The college campus stood on a plot of land far bigger in length but shorter in width. The road and river went past either side of the college campus. Once the college premises ended, the road and river ran alongside each other.

Most of the GCIT campus was rocky, without any grass cover, but there were two beautiful lush-green lawns — one, near the administrative and academic building, and the other, in front of the cottages. Out of the eight buildings, one was the main administrative building, where President Sir's office was located. One building was for faculty members and library. Of the remaining six, two were for academics; two were hostels - one for girls and the other for boys - and one was the faculty quarters; and one, which had a community hall. Some faculty members stayed in the cottages, and some in the faculty quarters building.

Yet, there was a vast vacant area where many more buildings will come up in the future, when GCIT would introduce more courses.

Our cottages were in little isolated pockets, opposite all the buildings where the main activities of the college took place. The only building which stood near our cottages was the faculty quarters, where rest of the faculty members stayed.

What caught my attention was the college's spanking new sports facilities. The college had a beautifully maintained football ground and a basketball court. It had been many years since I had touched a football or entered a football ground. I could feel a shiver of excitement at the very prospect of playing football again. But I was not confident whether I would be able to play with my current

weight and lack of physical fitness.

When I went inside Lhato Jamba's chamber, he looked a completely different person altogether, now looking like the head of a college, attired in the traditional Bhutanese dress, gho. His chamber, though, was not as spacious as we are accustomed to seeing in India. A sofa set was placed near the entrance of the room for the visitors. His desk was on the left-hand side facing the window. I was surprised to find that there was no place to sit in front of him, which was not very common. If anyone had to talk to him, Jamba needed to come to the sofa and sit with that person. But then, I thought, this man was different and unique in his own way.

As usual, Jamba greeted me warmly and gestured at the sofa.

"I hope you did not face any difficulty at night. No wild animals disturbed you at night, no?" he asked me with that mischievous smile, as he came and sat in front of me.

"No, Sir. Everything was fine," I assured him with a smile.

"Did Barma come to prepare breakfast for you?"

"Yes, Sir."

As Jamba poured out some tea for me and offered biscuits, there was a knock on the door, and two people entered the chamber, and politely greeted Jamba and me. Jamba introduced me to his personal secretary and the Dean, Academic Affairs, and asked me to complete the joining formalities.

I completed all the formalities that day. I was assigned two theory classes per day, apart from two practical classes. I sat with Tshering, the Dean, Academic Affairs,

who took me through the nitty-gritty of taking theory and practical classes and the timings. Since I was completely new to the profession of teaching, Tshering gave me some ideas about how to take classes; he briefed me about the students and other faculty members. He also informed me about the rules and regulations of the college. I then talked to Lhendup Dorjee, Dean, Students Affairs, who explained to me the requirements of the students.

Like Jamba, the men were dressed in their traditional dress, gho and the women wore the kira. The gho and the kira are Bhutan's national dress. (Bhutan's traditional dress is one of the most unique and noticeable features of the country.) Bhutanese people invariably wear their national dress in schools, government offices and on formal occasions. Their traditional clothing is made from Bhutanese textiles in different colourful patterns.

Gho is similar to the Tibetan chuba, a knee-length-long robe and it is wound tightly around the waist with a woven cloth belt called a kera.

The kira, worn by Bhutanese women, goes right down to their toes. This is a brightly coloured dress that is wrapped around the body over a Tibetan-style silk blouse called wonju. Toeg, a short, open, jacket-like garment, is worn over it.

I asked Dorjee if I had to wear a gho. He told me it's not mandatory for non-Bhutanese people. However, I decided to buy a gho for myself, as I liked it very much. Since the college offered only one course - Bachelor's degree in Computer Application (BCA) — and that too, for only the first- and second-year students, I understood that I would not have much work load here.

I next went to see the library. I met the librarian, Pema Wangchuk. He was of average Bhutanese height, very thin

and with an oval-shaped face with high cheek bones and a prominent jawline. A soft-spoken man, Pema would not elicit respect from people by his gravitas. I later learnt that he was a highly talented musician, who could play all the traditional instruments of Bhutan and sing the traditional folk songs too.

Pema, like everyone I had met here so far, received me warmly with a smile. He showed me the different sections of the library. As it was a new college, the library did not have a lot many books. I suggested some books on computer science, some motivational books and some fiction books as well. He showed me some fictions which were already there. I picked up Zeppa's Beyond the Sky and the Earth: A Journey into Bhutan, as I wanted to know more about Bhutan. He told me that like everyone else, he stayed in the college campus; his cottage was next to mine. I was happy to find an affable man as my immediate neighbour.

After coming out of the library, I sat for a while on a bench in the green meadows in front of the administrative building. There was a sense of tranquility pervading the place. The beautifully designed Bhutanese buildings looked lovelier with the exquisite mountains in the background. Bhutan is all about keeping its own indigenous culture and tradition alive, which included the traditional architecture. All the buildings were constructed with multi-coloured wood frontages, small arched windows, and sloping roofs.

Given the large influence of Buddhism in the country and its long history with Tibet, the main architectural style of the buildings was in Tibetan-Buddhist style.

When I was returning to my cottage, I heard someone calling me from behind. Turning around, I saw Barma.

He came running up to me and asked, "Going to your room Sir, la?"

"Yes."

"Sir, I made lunch, la… rice, egg curry, kewa datshi," Barma informed me in his own English.

"Thanks a lot, Barma."

"Sir, go with you, la. I give food for you, la," Barma told me, expressing his desire to serve me lunch.

He started walking beside me before I could say anything.

Barma cooked really well. The egg curry was more in Indian style, as he told me he could cook Indian food very well. I also liked the kewa datshi. I had come to know from Barma that Bhutanese did not use spices and liked to mix cheese in curries.

"Don't you people eat fish or chicken?" I asked Barma, curiously.

"We eat, but not fresh fish or chicken, la," Barma answered.

"Why?"

"Because here we not kill animals, Sir. So, we not kill fish or hen or goat. All come from India. Kuri Chu river… lot of fish… but we not kill fish in the river."

I asked Barma if the market was very far from the college. Around 2km from here, Barma told me. We decided to go to the market in the evening to purchase some basic household items.

Barma came at 5.30 p.m. to take me to the market. It was a pretty good market situated at the northern side of the college, near the hills and almost everything was found there. I bought some vegetables, groceries and some daily

essentials. I also purchased a pair of boots, two shorts, two jerseys and a gho. Barma told me that he would help me in wearing the gho, as wearing it was a difficult task for any beginner.

I decided not to appoint a cook. Since Barma was relatively free as Jamba Sir stayed most of the time in the campus, I made an arrangement with Barma that time permitting, he would cook for me, and on days that he was busy, I would cook myself. Barma also promised me that he would teach me to cook Bhutanese food. I had never really cooked properly. Both Ma and Sushmita could rustle up delicious dishes and there never was any need for me to learn this particular skill.

I had my dinner alone that night after Barma left. I snuggled down for a while with the book on Bhutan by Zeppa. Before going to sleep, I opened the packet that held my new football boots. I took out the boots and held them in my hand for a while, and then lifted them close to my face; I inhaled deeply. The whiff of my new boots felt… oh, so good! Within seconds my mind travelled back to those good old football days. I felt something positive stir within me. I yearned to get back to the football ground once again.

Though I was looking forward to making a comeback in life, something was still torturing me from the inside. The incidents of my past were pulling me back and obstructing my march forward. All the bad memories of the previous year returned to agonise me, especially, at night. The thoughts of my parents, Sushmita and all the past events did not allow me any peace.

My initial interaction with my students went off well. Since the medium of instruction in schools of Bhutan is English, most of the students understood English well. Students, dressed in gho and kira, were mostly well behaved and respectful, and in no time, we established a

rapport.

After a couple of days, I asked Pema about the timings of football practice. He took me to the administrative officer, Kelsang Namgyel, who was in-charge of the college football team. Kelsang was a 25-year-old physically fit, handsome man, who was also a good football player. He invited me to come to the football ground after classes were over for the day.

When I returned to my cottage, I put on my brand-new football shorts, jersey and boots. I had last worn football boots almost 19 years ago. I was extremely nervous — I was not the 15-year-old Siddhartha Lahiri, who was very thin, agile and bubbling with energy. This Siddhartha Lahiri was different - he was overweight, physically unfit and mentally depressed. The Siddhartha Lahiri of the past was full of dreams and busy in chasing success. But this Siddhartha Lahiri had no such things; he only wanted to get over his mental troubles and lead a peaceful and happy life.

After putting on the boots, I found myself tottering — not because the boots had spikes, but partly because I was overweight and bulky now, and partly because of lack of practice. My situation, I thought, was like my childhood hero Maradona, who, too, because of his unhealthy lifestyle, alcohol and drugs, had become terribly overweight.

With a lot of doubt, I somehow walked towards the football field. The picture of Mayna Sir and his parting words came to my mind and ignited the desire in me to turn to football in order to bounce back in life. 'Football teaches you that you can always make a comeback in life. It is never late to make a comeback.'

As I was about to step into the football ground, I could almost hear that roar from the gallery, which I had last

heard in that final match, in which I had given my best and won the man of the match trophy. In my mind, I could hear someone shouting 'Come on Siddhartha, you can do it!' I took the ball in my hand and touched it reverentially. My heart was pounding with excitement and anticipation. I kicked the ball after a long time. I cannot express how good I felt after kicking the ball! I felt a surge of positive energy within me, when I heard the thrilling sound of my boots striking the ball.

After that, I took part in the warm up exercise with the students under Kelsang's supervision. But soon I found that it would not be an easy task for me. I was feeling slothful and lethargic. I was out of breath. My whole body was in pain after about a mere 5 minutes or so. A voice in my head kept telling me that it would be an impossible task for me to play again. Shaken, I wondered if I should leave the ground and sit outside.

But then again, I summoned courage, thinking about the final match 19 years ago in which I had scored despite my injury and we had won the match coming from behind against all odds. I gathered confidence from the fact that nothing was impossible in life. I just needed to hold on here and have patience, I thought.

When we started playing a practice match after the exercise, I could play for just 10 minutes and then strained my thigh muscles. It was a bad injury. I experienced a severe pain in my left thigh. In agony, and virtually screaming, I was taken out of the ground to the side-lines. Some boys came with ice cubes and applied it on my left thigh. My face contorted in pain, I sat despondent outside the ground, and doubts sneaked into my mind again. I thought that with that level of fitness it would be impossible for me to play again. Getting back to full fitness seemed impossible. Playing football was something beyond me now, I despaired.

Suddenly, I looked up and saw Jamba Sir standing there; I hadn't been aware that he was watching me play.

As I was moaning and groaning, Jamba Sir came to me and asked, "How much is it paining?"

"It's paining a lot, Sir," I whimpered through gritted teeth.

"Imagine your leg was broken or chopped off. Is this more painful than that?"

"No, Sir," I moaned.

"Dada, remember one thing: Pain will be there, but how much you suffer is up to you, up to your mental strength," he said, nodding his head wisely, and then with his typical smile, "anyway, nice to see you play football."

"Yes, Sir. I used to play in childhood, but then I quit it for my studies."

"You quit football to study? You know football helps us in so many ways in life? You should not have quit football. I want all my boys and girls to play football regularly. Football teaches us so many life lessons which are no less important than maths or science. I take my students to different places to play football. We had a very strong team at Gedu, my previous college. I'm trying very hard to build a very good football team here also. You play with them regularly."

"Yes, Sir, I will."

"But you need to be in shape first. Start practising twice a day. What I saw in a short span of time, you have good football skills."

"Thanks a lot, Sir. I will start practising regularly from tomorrow."

Jamba went away.

Surprisingly, my pain also lessened after Jamba's pep talk.

I realised that Jamba Sir was probably right. How much we will suffer in life is all in our mind.

I continued to watch the game from the side-lines; the boys were swift and agile. They came to meet me after their practice match was over. They were all happy to see my skills in the short period that I played with them, and enthused me to play regularly. I, too, was impressed with their skilful ball control, especially, of Kelsang and some boys like Ugyen Jamtsho, Karma, Tshewang Tashi, Tenzin Kelzang, Phuntsho Wangyel, Dawa Tshering. Our goalkeeper, Jombay Dorjee, whom everyone called affectionately JD, was also very agile and adept.

My pain had reduced considerably. I felt inspired, watching those boys play. I could not wait to make myself fit again, so that I too could start playing with them. For some time now, I had wanted to turn around my life. I wanted to embark on a fresh new journey. I wanted to win my battle against myself. But I had never thought that one day it would be football – and that too, amidst the far-off mountains of Bhutan, which would open up the path to Life.

Life, in fact, had taken a full circle for me. My journey towards salvation had started from a football ground in the tiny Himalayan nation known for its happiness.

For the next few days, I could not practice because of my injury. In the mornings, I would just walk, or to be very precise, limp, with Jamba Sir, who kept inspiring me to practise regularly. While we were walking, Sir wanted to know about my family. I told him about my past, all my

troubles, losing my job, my divorce, the back-to-back deaths of my parents and my depression-related problems. He suggested that I should not think too much about the past, but instead, focus on what I had loved most in my childhood.

"Once you start playing football, you will be happy again, because that's something you love the most. All your troubles will go away gradually. The troubles you have faced in life so far were because you did not follow your heart, did not pursue your dream, or rather you were forced to abandon your dream. Your dream was to play football and become a footballer. But you could not chase it. Instead, you followed the dreams of your parents and your teachers," Jamba Sir pointed out gently.

Then on, every day I got up at 5 a.m. and did all the physical training and running that I needed to lose weight and become fit. In the mornings, I first started running on the hilly road of Gyalpozhing. First one km then two... three... and then, up to 5km. In the initial days, to put it mildly, it was very painful. But whenever I was in pain, I would recall Jamba Sir's words that pain will be there, but how much I suffer would depend solely on my mental strength. "I have to be mentally very tough," I would keep telling myself, "I cannot afford to lose this battle."

Actually, the pain during any physical exercise is an integral part of one's transformational process. Initially, there will be pain and discomfort. But pain is a part of the whole process — to feel good in the long term. There comes a time when one enjoys this pain, or, rather, if one does not experience this pain, he will think that his exercise is incomplete. All good things in life come only after experiencing this pain.

After running on the road, I would go straight to the football ground where I would do stretching and core exercises to regain my physical strength.

After one and a half months, I began to feel a lot better physically. My body had finally started on its journey towards getting back to full fitness.

I practised football with the boys after college hours. My balance, my football skills were also gradually on the path of recovery. This went on for the next two and a half months. I lost around 10kgs in four months' time.

Mentally and emotionally, too, I was feeling much better than when I'd first come to Gyalpozhing, on that dark night four months back. I realised that physical transformation was essential for mental transformation. Both are connected with each other. Without changing your body, you can't change your mind, as body and mind work hand in hand. My confidence had increased ever since I entered the football field again. My depression-related problems had been pushed to the back burner and had very little effect on my mental strength. I would forget everything whenever I was in the field or whenever I would spend time with my students in class or in the campus.

My bonding with the students who played football had developed in no time. Our college team started playing very well. In some practice matches at our football ground, we beat some of the local teams. While all the boys were superb players, I was especially impressed by the deftness and agility of our goalkeeper JD; mid-fielders, Ugyen Jamtsho, Karma; forwards, Tshewang Tashi, Tenzin Kelzang; wingers, Phuntsho Wangyel, Dawa Tshering; and defenders Kelnam Gyeltshen, Pema Rigzin, Phuntsho Dhendup and Pema Tashi. Since Bhutanese boys were nimble-footed and skilful in ball control, they loved to play with short passes, much like the Spanish football style — Tiki Taka style— of play. The understanding between our team members was so good that they would play in that style to perfection and beat the oppositions in style.

At first, I had found teaching a bit boring as I had always worked in the corporate sector. But after a couple of months, I discovered the charm of teaching. There was nothing more interesting in helping young minds to learn new things and help them grow as a person. I tried to motivate these young boys and girls with my knowledge and experience in life, both in the professional and personal fronts.

Sometimes, I would go for a tea break with some students or other faculty members. Rakesh Singh, a faculty and cyber security expert from Uttarakhand was one of the two Indians, other than me; the other person was a very senior professor from Kolkata, Dr Priyotosh Khan. Dr Tikoo, an Ethiopian, and Dr Brent Bass, a 45-year-old American, were faculties in the computer sciences department. Bass was a Fulbright Scholar, who had signed up with GCIT for his research and teaching assignment for two years. The Bhutanese faculties – Yoenten Jamtsho, Ugyen Choden, Sonam Wangmo, Rebbeca Tirwa – were all very competent and well-mannered.

Rakesh was a jovial man and played football with us. Jamba also liked him for this, and he gave Rakesh the responsibility of developing the women's team.

Most of the students of the college liked me and respected me. I had no one close left in this world. I needed a family, and I had probably found 'my family' in them.

In the company of my students, the college football team, Jamba Sir, Pema, Kelsang, Barma and all, I always felt positive and better, but whenever I was alone, a sudden fragrance, a word, or colour would act as a trigger and my mind would instantly travel to the past, and painful memories would overwhelm me.

....

One day, in the beginning of January, the temperature had gone down considerably at Gyalpozhing and it was freezing cold in the morning and at nights. The entire college campus, the mountains and Kuri Chu river would be covered in fog, both in the mornings and at nights. Sometimes, I did not feel like waking up early.

One morning, I was feeling cold and decided to sleep a bit longer. At 8 a.m. when I was still sleeping, I heard someone knocking on my cottage door. I thought it was Barma. But I was surprised to see Jamba Sir there. I requested him to make himself comfortable in my living room while I freshened up. When I came out, I saw Jamba Sir, much to my embarrassment, had already prepared tea for me in my kitchen.

I sat in front of him on a chair. He handed me a cup of tea and took one himself.

"Why did you miss today's practice?" Jamba Sir's expression was stern.

"It's so cold. I didn't feel like getting up."

"Dada, don't do it again. It's very easy to fall into the hole than coming out of it. You have made huge progress in the last few months, but you have to be very careful. It's very easy to go back to your old habits, if you allow the slightest of complacency to creep in." Jamba's tone was grave as he cautioned me, "Everything is a habit. Every good practice is a habit. It is rather a result of hard work and mental toughness. Working hard is also a habit and so is keeping promises. You suddenly can't do these things if you are not accustomed to it. You have to be mentally very alert to keep the good things going for you. Don't allow it to slip away from your hands."

I kept quiet. I was feeling guilty by then, as I was on the

path of revival, which was always difficult and hard. One mistake and I would be back in the hole again.

"Dada, I want my team to be the best. Kelsang and the boys are very happy with you. I want you to guide them."

From that day, till today, I have never bunked any practice session. I never got up late for a single day, whether it was freezing cold or blazing hot. I have seen the worst in my life; I didn't want to go back to those dark old days.

Occasionally, we would go to the Gyalpozhing Stadium to play matches with other local teams at night. This beautiful stadium, surrounded by the majestic mountains, was equipped with floodlights. Playing football at night under floodlights, in the chilling cold, was a unique experience. Jamba Sir told me that all the towns in Bhutan had one such stadium which was rented out to different teams for practice matches and tournaments.

Sometimes, Jamba Sir would call me to his office or take me to the canteen and discus the academic performances of the students as well as the performance of the footballers. He was keen on providing his students hands-on training or practical experience rather than mere bookish knowledge. I started giving my students more project-oriented work and practical problems to solve. Jamba was impressed with the students' progress under my guidance.

I don't know the reason, but Jamba Sir had taken a liking to me from the very beginning and he became fond of me after my close involvement with the football team. He was so impressed by my performance in the football field that he formally gave me the responsibility of coaching the college football team.

Though I worked hard throughout the week, both on and off the football ground, on Sundays, I took it easy. I

would give my overworked muscles a rest day to heal, which was an important part of training. My routine would be completely different on Sundays, though I would still wake up early at 5 a.m., since I made it a habit, especially, after Jamba Sir's reprimand. I would go for a morning walk with Jamba Sir on the main road, walking along River Kuri Chu, towards the dam.

In the morning, the river looked spectacular against the hills, which would be covered with thick mist in winter. We would walk and talk about many things related to college, football and life. Sometimes, we would go down, close to the river, and sit on the big stone on the bank and watch the sun rise through the mountains. We would also discuss Bhutan and Bhutanese culture, heritage and its people.

Jamba Sir and I would have tea and breakfast after our morning walk at his beautiful one-storeyed elegant cottage. We would sit in the balcony of the cottage looking at the majestic mountains. Jamba Sir had two big goats, Chimi and Chiku, at his house, who would invariably come to me whenever I would start having my breakfast and would not leave until I gave them a bit or two.

Whenever I finished my tea, Jamba Sir would always be ready to pour some more tea into my cup.

'You need more?' he would ask amiably.

This is a typical Bhutanese way of serving tea. In India, tea is served in a cup and there would be no one to ask if you would need more tea, like people offer more rice or chapati. But this was a unique way of the Bhutanese people to feed you more. It did not matter whether they were rich or poor; they would be ever-ready to feed you to your heart's content.

Sometimes Jamba Sir would call me for dinner with

his family on Sunday evenings. I liked having dinner at his place as his wife was a very good cook. I quite enjoyed the traditional Bhutanese home-made food, whether it was at Jamba Sir's place or Pema's place or at Barma's house. Jamba Sir's son Kinga, who learnt traditional guitar from Pema, studied in Class XI at the Gyalpozhing Government Higher Secondary School. Schools, colleges and hospitals in Bhutan are run by the government and are free for all.

On Sundays after breakfast, GCIT students would go for community work. Most of the times, I would accompany them, as this gave me an opportunity to know Gyalpozhing well and see the villages of Bhutan. They would usually go to different places of Gyalpozhing and clean those areas. Community feeling was very strong in Bhutan. They did not live for themselves only, or selfishly, like we did. Rather, Bhutanese people live for each other and die for each other. And when people live for each other, no one can stop them from being happy.

One thing I found unique in Bhutan was the lack of variety in names. You would find some very common names all over the country. So, there were more than one Karmas, Tsherings, Sonams, Sangays, Pemas in our college and these could be names for both, boys and girls. Though the surnames were different for males and females, so many similar first names would surely confuse anyone new in Bhutan. Initially, I too would get confused - it was awkward and embarrassing for me — but as time passed on and our interactions increased, I could recognise them all.

I also did my utmost to learn the local language from my students, but I found it very hard to master. Though Dzongkha is the national language of Bhutan, people of this region use Sharchopkha as their main language for communication.

One Sunday we went for a trek on the Yongko la with

Rakesh, Brent Bass and his wife Cathy, Tikoo and Barma. Bass was an interesting American with a very humble living style. He and his wife seemed to be in love with Bhutan and its people. Unlike most Americans, Bass was hardly a person attached to material possessions and was fascinated by Bhutan and Buddhism. Cathy tutored the underprivileged children of Gyalpozhing in the evenings, after their school hours. The American couple seemed to be joyfully living their lives in Bhutan.

Barma was our guide on the trek to Yongko la. We could see the whole Gyalpozhing town from the mountain – the market, football ground, our college, River Kuri Chu – in miniature forms.

We became exhausted while climbing through the least-travelled routes of this mountain, and decided to rest for some time; there was a huge rock there, and some members of our little group leant against it, others sat atop it.

After some time, I asked Brent, "Of all countries, why did you choose Bhutan?"

"Because I was fed up with the American lifestyle. I heard a lot about happiness of Bhutan. Moreover, I have a serious inclination towards the doctrines of Buddhism," Bass replied, while sipping water from his bottle.

"But being a Christian, how do you relate to Buddhism?"

"Buddhism is not treated as a religion – it's a way of life here. Anyone can follow it. You don't have to be a Buddhist to follow it. You can be an 'engaged Buddhist' and follow the path of happiness and peace."

"Do you think all the people of Bhutan are happy?" I observed him keenly as I asked Bass this.

This is the question I kept asking everyone. I was

curious to know if everyone in Bhutan was happy.

"Look, it's not possible for everyone to be happy. But what attracts me is that happiness is a human goal here. It's not the case in other countries where material and personal comforts are more important than achieving peace and happiness," Bass said, and Cathy nodded in agreement.

I liked listening to Bass. He explained everything very clearly with reasons. Since I did not have much knowledge about Bhutan and Buddhism, I kept asking him, Jamba Sir or Pema a lot of questions on happiness and Bhutan.

"But why can't other countries pursue happiness like Bhutan?" I asked him again.

"In most of the Western countries, we give more importance to developing Intelligence Quotient or IQ, which is more related to developing the power and capacity of the functioning of human brains. But we ignore a vital element in life, that is Emotional Quotient or EQ, which helps us understand, use and manage our own emotions in a positive way, so that we can empathise with others, overcome challenges and conflicts with others. In Bhutan they stress on nurturing EQ. Don't you think EQ is more important than IQ?" he asked me in a serious tone, as always.

I agreed with Bass. Earlier, I hadn't understood this, but ever since Rathin Sir had lamented about his son, I had started to believe in nurturing human empathy and compassion.

"That's why I have come here to learn about life in Bhutan, the happiest country on earth. I have come here to learn about nature, to see how people can peacefully co-exist with nature," Bass continued.

All of us listened quietly as Bass enounced.

Bass was probably right in every assessment. We Indians, too, are never taught in school or colleges to be happy in life or to consider happiness as our goal. We are not trained to manage conflicts. I sincerely repented having done all the wrong things in my life. I wished I had known how to manage conflicts. I wished I had known that happiness was the most important thing in life.

"Bass is right. Bhutan is different from the rest of the world," said Tikoo, joining the conversation.

"You also love Bhutan as much as Bass?" I asked Tikoo, curiously.

"Yes. It's such a beautiful country with so many innocent people. You will also fall in love with this country after a while," Tikoo smiled.

"I have already begun to fall in love with this country and its people," I said, smilingly.

Rakesh, who was attentively listening to Bass and Tikoo, also said the same thing.

"If I ask you one thing you like most in Bhutan, what will that be?" I asked Tikoo.

"The one most important thing here is that nobody treated me as a black. I have been to many countries and everywhere I faced racial discrimination in some form or the other. But I did not face it here," said Tikoo.

It was a very satisfying trek for all of us. We explored several unknown places in the mountain that day and talked about so many things on Bhutan and its happiness quotient. While coming back, I felt that my love for this beautiful country was increasing day by day. And as my attachment to this country and its people grew, my personal problems seemed to become less legible to my consciousness.

....

My love for Bhutan had increased manifold after I had completed reading the fascinating book, A Journey into Bhutan. The author, Jamie Zeppa, was a Canadian, who had come to Bhutan on a teaching assignment in the late Eighties. She stayed in Bhutan for quite a long time, converted to Buddhism, and married a Bhutanese, one of her former students. Zeppa's description of Bhutan and its innocent people is so vivid that simply by reading this book anyone would fall in love with the country.

After completing that book, I restarted Paulo Coelho's The Alchemist, which I had started reading after my mother's death, but couldn't complete it because of my father's death.

The theme of the book – 'When you want something, the universe conspires in helping you to achieve it' – resonated in my life, I thought. Yes, I passionately wanted a turnaround in my life. And I could sense all the good omens. I could feel that things were getting better for me with each passing day. Sometimes, I wondered how everything had changed for me within a few months. I was on the brink of the precipice. I could see no light at the end of the tunnel. I had considered suicide. My journey to Bhutan from the jaws of death was nothing short of a miracle. But miracles happen when you honestly want something with passion.

Some evenings, when I felt lonely, I would spend time either with Pema or Barma. Sometimes, Barma would take me to his small two-room bamboo house where his whole family – his parents, wife and two daughters – lived happily together. I asked Barma one day, if his family ever quarrelled amongst themselves. He laughed at my question and answered that they adjust with one another so well that there was no question of any arguments or fights.

Sometimes, I would go to Pema's cottage. There too, I would see the same thing. Pema's parents lived happily with his wife and two sons. I had never heard anyone shouting or any family arguments despite their cottage being so close to mine.

Pema could play a number of musical instruments like the typical Bhutanese instrument yangchen, which has strings like the santoor; the flute; drangyen (the traditional guitar), and many more. Pema's flute or yangchen would often cheer up my sagging mood. Sometimes, I would sit with Pema at the back of my cottage, facing River Kuri Chu and listen to his music.

Once we went to the river bank on a moonlit night and sat on two big stones, which were lying side by side. Taking out his flute, Pema played a traditional Bhutanese tune of nomadic yak herders, who lived in the highlands, breathing in joy to the absolute serenity of the place. As the moonlight reflected on the water of the Kuri Chu river and illuminated the Yongko la mountain, the entire place looked like heavenly. The mesmerising sound of the flute reverberated in the water of the river and the hard rocks of the mountains, and made me forget everything. It was so surreal that for a few moments I lost track of my own existence and forgot all about my past or future. I completely surrendered myself to Nature.

For the first time in life, I rued that I didn't know how to sing or play any instrument. Here in Bhutan, a lonely Siddhartha learnt that everybody should learn how to play at least one musical instrument. I asked Pema to teach me the yangchen, which simply mesmerised me and lifted my mood anytime of the day.

Pema also taught music to all the GCIT students. Jamba was rather keen that every student should learn at least one musical instrument. During their cultural programmes,

everyone would take part in some individual or group music or dance performance.

One day, while listening to Pema's soulful music, I asked him, "Why is music and dance so important in Bhutan?"

"Traditional music and dance matters in Bhutan, since through that people fully learn and experience with their whole mind and body what it's to be truly a Bhutanese. By participating in music and dance from childhood to college, Bhutanese people experience very strong cultural and spiritual values."

"That means it is a part of Bhutan's community programme?"

"Yes Sir, la. Through music we experience how we relate to nature, how we relate to community, how we relate to the world and cosmos. Music and dance throughout Bhutan not only shares many common traces and values, it connects to local languages and the way of life. What we learn by participating in song and dance can't be taught through books or by teachers."

The more I learnt about this country, the more amazed I was at their ideas and thoughts.

"Experiencing and preserving our culture is one of the four essential pillars of Bhutan's Gross National Happiness – or GNH – programme. Promoting contentment and peace in the country is directly related to promoting Bhutan's indigenous culture," added Pema passionately.

I had observed this common trait in everyone I met there. When they spoke about their country, they would be very passionate and emotional. I wish we had something similar in India, unlike the usual chest thumping.

"What are the three other pillars of GNH then?" I asked Pema.

"They are: sustainable and equitable socio-economic development; environmental conservation, preservation and promotion of culture; and good governance."

Pema remarked that they should preserve their music and pass it on to the next generation, so that it survives down the ages.

There was so much to learn from this small nation. Their feeling for preserving their culture and tradition is so strong. How I wished we had learnt all these in our childhood. I regretted that our students were learning so many subjects but missing out on these vital aspects of life.

....

An hour passed since Ranjit had said something. He had been so engrossed in the story that he had not disturbed me even once. In-between, he had laughed, sometimes, at Jamba Sir's words or some actions. He had taken notes, wherever he felt it was necessary for his special newspaper story on my life.

I could sense that he was much more relaxed, now that my life was finally beginning to settle down after those terrifying days — as if, he was witnessing a fresh morning after a stormy night.

"Ranjit, please have lunch now..."

"No, Sir, I want to listen to the entire story in one go and then have lunch," Ranjit answered firmly. "I have a question, Sir."

"Go ahead."

"Why and how did you leave Bhutan and land in Buxa?"

"That's a most fascinating story, and I will tell you about it now. When you seek something with full faith, you will get that. Miracles do happen when you want something badly. I have experienced this in my own life."

"Sir, please continue. I can't wait more," Ranjit said.

I started narrating the concluding part of my journey.

****

9

I shed around 25kg after seven months. My football skills too improved considerably. Just as Jamba Sir had told me initially, if I played football regularly, my mental agony would gradually go away. Though I was not totally out of the woods with regards to my tormenting past, it did not feel that unbearable anymore. As if I had the strength of some kind. Rather, it was an ache that gave me anxiety sometimes. More importantly, it would not allow my mind to be fully free and achieve complete peace in life.

In addition to that, I was experiencing a completely new feeling. There was a strange void in my heart. Sometimes, when I was alone, I felt the futility of daily routine life. My yearning for doing something meaningful in life had also grown manifold. I was becoming restless.

With the little exposure that I had had so far about the Bhutanese way of life, I was pretty clear that the social and cultural life of the Bhutanese people and their happiness was deeply rooted in Buddhism. Hence, I felt the urge to know Buddhism from close quarters.

I shared my overall mental state with Jamba Sir. He listened to me carefully but did not say anything. In his typical style of keeping things in suspense till the last moment, one Sunday morning when we were in the midst of our morning walk, Jamba Sir asked me to get ready as soon as possible for a tour to Bumthang after the walk.

We started for Bumthang at around 7 a.m., driving on a very scenic road. It was my first tour to the hinterlands of Bhutan. En route, I felt as if the whole country resided in forests and hills. We crossed some orange orchards and apple orchards in the valleys. The journey was peaceful and throughout we came across very few vehicles.

We passed some small hamlets but everywhere there was pin-drop silence. I could only hear the constant chirping of crickets and the twittering of different birds. I could see some people, but they seemed to be happy and busy in their own way, in no hurry at all.

Along the road, in some places, villagers were selling their home-grown corns, bananas, apples, oranges and some local vegetables. But there were no restaurants, tea or coffee shops in the entire route of around two and a half hours.

We crossed several mountains and valleys, sometimes descending down a winding road only to go up another, sometimes past a flattish plain, sometimes with sombre tall trees, shrubs and bushes bordering deep ravines.

The valleys were full of paddy farms. The entire valley was draped by a green sheath of paddy. I saw some farmers in far-off fields, as well as young lads with their cattle walking aimlessly near the road.

It was so serene and peaceful that no one seemed to have any complaints about life. It seemed that the entire universe had stopped moving here; no one was in any urgency.

The entire landscape looked so picturesque and quiet that I felt like staying in one of these hamlets and live there forever, far away from the clamour of the rest of the world.

Despite the pleasant journey, I was, somehow, relieved when we reached Bumthang, one of the important tourist

places in Bhutan. I was eager to see this place after what Jamba Sir had told me about it on the way. He said Bumthang, which consists of four main valleys – Chokhor, Tang, Chhume and Ura – is a highly religious place in Bhutan. Most of the important monasteries and temples of Bhutan are located in Chokhor Valley, which is also the biggest of all these. Among the four valleys, Chokhor Valley is generally referred to as Bumthang.

Jamba Sir explained that in Tibetan Buddhism, which is followed by Bhutanese people, chokhor means prayer wheels. Prayer wheels are common in the monasteries. According to the Buddhist belief system, when one spins the wheel, one accumulates wisdom and merit. This also helps in purifying negativities.

Chokhor Valley is a must-visit for anyone who is deeply religious. But for someone like me who was not a religious person, it was certainly worth seeing these Buddhist temples for their unique architecture, legends associated with them, huge, colourful and intricate paintings and murals that adorn the walls of these Dzongs.

We first visited Kurje Lhakhang, which is also known as Kurje Monastery. It's a very popular destination and one of the important places to visit in Chokhor Valley. Located on the banks of Chamkhar river, this monastery consisted of three temples which were surrounded by 108 Chorten walls. The first temple was built on a rock, where Padmasambhava, also known as Guru Rinpoche, an 8th-century Buddhist master from India, meditated. Behind one of the temples there was a large tree which is believed to be a terma (hidden treasure) that was left there by the Guru. We went inside the temple. Sir offered prayers to the various small idols in the temple: Buddha, Guru Padmasambhava and other disciples of Buddha.

Though I was an atheist, my stay in Bhutan had somehow

softened my stand towards religion and spirituality. For the first time in my life, I felt a strong spiritual connection in Chokhor Valley. Except for the mild clicking sounds of prayer wheels from different monasteries in the area, there was absolute tranquility in the entire valley. I felt upraised and blessed. The serenity of the place stirred in me some unknown, hitherto unfelt, feelings for a few moments. It was like a clarion call from the eternal power. For the first time in life, I felt spiritually inclined after coming to this place.

After visiting several other monasteries, we visited the Lhodrakharchhu Monastery. This was a huge monastery with more than 400 monks, many of them children and young adults, residing.

"We owe India a lot for teaching spirituality to the entire world," Jamba Sir told me while coming out of the monastery.

When Jamba Sir talked about Buddha and Guru Padmasambhava and their Indian connections, I felt proud as an Indian for the first time in my life.

Looking back, I feel that I was destined to tour Chokhor Valley at that stage of my life when I was feeling that strange void and searching for the unknown. That day in Chokhor Valley and the subsequent events after that changed the trajectory of my life completely. I never looked back. I simply kept following the sounds of chokhor after that.

....

Barma had just started our vehicle, when I saw a Westerner, attired in the maroon robe of a Buddhist monk, approaching our car. He leant forward and spoke to Jamba Sir, who was sitting on the front seat of our vehicle.

"Sir, can I come with you?" the tall and fair monk politely asked.

"Why not? It will be our pleasure. Please get in," Jamba Sir replied cheerfully.

I opened the left door of the back seat where I was sitting. He got in and sat beside me.

"Where are you heading to?" I asked him.

"Gyalpozhing Monastery," he answered calmly.

"That's good. We will also go to Gyalpozhing. That's near our college," said Jamba Sir.

I was surprised to find a Western man in Buddhist monks' robe. I had heard of Westerners getting attracted to Buddhism and Hinduism, and though Westerners in ISCKON attire were fairly common in India, I had never seen any Western monks during my stay in Bhutan till then.

Curious, I glanced sideways at the monk; he was silently looking outside in deep meditative contemplation.

I thought of talking to him but decided against it, as I felt it wouldn't be right to disturb his peace.

Our car was descending now, the Chokhor Valley behind us at some distance; all the monasteries gazing over the region. Jamba Sir, as usual, nodded off reminding me that 'there is so much to see in this world'.

I was trying to keep my thoughts on the beauty of the journey, but many questions regarding this Western monk were running simultaneously in my head. From where had he come, and of all the countries, why had he chosen Bhutan, why had he become a monk, and many more.

I again looked at him from the corner of my eyes and

found him gazing at the passing nature, peacefully.

"Excuse me, Sir! May I know which country are you from?" I finally asked him, unable to control my curiosity.

"I am from London," he replied in a polite and soft voice, in a typical British accent, looking at me.

There was a sense of pleasantness on his face which, I felt, could be acquired through meditation and renunciation only.

"Where are you staying?" I asked him hesitantly.

"I stay, or rather, was staying, in Lhodrakharchhu Monastery, but from now on I will be staying at Gyalpozhing monastery."

"I also stay in Gyalpozhing." I couldn't contain my excitement.

"What do you do in Gyalpozhing?"

"I teach in the Gyalpozhing College of Information Technology. May I ask you something?"

"Yes, please," he said.

"When did you come to Bhutan?"

"Five years back," the monk replied gently.

My curiosity had gotten better of me and though I was hesitant about asking such personal questions like a probing aunt, in our first meeting, I found myself asking him what inspired him to settle down in Bhutan.

He simply smiled at me and said, "That's a long story. It will take some time to tell." He paused, smiled again and said, "Actually, I came to Bhutan to study Buddhism and the concept of happiness."

Since there was no hint of irritation in his voice or face in answering my questions, I asked him some more. I was finding him very interesting.

"What made you study Buddhism and happiness?"

"After completing my bachelors in economics, I did my masters in Regenerative Economics with specialisation in Buddhist Economics," he said civilly, without any hint of bragging or pride in his tone.

"Buddhist Economics! Is there a subject like that? The term sounds very interesting! There is a course on this?"

"Yes, I studied this in Schumacher College in London. Buddhist Economics is really a very interesting subject. The term was coined by the well-known economist E.F. Schumacher in his famous book, Small is Beautiful."

I requested him to explain a bit.

After a short pause, he started speaking in his soothing voice.

"It's an alternative to GDP-based economic model. Traditional economics is all about consumerism. It tells us to consume more and more to be happy. Here you will chase happiness but you will never be happy. In mainstream economics, people don't matter, generating capital does," the monk elaborated, as we passed by some gorgeous green-blue mountains.

"On the other hand," the monk continued, "Buddhist Economics is 'happy economics' as it makes people happy. Here, not only people but even animals and Mother Earth matters. In fact, nature in its entirety matters."

Though I did not understand the concept very clearly, I asked him, "Does Bhutan follow the Buddhist economic model?"

A beatific smile engulfed his face as though he had heard this question many a time.

Gathering his thoughts, he said, "If any country which has adopted and implemented the concept of Buddhist Economics in letter and spirit, it is this tiny Himalayan nation." Then he added, "When the rest of the world was busy calculating GDP or GNP, Bhutanese was engrossed in promoting happiness in their country through their policy of GNH or Gross National Happiness."

As our vehicle zipped through the remotest parts of this remote country, I was being initiated into Buddhist Economics, a subject I had never heard of, nor did I know how many people had ever heard of it.

"Ever since I came to Bhutan, I have seen people talking about GNH a lot. You are an economist. Please help me understand the concept of GNH from the perspective of economics," I requested him.

"Yes, that's very important. Economic activity of a country is very important in understanding happiness. Bhutan is unique in a way that when every other country calculates GDP to understand its economic growth, the Bhutan government measures the well-being of their citizens through happiness. Isn't that interesting?"

"Yes, that's very unique."

"In 1979, when every other country was adopting the conventional economic method for their country's development model, Bhutan rejected the concept of GDP or GNP. This was because the then king of Bhutan, Jigme Singye Wangchuk, was convinced that GNH was more important than GNP."

"But what was the reason that he gave for not adopting the GDP-based model?"

"The king of Bhutan doubted that the GDP or GNP models of growth provided a good economic model for them, as it would destroy their country's bio-diversity and ecological balance. The policymakers in Bhutan thought that the much-hyped economic model of globalisation promoted only greed and consumerism – the concept of 'more is better'. It promotes the illusive idea of getting happiness through consuming more products."

"Was his doubt a valid one?"

"Yes, hundred per cent! It has been seen that the culture of consumerism leads to individualism, which is the root of unhappiness. It creates a huge gap between the rich and the poor."

"That's a very commendable approach by the king," I said in an appreciative tone.

The monk continued in an affable manner, "Really commendable. That's why this country is different from the rest of the world. In a world where everyone wants to cling to power by any means, the current king of Bhutan, Jigme Namgyel Wangchuk, the son of the retired king Jigme Singye Wangchuk, relinquished power on his own and allowed democracy to take its root in his country in 2008. Have you ever seen that anywhere in the world?"

"No, perhaps not," I shook my head.

"You see, the GDP-based model is based on self-interest and desire for maximum profit whereas, the Buddhist Economics is based on 'compassion' and follows the Buddhist mandate of 'minimising suffering'. Though Bhutan is a deeply spiritual country, these concepts have some similarity with socialism. But with a tinge of religious flavour. It's a spiritual approach to economics. It's based on Buddha's eight-fold path approach to life."

"What is the eight-fold path?" I was fully absorbed in the monk's explanation.

While I had learnt a lot about GNH from Jamba Sir, Pema, Bass and others, the spiritual and economic aspects of it was not quite clear to me.

"Some of the basic features of the eight-fold path are right livelihood, ethical career choice, interdependency on people and things, and compassion for all, among others."

"How is right livelihood connected to GNH?"

"Right livelihood and GNH are very much connected. What you choose as your career is important in getting happiness."

"What kind of career should we choose then?" I was perplexed. Wasn't career related to earning a stable and handsome income?

"Can you get happiness when you are into a job which involves cheating people? Can you find happiness if your job takes you far from your close ones? Can you get happiness if your job requires you to harm anyone? As without interconnectedness, there is no GNH."

I nodded and listened quietly as he spoke.

The monk continued, "The West is suffering because their society is individualistic. GDP is based on ego, while GNH is based on compassion, kindness, sharing, caring and serving others."

While we were discussing, Jamba Sir's rhythmic snoring continued in the background.

"Which country have you come from?" the monk asked me.

"India."

"I have an Indian connection too."

"How come?"

"I stayed in the Ramakrishna Mission in Delhi for five years before settling down here," the monk said.

"Really! I lived in Delhi before coming here," I said, trying to make a bonding with him. "You told me that you were interested in Buddhism. But then why did you go to India first?" I asked him.

"I'm interested in all the religions of the East and their concept of spiritualism. But I was interested to learn about Indian philosophy first, and Buddhism is a part of it," he said smilingly.

"But as an Englishman, how did you get interested in Eastern religions and Indian philosophy?"

"When I was studying for my bachelors at the London School of Economics, I read a book called The Razor's Edge, by Somerset Maugham. Maugham's book inspired me so much that I started studying Vedanta and the Upanishads. I also read about Swami Vivekananda. Then I read The Autobiography of a Yogi, and was so fascinated by it that I decided to study Eastern philosophy and spirituality. That's why I went to India first. Since Vivekananda's ideas inspired me a great deal, I decided to stay in the Ramakrishna Mission Ashram."

The monk's education and knowledge were pretty evident. I thought, he must have been a brilliant student to have studied in the London School of Economics, one of the best places in the world to study economics.

This man was from London and still he knows so much about our religion and philosophy, I thought. Despite

being an Indian I was so ignorant of my own country and its cultural roots. I felt a deep sense of shame. Jamba Sir had by then woken up from his deep slumber, and he asked the monk if the journey had been comfortable. Jamba Sir mentioned the names of a few monks in Gyalpozhing and asked him if he knew them. The monk answered in the affirmative.

Finally, we reached Gyalpozhing Monastery and dropped our travel companion there. We bade him good bye.

Before leaving, he asked me to visit him any time.

"I will meet you in the evening tomorrow," I told him, thanking him for his invitation before we went our way.

I thought, finally, I have got the right man I was looking for to tackle the void in me. I was looking forward to learning more from him as he was now part of the same community and place.

After coming back from Chokhor Valley that day, I remained in my cottage, thinking about the monk from London. The way he talked to me, his calmness, his composure — everything attracted me so much that I could not think of anything else for the next couple of hours.

I've never been spiritually inclined, but at that time it struck me - which got reinforced every time I recalled my time spent at the Chokhor Valley and my conversation with the monk — that I needed to change the way I saw life or approached life. I needed to unravel the mystery of life.

....

The next day I went to college but found myself waiting impatiently for the classes to get over so that I could keep

my promised rendezvous with the English monk at the monastery.

Gyalpozhing Monastery was towards the dam and about 5km from the college. I headed to the monastery after my classes were over for the day. The monastery was situated at a slightly higher altitude in the Pongtua la mountain. From the main road I walked up a steep road on the right, about half a kilometre, to reach the monastery.

When I was close to the monastery, I suddenly realised that I hadn't asked the monk his name. Feeling annoyed with myself for this blunder, I went inside the monastery. But I could not see anyone.

After sometime, I saw a monk coming out of a room. I went up to him and, feeling a bit silly, asked him if he knew a Western monk who had come there the previous day, and described him.

"Yes, I understand, you talking about Jennings," said the monk in broken English.

He asked me to wait and went back to the room.

In the meantime, I roamed around the beautiful monastery. River Kuri Chu was clearly visible from there. The monastery comprised a few buildings. A big idol of Buddha was enshrined in the main temple, which had a huge prayer hall. There were two more buildings in the monastery, probably the monks' residential quarters. One big prayer wheel and some small prayer wheels were located adjacent to the main temple.

Apart from that, prayer flags of different colours were strung all around the monastery, and were fluttering away merrily, in harmony with the pleasant breeze that drifted up from the river. There was something completely peaceful,

completely healing in the prayer flags and in the flapping sound that they made as they fluttered in the wind.

Prayer flags are everywhere in Bhutan – in monasteries, temples, religious sites, places of spiritual importance, in front of homes, hotels, shops. They can be found on rooftops and near roads, in the valleys, on hillsides, bridges, over rivers, and at mountain passes. These flags are a part and parcel of the Bhutanese daily life and part of their religion.

The Bhutanese believe that the flags carry within them prayers and blessings, which bear fruit when the prayer flags dance and swing with the breeze. As the flags flutter, these blessings are carried through the air in a spiritual vibration over the entire region, blessing one and all. All sentient beings benefit from the prayers and blessings that are thus 'scattered' by the wind.

After 15 minutes or so, the English monk came out. Now, I could see him clearly. Yesterday he had sat beside me in the car, because of which I could not get a full glimpse of his stature. It seemed he was around 45 years old. He was a well-built, tall, fair and handsome man who looked more like a Hollywood hero than a monk. As he walked towards me, attired in maroon robes and shaven-headed, a kind of aura seemed to emanate from him.

"I was expecting you," he smiled at me warmly, his voice soft and melodious, as he came close to me.

There was something extraordinary about this Western monk who had deep, thoughtful blue eyes set in a square-shaped face. With a prominent nose and chin, broad forehead and a strong jawline, he had a surprising facial similarity with the former England football star, David Beckham.

Jennings was barefooted and he politely requested me

to take off my shoes and walk barefoot with him on the green grass of the monastery.

"Let us walk and talk," he said, indicating with his hands to walk alongside him. "You will feel good walking barefoot on this grass. It's a very soothing experience. "By the way," the monk stopped and asked, "I forgot to ask your name yesterday."

"My name is Siddhartha."

With a serene smile on his face and twinkle in his eyes, he exclaimed, "Siddhartha means Buddha!"

I have met so many people in life, but nobody has ever told me this after hearing my name.

"I too forgot to ask your name, but the monk I met today told me your name is Jennings," I said apologetically.

"Yes, it's Christopher Jennings," he said.

We were walking barefoot on the green lawn of this elegant monastery. Kuri Chu was flowing smoothly downhill. The afternoon sun was already slanting towards the hill. The sunrays glistening on the river created a reddish hue on its surface. There was a pin-drop silence in the monastery, apart from the occasional twittering of a cuckoo from the distance.

"May I ask you a question?" I asked him breaking the silence of the monastery.

"Yes, please."

"Yesterday, you were speaking about happiness. You are a monk, it's easy for you to be happy, but can we – who haven't taken up monkhood – be happy all the time?"

"Why not?"

"Because we have so many problems in life, so many issues to face in everyday life. Even if I want to be happy or peaceful, something in my home or workplace can easily disturb my equanimity..." I elaborated.

He smiled serenely after listening to my question.

There was something in his smile which would soothe anyone at once. You could get absolute peace just seeing his smile.

"Look Siddhartha, happiness is a state of mind. What's happening outside has nothing to do with our inner happiness."

"But still..." I tried to argue.

He paused a bit, smiled and continued, "I know it's difficult for anyone to understand it at first. But with practise you will gradually understand that happiness depends on how we respond to any situation."

"But how would I respond happily to a bad situation?"

"If your mind is peaceful, you will be happy regardless of your circumstances or the people around you. The Buddha advised his followers that if they desire true happiness, they should concentrate on cultivating inner peacefulness."

"But despite trying my best, I can't get over my past completely. How can I get inner peace?"

"What is it that's bothering you?" he asked me gently.

We both stopped and faced each other; I told him about my past in a nutshell.

He listened to me with his eyes closed, as if he was watching my past in his mind's eye. After I finished my

story, he opened his eyes after a while.

For a moment, he went into a meditative mode and then started speaking in his soft but firm voice, as if he knew how to solve every issue that I was facing.

We started to walk again.

"I will come to your problems one by one and try to solve those," he said gently, but there was an underlying confidence in his voice which assured me hope.

My gut feeling told me there and then that Jennings would be able to solve my problems and show me a new path that I had been searching for.

He said, "Look, the mind suffers primarily because of two things: when it does not get what it wants or, it gets what it does not want. That's pretty much the bottom line. That leads to the state of mental suffering.

"Anxiousness comes not from the real threat, but when we think anything negatively and repeatedly in our head. That is why we worry."

"I'm trying so hard not to worry. Yet, those things come back to haunt me again and again," I told him. "I want to completely overcome those demons in my mind. I'm just not getting the absolute peace that I'm looking for..."

Jennings smiled again and said earnestly, "Look Siddhartha, it won't happen overnight. This is something you have to learn with practise. For this, you have to learn how to live in the present and let go of your past."

He stopped again for a while, stared at the setting sun and the mountains. I also stopped with him and looked at him in wonderment. He must have felt my gaze, as he turned to look at me, and then he resumed walking. I followed him as he started to speak again, choosing his

words carefully.

"First, you have to learn how to not hold on to your past. The past is like a heavy baggage on your back. If you keep carrying it, you will soon be sick, tired or exhausted. That's what you are experiencing. Am I right?"

"Yes."

"That's why you have to free yourself from the past events, because you will only get peace and happiness when you stay in the present. Present is what matters, Siddhartha. That's why we have to learn to live in the present."

"But how do I stay in the present, when I'm tormented by the past all the time?"

"Don't worry, Siddhartha. I'm coming to everything gradually.

"Everything is connected to each other. Learn to live in the present means accepting things how they are. Take things as they come. You can't run away from problems. Rather, you have to learn to accept it and resolve it with a calm mind," Jennings said.

"But how can anyone accept problems? We all look to avoiding problems!"

"Yes, you are probably right. We all look to avoiding problems, because we don't know how to solve these problems," Jennings said, while continuing to walk.

I listened to him silently, walking beside him.

"Take any problem, be it your personal problem, be it a disaster, epidemic or natural calamities — these problems actually teach you many life lessons."

He stopped again, paused and said, "Take the example

of your depression or sleeplessness. When you suffered from those, they became your teacher. They taught you so many things like the importance of leading a disciplined life, how to focus your mind on good things or the importance of staying away from negativity."

When we were discussing my problems, I suddenly remembered Sushmita. How was she? Where was she? What was she doing? Did she get married again?

Silence fell on us as I thought of my estranged wife. Perhaps Jennings understood that I had drifted to the days gone by, he stopped speaking and gazed at me. When I realised that he was silent, I gathered myself.

"What were you thinking?" Jennings asked me politely.

"Some people whom I have hurt in the past," I admitted.

He continued, "Most people run away from problems and that's why they can't solve those problems. So, they can't get to the root of the problem. Instead, they start blaming others or circumstances for their problems."

That's me! I thought.

"Siddhartha, remember one thing, everything has a reason. Every incident in your life happens for a reason. Who knows these problems may help you achieve greater things in the future?"

As we walked on the green grass, I would occasionally look at him while he instructed me on these valuable life lessons, his face serious and peaceful.

"Take your example. Had you not faced those problems, you would not have come to Bhutan and would not have searched for happiness or peace. So take it positively. Maybe you have some other roles to play in life. That's why you experienced those troubles."

These words from the monk really soothed my nerves. I was feeling a lot calmer within. His way of talking was like that of a psychiatrist, who knew how to resolve your issues while holding your hands.

"But if someone provokes me, if someone ditches me, how can I remain calm?" I asked him.

"That's why you have to understand the 'law of karma' first," he said very politely.

There was no domination, no argumentative approach in his voice. Rather, his style of making me understand was such that you could not counter him in an argumentative voice.

"What's the law of karma?" I asked gently. I have heard Jamba Sir using the word karma many a time, but I still did not understand the concept properly.

"Eastern philosophies or way of life, like Buddhism and Hinduism, are based explicitly on the philosophy of karma. Karma or actions have consequences. Good actions (karma) mean dharma, which have its merits, meaning punya. Good karma brings happiness (sukha). Bad action (karma) means adharma, which are basically demerits. Bad karma brings paap. The result of paap is dukha or unhappiness. Each of us faces the consequences of our good or bad karma."

"So, every single problem that I've faced was a result of my own karma, my own actions?" I felt sick as this realisation dawned on me.

"Probably…" he told me with a meaningful smile.

Then he started to explain, "Siddhartha, happiness comes from never-ending compassionate activities. Unhappiness comes from never-ending selfish activities,

meaning bad karma. Your alcoholism, your unhealthy and selfish lifestyle were your bad karmas, which brought forth your disaster. And, you have faced the consequences of that.

"But if you accept your faults, you will be able to change your present as well as your future. Otherwise, you will spend the rest of your life blaming others. You will dislike this one and that one; hate this one, complain about that one. Your whole life will go on like this. And you will never find the reason to make a comeback to live your life."

"That means karma is fate?"

"Karma is not fatalism or destiny. Karma is taking complete charge of your life. It's like becoming the master of your own destiny," Jennings said gently, but firmly.

"But my question is, if someone hurts me or harms me, what should be my approach in dealing with it?"

"If someone hurts you, that's his or her karma. That's their problem. It's not your problem. We should concentrate on our karma only and need to learn how to be peaceful in difficult situations."

"But it's very difficult to be peaceful in adverse situations..."

"Yes, it's difficult, but you can achieve that with practise. That's why you need to understand Buddhist teachings. In the Buddhist way of life, we accept everything in our path. That's reality. We don't push anything out of reality, because that hardly helps us in dealing with the problems. We include, not exclude," Jennings said earnestly.

"Then how do I proceed?"

"It's an incremental manner of practise, so that we take discomfort into our path. In that process, we gather

experience and wisdom."

I nodded in agreement as he continued. "Siddhartha, you should know three things that will help you achieve peace. One, you need to learn how to be calm; two, you have to recognise the impermanence of life; and three, you have to work for others selflessly."

As he said this, the sun was all set to vanish from our sight, bringing to close an amazing day. The day had been a bit warm, but the slightly cool evening breeze from River Kuri Chu was gently touching my face, which was soothing and relaxing.

Looking at me thoughtfully, Jennings said, "I have to go as it's time for puja."

I was so engrossed in what Jennings was telling me that I felt a bit disappointed at the suggestion of stopping there.

Jennings had probably read my thoughts as he said, "I know you have a lot of questions left, Siddhartha. We will continue our discussion when you come to meet me again. I will be busy the next seven days, as the highest spiritual leader of Bhutan will be staying here, in this monastery. Please come after that," said Jennings.

Yes, I still had many questions in my mind which needed to be resolved urgently. At that moment, I was able to understand the things I needed to do to get peace, or to find true meaning in my life. But I was still not sure how to implement those things in my life.

Unable to come out of the hangover of the discussion we had, I silently watched Jennings who was calmly walking back to the prayer hall.

Suddenly, clouds covered the entire area. As I walked

back to the college, it started raining heavily, accompanied by lightning and gusty winds. But I kept walking amidst the dark road with the rain drenching me completely. I was oblivious to my surroundings. I could not feel anything. Jennings' words were resonating in my head. A peculiar feeling of blissfulness engulfed me.

Lying in bed that night, I only kept thinking about the evening. Something was triggered inside me. I was excited and felt restless by whatever this English Buddhist monk had said to me. I was also moved by Jennings' magnetic personality – his way of talking, his knowledge, his wisdom, his radiant face and glowing blue eyes.

That evening, I had unknowingly embarked on a voyage towards new shores, holding Jennings' hand. I had never been to this territory before. But I must confess, it was a blissful place – far away from the land of ego, fear, anger, jealousy, selfishness and greed.

....

I anxiously waited for the next seven days to pass by. Those seven days seemed like seven months! My queries kept troubling me more and more. I was looking forward to meeting Jennings again, to learn from him the secret of attaining peacefulness and happiness.

I went to meet Jennings after seven days.

When I reached the monastery in the afternoon, Jennings welcomed me warmly.

"So, how were your days?" Jennings asked me, a beatific smile on his face.

"Actually, I was anxious about our meeting," I confessed. "That day we could not complete our conversation. I have so many questions!"

Jennings asked me to walk barefoot with him on the grass, again, "What do you want to discuss?"

"You were telling me about how to be calm and work selflessly for others…."

"That means you have not forgotten," he said gently, appreciating me. "Yes, if you properly follow those things, most of your troubles will vanish.

"For me, the actions which come from selfishness, greed and anger are bad karma. Selfishness, greed and anger lead to an unfocused mind. If you always have your own interest in mind, it will definitely lead to anxiety and frustration," Jennings said.

I nodded.

"On the other hand, the unselfish mind, or the mind filled with love and compassion, is a relaxed mind. So, the more you work for others – for extended family members, for your community, for your country – you will feel more relaxed. The mind with love, compassion and selflessness leads to a better-focused mind," Jennings added.

"That means the source of action is the main, important factor?" I asked him.

"The purpose behind the work is important. I am not interested in what you do, I am not interested in what you say; I am only interested in knowing your purpose behind every work you do. So, what you do, how you do… that is not that important. Why you do it is the most important thing."

"But selfishness, greed and anger are bound to be part of us, as we are human beings…."

"Yes, it is bound to happen. But there are people who manage to avoid those too. And, that's why and how, they

remain blissful," Jennings pointed out.

I nodded.

"That means we accept that selfishness, greed and anger are avoidable because some people can avoid it. But the question remains, how to avoid those. No?" asked the monk, as if guiding me to the logical next step.

"The answer is, first, we have to recognise which are the things that you should avoid. If you are aware of your problems, it's the first step towards the solution."

I nodded.

"Though you know it is difficult, you still want to get rid of those things because they, bad things, lead to suffering. Tell me, does anyone want to suffer intentionally? Or, they want to be happy and peaceful?" the monk asked me.

"Everyone wants peace and happiness," I said, realising that it was a rhetorical question.

"So, if you want to be happy and blissful, you first need to develop a strong mind which will keep those 'bad things' away," he said.

"Is there any particular way to make the mind strong?"

Jennings looked at me carefully and said, "You have to be determined enough not to repeat your mistakes and be able to direct your energy to an unknown path. But for that, you first need to have a great motivation to live by."

I kept quiet. Probably my blank eyes told him that I did not get the meaning of the word motivation in this context.

So, he started explaining it further, "If your motivation is to love everyone and have compassion for all the sentient beings, you will act accordingly."

"That means I need to have the right motivation first..."

"Yes, that's the most important thing. If your motivation is to have love and compassion for all, that itself will give you profound feelings of integrity. And living with integrity creates a strong as well as a calm mind. We can rather say that a calm mind is actually a strong mind," Jennings said. "Integrity of mind means that you have the mental strength not to commit bad karma or fall into the trap of any temptation again. Suppose, you have quit alcohol, but when someone invites you to a cocktail party, you are still tempted. No?"

I nodded.

"Then you have two choices in front of you: one, either you say 'no', or, you succumb to the temptation and again start drinking and go back to your old habits, which you had overcome after a hard battle with yourself."

I was listening to him with undivided attention.

"When you say 'no', that means you have developed integrity. Integrity instils confidence in you, which helps you develop a strong mind. A strong mind with integrity leads to a calm mind, because you have attained the capacity to keep those bad things at bay, which create distractions for your mind."

I was just about beginning to get an idea about what he was driving at.

"Now, I can understand that. But can the mind be calm all the time?" I asked him again, as we walked side by side.

"Yes, by practising breathing exercises and meditation, you can create a permanently calm mind," Jennings said.

"But one has to learn these things...."

"Yes, you need to learn the correct breathing technique." He paused for a moment and added, "Breathing is a bridge between the physical body and the mind. Breathing is linked directly to the human nervous system. But it is not necessary to meditate formally, in the initial stage. There are many methods of meditation and breathing practises."

"I have never done any breathing exercise before. Is breathing practice so powerful?" I asked him, fascinated.

"Breathing is the fastest way to impact your nervous system. The human nervous system is the landscape on which you experience anxiety, stress and calmness. Breathing is the fastest way to reduce your anxiety. You have to do something, which gives you instant calmness. When you are facing emotions like anger, you have to pause or, take a deep breath."

I nodded in agreement.

"So, it is an immediate, on-the-spot solution to your anxiety. It's an immediate antidote to all your problems," Jennings reiterated. "We need to do conscious breathing, because it affects our nervous system. You can practise that anywhere, anytime," he added.

"Can just having conscious deep breathing solve all my problems?" I was becoming curious about the outcome of breathing exercises, as there was a time when I disliked yoga and meditation. My take on these things was that they were devices to delude the already deluded.

Jennings smiled. Perhaps, he had got a hint of my mind set. The reflection of the rays of the setting sun on his face made him even more radiant. He looked like an angel, a message bearer, who knew and was willing to show me the path.

"Nothing can solve your problem, if you don't want to solve it consciously. Once you have calmness 'within', you have the clarity or the conscious approach. When you have clarity of thoughts, you can make a conscious choice. But we need to have a meditative or still mind for that."

"Please, tell go on."

"Meditation is food for the heart and spiritual health. We only concentrate on our physical or external body, but we don't care about the internal health. Like you play football, which helps you to be physically fit. But despite being fit, you are not getting any mental peace. Isn't it so?"

I nodded hesitatingly. As if Jennings was prying open one after another secrets of my mind.

"But a balanced individual is one who takes care of both her external, as well as internal health. When your mind is unfocused, your capacity to help others reduces. At the end of a meditation session, the mind is so clear; your actions would automatically result in being good.

"But you have to remember all the time that the root of getting happiness is in helping others. And, you need to train your mind for that," Jennings added.

I was silent. The directness and simplicity of the idea struck me.

He continued after a pause, "When you have finally decided to work for others, you start maybe with a single person. Change his life. Once you have this in you to help others, help more people and change their lives. Gradually, you increase your scope of work to larger social arenas."

"But I don't know how to meditate or the correct breathing techniques. I have tried to do something sometimes on my own, but I couldn't concentrate. Please,

would you teach me the correct technique?"

"For that, you have to come with me and sit in the meditation hall."

I followed him into the meditation hall, a large room with different idols of Buddha and Padmasambhava. The walls were also decorated with different religious paintings. The hall was in complete silence.

Jennings sat down on the floor, cross-legged and asked me to sit likewise, in front of him and follow him.

Sitting in front of him, I looked at his eyes, and I was mesmerised by the depth of his blue eyes. I realised that spiritual training not only changes your heart, it changes one's eyes too, making it a platform, which can speak on behalf of one's heart easily.

Before showing me the meditation and breathing processes, Jennings gave me some instructions regarding what to think before and during meditation and breathing exercises.

"According to Buddhist and yogic teachings, before starting meditation, you should be aware of your karma consequence about which I have told you earlier.

"Your motivation should be: 'good work leads to happiness and evil work leads to suffering'.

"Your method will be those that bring happiness.

"There are six parameters of method: generosity, ethical conduct, patience, enthusiastic diligence or not giving up, meditative concentration and wisdom."

"That means meditation is one of these six parameters..." I said, trying to show that I understood his words.

"But here is a trick. Without focus or meditative concentration, you can't achieve the other five qualities, that is, generosity, ethical conduct, patience, enthusiastic diligence and wisdom. You can only work for others when you have a meditative or focused mind. When the mind is distracted or unfocused, it is vulnerable to anger, desire, selfishness and greed.

"I am coming to the breathing practice now.

"First, I will tell you about the four parts or cycles of the basic breathing exercise.

"Two of them are moving and two of them are still.

"Now you follow me and do the exercise with me."

Jennings then proceeded to show me the correct technique of breathing exercise.

"This is the first and simple breathing process: do this for a couple of weeks. And then, I will show you some more processes," Jennings said, his voice becoming softer and gentler, as he began to teach me the art of meditation.

"As you are sitting cross-legged, your right hand will rest on your left hand."

"Close your eyes and inhale deeply."

"Then hold your breath."

"Then exhale."

"Then hold your breath again for a few seconds before inhaling."

"It's a simple process of inhaling, then a natural pause, then exhaling and then again a natural pause."

"Continue this simple process."

As he was showing me the breathing process, I observed him keenly. His dedication and his peace of mind were reflected on his face. It was clear that this man had attained the elusive happiness and peacefulness which all of us were in search of.

Though his eyes were closed, there was a blissful radiance on his face, which I saw before closing my eyes.

As I closed my eyes, Jennings softly said,

"Notice the four parts of breathing. The movement parts will be longer. Between inhaling and exhaling, you have to pause for a few seconds.

"Do it for ten times at first. You will feel a lot more calm and relaxed."

I followed his instructions meticulously. I had never taken a deep and longer breath so consciously in my life. When I took a deep breath for the first time, I felt a positive sensation in my head, and when I released my breath, there was a soothing feeling of relaxation which ran through my whole body. After doing this ten times, I immediately found some changes in me. I felt a strange sensation in my head. I was feeling a little dizzy, but I was feeling a lot more relaxed and calm.

"Don't open your eyes yet," Jennings cautioned quietly in his usual gentle but firm voice.

That was fine with me – I didn't feel like opening my eyes yet!

In a low-pitch tone, Jennings continued to instruct me what to think in my mind.

"What you are thinking during the exercise is very important. While doing this exercise, see yourself in the larger context.

"Bring your focus around your breathing.

"Imagine that the goodness of this practice is immediately touching everyone.

"Feel the joy that others feel.

"If you practise it regularly for half an hour, the breath becomes longer, the pause becomes longer. It will naturally happen over a period of time.

"Now, do it as long as you want," Jennings prodded in a soft voicc, which I could hear faintly.

I don't know for how long did I stay like that. I don't know where I was at that time. I was in deep contemplation. I was in a trance. I felt hypnotised. It seemed that I was going inside a deep black hole where there was no one except Jennings and me. I felt he was taking me to a wonderland where only peace and happiness exist. I was only able to hear Jennings' soft, melodious voice and nothing else. That blissful voice seemed the voice of an eternal power. I could sense that the voice and the journey were catalysing something positive within me. It destroyed every idea, every belief and every act of my past. It was transforming me fully from the inside for the rest of my life.

"Now you can open your eyes slowly," Jennings' voice suddenly took me out of the stupor.

When I opened my eyes slowly, an unusual sensation gripped me from the toes to the top of my head. There was a sense of calmness, peace and happiness inside me. Everything looked beautiful, positive and energetic. I was feeling a lot kinder and more compassionate. A strange sense of detachment overpowered me.

I saw Jennings' arresting, glowing face and his blue, deep and penetrating eyes. He looked like a Greek god who

had just saved me from the jaws of death. He somehow overwhelmed me mentally.

I had never ever experienced what I felt that day. I felt empathy for every sentient being. I was feeling a lot closer to nature; the hills, the trees, the Kuri Chu river, all seemed a part of me. It seemed as if I was successfully swimming through all the blockages of the past. I felt less angry, less greedy and less selfish. The 'I' in me was turning into 'we'. I never felt so pure and so powerful from inside. I had never realised such peace and happiness within me before. It was a completely new experience for me.

That evening changed me forever.

I suddenly realised my face was wet. It was a feeling of ecstasy and joy of something, which was indescribable, inexpressible and of a much higher level. It was a feeling of finally discovering the meaning of life, like finally finding the hidden treasure that I had been searching for some time.

****

10

When I woke up the next morning, I felt extremely powerful, determined and, at the same time, a lot calmer and relaxed. The first thing I did was to practise meditation and the breathing exercise in my daily routine. I meticulously followed all the instructions given by Jennings.

From that day on, I became a devoted practitioner of meditation and breathing exercise, so much so that I have never missed this practice even for a single day. It has become a part of my life. Every morning, on waking up, the first thing I do is 45 minutes of meditation and breathing practice and then, go for my physical training or play football.

I attended many more sessions with Jennings in the next four months. He taught me many more forms of yoga and meditations which he had learnt from his guru.

My Sunday routine in the evenings had changed a bit. Every Sunday afternoon, I would have my learning sessions with Jennings. He gave me the much-needed direction to lead a meaningful, peaceful and happy life. He answered my queries. I realised that happiness is found when you look inwards. When you are content, nothing could disturb your peace. Gradually, all my anxieties, restlessness, troubles, suffering melted away.

One day, Jennings told me in passing, "All your tragedies and problems were because of your ego, your cutting off from your roots and detachment from what you really loved — football. Once you snapped your ties from your true self, you lost your own identity."

On yet another Sunday, he said, "You only thought about yourself. You never thought about others. You never thought about the welfare of other human beings despite having all the resources to serve others."

In that session Jennings also said, "When you faced roadblocks because of your own bad karma, you took refuge in temporary solutions or temporary happiness like alcoholism. But that did not work for you in the long run."

In one of our sessions, Jennings told me, "You considered pleasure as happiness, never knowing that it would actually take you far away from happiness and peace. You considered life to be an everlasting affair, forgetting that your existence - like that of others - on this earth is temporary."

It all made sense now.

"Suppose, some criminals are kept in a place and are told that they would be hanged to death after a few hours. What will these criminals do in the next four hours?" Jennings asked me.

"They would lament or repent in each other's company," I answered.

"Will they talk about committing a crime again or harming anyone in the next few hours?" Jennings continued.

"Obviously not."

"Why?"

"Because they know they will die after a few hours," I answered.

"Right," Jennings agreed, and added, "our situation is no different from those criminals. They know they will die after a few hours, but any of us can also die before that. We can die anytime. Is it not so?"

"Yes."

"When you are aware that death is imminent, or this life is temporary, you will never do anything bad."

"Rather, you will naturally concentrate on serving others. That's why we have to remember that death is the ultimate truth in life."

"But is it not a negative feeling?"

"Thinking about death is, rather, a positive feeling. This constant thought of death as the only reality can give you the much-needed freedom from selfishness, greed, anger and ego," said Jennings in his customary style of softness, blended with strong logic.

"I never thought of life in this way," I confessed to him, self-consciously.

"This principle of impermanence is the main theme of Eastern philosophies," Jennings said.

On another Sunday afternoon, Jennings asked me, "Are you familiar with Swami Vivekananda's writings?"

"I've read only a bit when I was in the rehab centre."

"Didn't your school teach you about Vivekananda?"

"Not that much."

"That's the problem with India now. You people don't

know and don't appreciate your rich heritage," Jennings said regretfully. "People in India look to imitate the western model of education. That's the reason for all the problems in India. India should learn from Western technological advancements, but they should not forget their rich past. If India can merge these two seamlessly, as Vivekananda wanted, India could take the leadership in the world."

He was so correct in his assessment, I thought ruefully.

"Vivekananda said worship the living god by helping people. Vivekananda loved Buddha. Like Buddha, Vivekananda worked for human beings to alleviate their sufferings," Jennings told me.

"Yes, I know that Vivekananda said worship the living god by helping people," I said, remembering something from the few books by Vivekananda that I had read.

"Yes, I'm deeply inspired by Vivekananda. That's why I've been working for poor Bhutanese children. I, along with my friends in London, run a project – 'Little Buddhas of Bhutan' – to help the poor children here. I raise money by giving lectures on spirituality, yoga and meditation in different parts of the world. I have spoken at different TEDx platforms on my experience of becoming a Buddhist, and a monk. Several organisations around the world invite me to give lectures. Whatever I earn from my lectures and from the sale of my books on Eastern philosophies, I use it here to serve people," the monk let in a few things about himself, at last.

My respect for this monk from London grew even more after hearing this. Jennings was really living a meaningful life.

And, he declared that this century would be Asia's century, with India, as it would, with its rich culture and

heritage, guide the rest of the world.

"India taught tolerance and service to others. Siddhartha Gautama achieved enlightenment in Bodh Gaya, India, and became the 'Buddha'. It's from India that Buddhism spread to different parts of the world. India has the capacity to show the right path to the rest of the world. Vasudhaiva Kutumbakam, which means 'the world is one family', was propagated by the people of ancient India."

I was once again impressed by his knowledge on India and command over the Eastern philosophics.

"Do you know what Mark Twain said about India?"

I had no idea. I looked blankly at Jennings.

"Many years ago, Mark Twin said, 'India is the cradle for human race, birthplace of human speech, mother of history, grandmother of legend and great grandmother of tradition. Our most valuable and instructive materials in the history are treasured here.'"

During the course of these months, when I met him regularly, Jennings gave me some books that he had written on Buddhism and Hinduism. He also gave me some books of Vivekananda and the Autobiography of a Yogi, which has inspired many people in the West and kindled their interest in Indian philosophy.

Jennings had changed my life, or rather my perspective towards life, in just four months of meeting him. Encouraged by him, I vowed to start a new life, which would be dedicated to serving people and society. But I had no idea from where and how should I embark on my new journey.

....

Jamba Sir called me to his office one day, and told me that he wanted the GCIT football team to practise with famous football clubs in India, like Mohun Bagan or East Bengal, so that the boys improve and get a chance to learn by interacting with some of the finest footballers of India. He had fixed the time of the event after our final semester in November.

I called Sushanta and told him about Jamba Sir's wish and if he could help so that the boys could play in a practice match with players of Mohun Bagan. However, Sushanta told me he could arrange the match only with the academy teams. He also said that he would not be in Kolkata after November. If we have to go there, we have to go before November.

When I informed Jamba Sir about this, he said, "Tell your friend, we can make it in October."

"Sir, our final exams are scheduled in the first week of November. How is it possible before the exams?" I said in a strained voice.

"It's possible. We can't miss this opportunity. It has been my dream that my students will practise with Mohun Bagan or East Bengal."

"But it will hamper their studies before the final examinations..."

"Playing football is also an education, Siddhartha. Please request your friend to prepare a moderate accommodation for us. We will go in the middle of October."

I had no option but to agree with this man, who, I thought, was one of the unique people I had ever met on this earth. Which head of a college would take his students for a football tour with less than a month before the final exams?

But that was Jamba's way of imparting education to his students.

We started for Kolkata in our college bus. Sir, Kelsang, Barma and I accompanied our team. Since Jamba Sir preferred that we cook our own food, we carried with us necessary utensils as well as non-perishables like rice, pulses and other items. We would buy the vegetables, fish or chicken on the way.

"Is it necessary to take this difficult journey? We could have taken the train from Assam and reached Kolkata easily," I told Jamba Sir on the way.

"Yes, I know, but this journey is important as this is a valuable lesson for these boys. They have never taken this kind of a long journey before to another country. I have planned this tour in such a way that they will learn how to cook, how to adjust to new situations that may come up, difficulties and challenges, in their future. It will help them once they leave college and enter the professional world.

"Football has the enormous power to bring together people on to the same platform and teach them many life lessons. That's why I take my boys to play in different places. It gives them that much-needed exposure to tackle unexpected happenings in their lives," Jamba explained patiently.

I was really impressed with the 'football method' of Lhato Jamba.

We finally reached Kolkata on the third day, in the evening. Sushanta had arranged our accommodation at a youth hostel near the Mohun Bagan ground. Though Sushanta wanted to arrange a better accommodation for Jamba Sir and me, we preferred to stay with the students.

He came to meet me that night.

"You're looking super fit," Sushanta complimented me.

I just smiled.

"Yes, now I can recognise my friend who used to play with me. I was super scared when I met you in Delhi," he said, laughing heartily.

I smiled again.

"I knew you would be fine if you played football," Sushanta said with a rare sense of confidence.

"I'm really proud of what you have achieved," I told him. It was fantastic.

"But you know, I will be really happy, if I can give back to my roots. There are so many good players in our area. I have helped many players from north Bengal in getting into good clubs and finding accommodation in Kolkata."

"Well done, Sushanta. I'm truly proud of you," I said warmly.

"But that's not enough. We need to open a football academy in the tribal area of north Bengal because, if tribal children are guided properly, they can easily make it to the top. Even Mayna Sir asks me to do something for the unprivileged kids of the north. You know how much effort and pain Mayna Sir took for all of us," Sushanta said, with gravitas in his demeanour.

I liked his attitude. Even after becoming a famous footballer, he was rooted to the ground. He was thinking about those who don't have anyone to support them. I thought Mayna Sir had guided Sushanta not only to be a champion player, but to be a very good human being as

well – which, alas, many of our teachers in school could not do.

That's why Sushanta was 'successful' in the true sense of the term and Amit da and Sourav were not. You are 'successful' when you don't forget your roots, despite being on the top. You are 'successful' when you think about reaching out to those who helped you reach the top.

That evening we discussed many other things. Sushanta told me that his parents were happy and are still in Siliguri. His other siblings, who were running their own businesses – Sushanta had helped all of them set up their own business – were also doing well in life.

Sushanta asked me to stay with him at his apartment that night, but I gently declined the offer, as I preferred to stay with my students.

Next morning, we practised with the Mohun Bagan academy team. Sushanta came to oversee the practise session.

Our boys interacted with Sushanta, who gave them some valuable tips after the practice session.

He also arranged practise matches with other football club academies, like East Bengal, Aryans, Mohammedan Sporting, and Bhawanipore, clubs which were near the Mohun Bagan club.

Our boys played quite well and learnt first-hand from all this exposure. They won against Bhawanipore, Mohammedan and Aryans, but they had to settle for a draw against the Mohun Bagan and East Bengal academy teams.

It was a wonderful time but after three days Jamba Sir made a strange request to me. He asked me to talk to

Sushanta regarding a practice match with the Mohun Bagan main team.

"It's next to impossible, Sir!" I was taken aback, wondering if I had heard right.

"Why impossible?"

"Sir, they are one of the best teams in India. They may not want to play against a college team."

"No, no... they will play. Just do your best to convince your friend."

I knew Jamba Sir was a headstrong and stubborn person. He would not rest until he got it done.

"But will our boys be able to handle a defeat by a big margin?"

"I know our boys will get disheartened but they need that shock," Jamba Sir said with a mischievous smile. "They have played well against the academy teams. They have become overconfident! I want to break that."

I spoke with Sushanta about Sir's suggestion over the phone.

As expected, he scoffed and laughed at my proposal. But Sushanta called me after an hour with the good news that he had managed a practice match, somehow.

Jamba Sir was pretty excited to learn this.

He called the boys to tell them about the upcoming practice match; the students became tense on hearing the news but they had no option: they had to play the match.

"It's the biggest opportunity for you, boys. It's very difficult to get a practice match against a team like Mohun Bagan," Jamba tried to inspire the students.

When Mohun Bagan entered the ground, I myself was rather thrilled to see them. I was also excited to see Sushanta play after almost twenty years.

Suddenly Sushanta came running to me.

He wanted me to play for their Mohun Bagan team.

"What!" I asked in disbelieve.

"Yes. We will both play together for Mohun Bagan against your college team. Since it's a practise match, I requested my coach to allow you to wear our jersey," he beamed at me.

I simply gaped at him, flabbergasted, not knowing how to react. It was beyond my dream.

"Let's go to our bench and take your jersey from our coach," Sushanta suggested hurriedly. "We will play as strikers, just as we did in our school days."

It was apparent from his face that like me, he too was getting excited at the prospect of playing together.

The match started. There were some spectators occupying the green and maroon chairs, who were shouting out Sushanta's name and of the other Mohun Bagan stars.

Initially, I was not able to match my speed with that of the rest of the Mohun Bagan team as these boys were professional footballers. Our boys were also feeling the heat as the Mohun Bagan team was a completely different team in terms of skill, speed and understanding among the players.

Our college team had already conceded two goals within the first 10 minutes.

Our acrobatic goalkeeper JD and our defenders

Kelnam Gyeltshen, Pema Rigzin, Phuntsho Dhendup were playing extremely well and foiling most of the attacks by the Mohun Bagan team. Otherwise, GCIT would have been down with a greater margin by then.

Sensing that I was not able to match the speed of his team, Sushanta came to me and reminded me of those old days when we coordinated our play and speed with each other.

"Just follow me, forget everything... don't try to get every ball. You take your position, I will see the rest," Sushanta whispered.

I followed his advice.

And, in no time, I got back my old form.

Actually, more than skill, I was overwhelmed by the occasion.

Sushanta gave me a beautiful cross ball. I received the ball, dribbled past Kelnam Gyeltshen and Phuntsho Dhendup and shot it past JD with my left foot to score my first goal in twenty years.

I was over the moon and so was Sushanta.

All the Mohun Bagan players came and hugged me.

I could not control my emotions. Tears came rolling down my cheeks.

I had made a comeback!

'Life has come to a full circle for both of us,' I thought.

For the rest of the match, I completely forgot that I was playing for Mohun Bagan. I was just on the lookout for Sushanta as if we were playing for our school team.

I assisted Sushanta to score two more goals in the match. Our boys lost the match 6-0.

"You still have that old touch, Siddhartha," Sushanta told me, slapping my back, as we were coming out of the ground after the match. "But your college team put up a good fight. I never expected this kind of performance from a college team," Sushanta said appreciatively - and generously.

Before leaving, I asked Sushanta to meet me in the evening.

After the match, Jamba Sir told me, "I know the boys will be disappointed, but that's very important in life. We all have our good times, or successful periods in our lives. But how we manage our failures, determines our future. Their defeat and this experience of playing with such a star team is what will help them in their future."

In the evening, Sushanta came with his car and took me to Floatel, a floating hotel on River Hooghly, near the Kolkata High Court. We sat in the restaurant from where we could see the glistening, shimmering river.

"You have trained these boys so well," Sushanta remarked after placing our order.

"Whatever I learnt from Mayna Sir..." I shrugged modestly.

"Yes, the same with me. I've played under so many coaches, some of them foreigners, but what I learnt from Mayna Sir in childhood, was the best of all lessons. Whatever I am today is because of Sir," Sushanta said.

The more I saw Sushanta, the more I liked the way he was, the way he had turned out to be: a brilliant footballer and a wonderful human being. Despite achieving so much

as a player, he remained down-to-earth and humble. His heart was as vast and as holy as River Hooghly on which we were 'sitting' that day.

He had never been a good-looking boy, at least in the conventional sense. I realised that anyone would look good if he possessed a sympathetic heart because goodness has its own charm and aura.

Jamba's words came to my mind. Sushanta had done well in life and was very happy because he had followed his heart. He did not lose his identity because he had pursued his own dream.

"Sushanta, do you remember what you told me that day?" I asked him, a bit hesitantly.

"I'm not sure what you are talking about."

"You told me a few days back that you want to open an academy in north Bengal in a tribal area."

"Yes, I want to, but I won't be able to find the time at this juncture."

"What if I open the academy?"

"You! But how? You live in Bhutan! How will you manage?" Sushanta asked me, astonished.

"I'll leave my job and start the academy in any of the tribal areas of north Bengal."

"What!"

"Yes, I will stay in a tribal village in north Bengal and work for the villagers," I said.

"What are you saying?"

"Yes, I'd like to work for the underprivileged people and give back to my roots, so that no one has to struggle like you did," I told him, looking straight at him.

The last sentence made Sushanta emotional.

"You are right, Siddhartha. Apart from Mayna Sir, no one supported me. There were many nights when I went to bed on an empty stomach. I know the pain. I played with old, torn football boots. Baba's income was not enough to support me... you know all this... he wanted me to quit football... and I was about to, because of our financial situation. But Mayna Sir did not allow me. He requested my father to let me to continue with football. He virtually begged money from people, so that he could provide for my football kit. Siddhartha, Sir did not want you to quit football either. That evening when Sir finally told you not to come to the ground after your father insulted him, he was literally crying. You don't know Siddhartha, how much Sir loved you," Sushanta told me, his eyes moist, voice choking.

I could feel my eyes tearing up as well.

Blinking rapidly and taking a few minutes to control myself, I said, "Whatever happened has happened. Now, I want to rectify all the mistakes of my past and start afresh."

"But..."

"No ifs and buts, Sushanta... please. I have seen people regret at the end of their lives what they could not do. I don't want to do that. I want to lead a meaningful and fulfilling life. I will work for the helpless, the downtrodden and change their lives," I told him firmly.

There was a look of surprise in Sushanta's face as he heard me.